On the other side [of the]
village, on the cres[t of a hill, a]
wolflike figure lo[omed over the]
dying flames. Its f[ur was singed,]
a ragged gash from a splintered board
ran the length of the animal's side.
The wound would soon heal. The
anger would remain.

If he had escaped, there would be
others. To help them survive, he must
find them and bring them together.
He was the leader.

Derak pointed his muzzle to the
sky. The cruel teeth gleamed in the
moonlight. He tested the air. There
was the acrid smell of burning flesh
and fur. The bite of gasoline. The
sweat stink of the men. And there
was the familiar scent of the others,
those who had escaped . . . and
somewhere in the night forest . . .
his son.

Miles away, moving swiftly in the
other direction, Malcolm paused
and raised his head to listen to the
howling. . . .

THE HOWLING III

Gary Brandner

FAWCETT GOLD MEDAL • NEW YORK

A Fawcett Gold Medal Book
Published by Ballantine Books
Copyright © 1985 by Garrison Inc.

Library of Congress Catalog Card Number: 85-90723

ISBN: 0-449-12834-2

Manufactured in the United States of America

First Ballantine Books Edition: October 1985

Chapter 1

Sheriff Gavin Ramsay stretched out a foot and nudged the switch on the electric heater to OFF with the toe of his boot. The heater coils twanged as the red glow faded. The voters of La Reina County, all 4,012 of them, would be proud of their sheriff's economy moves.

Ramsay hoisted his foot back to the top of the desk and resumed his contemplation of the view from his office window. Out in front ran S31, a two-lane blacktop with a flaking yellow center stripe badly in need of repainting. S31 was also the main street of Pinyon, California, seat of La Reina County, Pop. 2,109, Elev. 3550.

Across the road from the sheriff's office was Art Moore's Exxon station, a Pioneer Chicken franchise, and Hackett's Pharmacy. On his own side of the road, out of Ramsay's line of sight, was Yates Hardware & Plumbing, the Safeway, the boarded-up Rialto Theater, and the Pinyon Inn. That was about it for Pinyon, except for the library and La Reina County Hospital, which were built off the road on the high ground between S31 and the mountains.

The storm that had hammered the town for two days had moved on in the early-morning hours, leaving everything wet and bedraggled. The landscape would need a couple of days of sunshine to dry out.

Gavin Ramsay was more than ready for some dry weather. The rain depressed him. Elise used to get poetic about the rain. Literally. She would go to her typewriter and turn out pages of tortured free verse whenever a few raindrops fell. Then she would show it to Gavin and ask what he thought of it. In the first year of their marriage he used to lie and say it was good, really good. After that first year he started telling her the truth. By that time it didn't matter anymore.

Today was the last day of March, and with luck there would not be another big storm until fall. Summer would bring its own problems—motorcycle gangs, irritable tourists, lost hikers, and campers with poison oak. Nothing that couldn't be handled as long as it was not raining.

Probably there would be fewer problems with hikers and campers this year. Thoughtful people were not eager to go into the woods since the Drago business. You couldn't blame them. It was peaceful now, but sometimes on a quiet night you could still hear it. The howling.

In truth, there wasn't a whole lot for a sheriff and two deputies to do in La Reina County. Well, one deputy and a trainee assigned here by the state, to be accurate. Right now the prospect of a quiet summer suited Gavin Ramsay just fine. After the double trauma of Drago and his divorce from Elise he could use the time to reassemble his life.

The people of La Reina County were happy to see things calm down again. Drago was enough excitement for several lifetimes. It was kind of fun for a while. Now the folks would just as soon not talk about it.

They still got a fair number of sightseers who detoured off Interstate 5 hoping to see something of the infamous village. They might as well have stayed home. There was nothing left to see.

The asphalt road connecting Pinyon to Drago had buckled

and cracked with the heat of the fire, and there were wooden barriers put up by Caltrans to block it off. Still, determined curiosity seekers could get through in a tough truck. Those driving something less rugged turned back to Pinyon, where they searched in vain for souvenir shops. Some of the locals used to joke down at the Pinyon Inn about printing up a bunch of Drago T-shirts with bite marks and red splotches, but those jokes got old in a hurry.

Gavin Ramsay had functioned with his usual quiet efficiency during the Drago business. In a way it was a relief for him to get away from home at the time. Now, like the rest of the people in town, he didn't want to talk about it. Not about Drago or Elise. That did not mean he had forgotten. Nobody who lived through Drago would ever forget. Elise, either, for that matter. You just didn't want to talk about it.

He picked up a paperback novel from the other desk in the pine-paneled office, the one shared by his two deputies. Ed McBain. 87th Precinct. It must belong to Milo Fernandez. The trainee. Roy Nevins's taste ran more to *Hustler*.

Milo was an eager kid, still excited by the idea of police work. Roy Nevins wasn't excited by much of anything these days, except finishing up his twenty years of public service and living the rest of his life comfortably off the taxpayers of California.

They should be returning soon. It was after four and getting dark. Ramsay felt a little guilty about sending them out on what he figured to be a wild goose chase, but he could see Milo getting restless with nothing to do, and Roy had been on the verge of falling asleep. They were not likely to find Abe Craddock and Curly Vane in the woods. Those fearless hunters were more likely holed up in some saloon down in Saugus, where everybody had a tattoo and a pickup truck. Still, Abe's wife *had* called to say she was worried about him, and it *had* been three days, so Ramsay was more or less obligated to look into it. Anyway, Milo would probably enjoy getting out of the office, and Roy could sure as hell use the exercise.

The gravel crunched outside and Orry Yates's panel truck pulled onto the parking area. YATES PLUMING was painted on the side in no-nonsense black letters. Orry claimed the misspelling was done deliberately to attract attention. Ramsay had his doubts.

Orry got out of the driver's side of the truck, and two teenagers, a boy and a girl wearing backpacks, climbed out of the other. Orry led the way toward the office.

Ramsay swung his feet down to the floor and waited for them to come in. A tightening in his gut warned that this was going to be trouble.

Orry held the door open for the young backpackers, then herded them over to Ramsay's desk. "Got a little problem, Gavin," he said.

"Oh?"

"These kids think they found a dead man in the woods."

"They *think*?"

"You know how sometimes the light plays tricks coming through the trees. A tree stump or a mossy log can look like something else."

The boy shot Orry a dark look. "If that's a log laying out there, I'm Beaver Cleaver."

Ramsay studied the young couple. The boy was thin and wouldn't be bad-looking if he shaved off the apologetic little mustache. The girl wore a UCLA sweat shirt and elastic jeans that showed off her firm little ass.

The sheriff cleared his throat and got businesslike. "Tell me about it."

"We were, you know, hiking," the boy said. "On a trail that leads off the old Drago Road, and Debbie goes, 'Hey, you smell that?' And I go, 'Smell what?' And she goes, 'Like spoiled meat.' And I go . . .''

"Never mind the dialog," Ramsay said. "Tell me about finding the dead man."

4

"That's what I'm doing, man."

"Could you speed it up?"

The boy looked sullen and Debbie took over. "We found him a little ways off the trail. A big guy, you know. Smelled really bad."

"How big?"

The girl shrugged. "It was hard to tell. He was laying down. Dead, you know." She looked at the boy and giggled.

"What did he look like?"

"Like a dead man," the boy said.

"His face," Ramsay prompted.

"Who knows?" the boy said. "There wasn't much of it left. Like something had chewed on it."

"Gross," the girl confirmed.

Ramsay levered himself out of the chair. "Think you can take me to him?"

They nodded without enthusiasm.

"You gonna need me anymore?" Orry Yates said.

"Not now, Orry. Thanks for bringing them in."

They walked out of the small wooden building that served as La Reina County Sheriff's office. It was built twenty years before as a sales office for an optimistic developer who thought there would be a migration of Los Angeles residents to the mountains. He was wrong.

Orry Yates climbed into the YATES PLUMING truck, waved, and drove off. Ramsay led the teenagers around to the back where the beat-up Dodge wagon was parked. His Camaro had gone to Elise in the settlement. La Reina County could afford only one sheriff's car, and the deputies were using it.

Ramsay wondered if the dead man was Abe Craddock or Curly Vane. If it was, he owed somebody an apology for mentally placing them in a saloon somewhere. However, if it was one of them, where was the other? An argument? Too much booze and a gun goes off? Better stop building a crime

5

until he had a look at the scene. He kicked the engine of the eight-year-old wagon to life and took off for the old Drago Road.

Deputy Roy Nevins stopped to pull his uniform pants free from the thorns of a wild blackberry bush. He knew this drill was one big waste of time. Craddock and Vane could find their way around these woods as well as anybody in the county. The only trouble they were likely to get into was when they came back to town and started drinking.

He knew Gavin Ramsay had sent him and Milo out here just to keep them busy. If it hadn't been for the gung ho trainee, Deputy Nevins would have sacked out in the back of the car until dusk, then gone back and told Gavin there was no sign of Craddock and Vane. That's what their search would add up to anyway. Zip. Only difference was now he'd get all wet and scratched up from these fucking thorns and his shoes would be ruined.

"Roy!" Milo called unseen from off to the left.

"Yeah?"

"Just checking our positions."

Yeah, great. Ten-fucking-four. Milo could be a pain in the ass sometimes. But what the hell. He was only twenty. When Roy Nevins was twenty he'd been gung ho, too. The kid might grow up to be a good cop. Not in La Reina County, where a couple of overdue library books was a crime wave. But it was a start. Three months from now the state would put him somewhere else. Nice gentle way to break in as a cop. Not the way Roy Nevins had done it, on the grungiest street in the grungiest section of Oakland.

Roy had been a cowboy back then himself. No more. Now he was sitting on a pension, just putting in his time. Couple more years and he could buy that mobile home down in Baja. Sit around fishing with a cool Carta Blanca in his fist. A man could still live pretty damn good in Mexico for

6

peanuts. Until then he would have to pass the days as comfortably as he could and put up with a certain amount of shit like slogging through these dripping woods.

"*Hey!*" he yelled in the direction of Milo Fernandez.

"*Yo!*"

"Let's take a break."

Roy stuck a Winston in his mouth and lit it. He eased his broad butt down onto a boulder that looked reasonably dry. Milo Fernandez, neat and slim in his uniform, pushed through the wet underbrush and joined him.

The younger man looked up at the patches of sky they could see through the thick tops of the pine and Douglas fir trees.

"Not more than an hour of daylight left," said Milo.

"Yeah."

"You think we'll find those guys before dark?"

"Craddock and Vane? No way. Not before dark, not before Easter Sunday. They gotta be lost before we can find them. Those two ain't lost. Shitfaced somewhere, maybe, but not lost."

"How do you know?"

" 'Cause I know them two assholes. Why Betty Craddock wants us to find Abe beats the shit out of me. Best thing that could happen to her, he falls down in the middle of S31 and gets run over by an RV."

"Well . . . we can give it a try, anyway."

"Sure. Old college try. You go to college, tiger?"

"Junior college, actually. I need two more years for a degree."

"Waste of time. You want to be a cop, don't you?"

Milo Fernandez nodded.

"They not gonna teach you that in college. Only way to learn about being a cop is to be one."

Roy was about to launch into a war story from his days as a real cop in Oakland, but the young deputy's attention strayed.

Milo looked around at the dark, dripping trees. "Roy, where's Drago from here?"

Nevins pointed off toward the south. "That way. Four, five miles."

"I'd like to see it sometime."

"Nothing to see. Dozen or so burned-out buildings."

"What was it like, Roy? The fire and all. Was it exciting?"

Roy shrugged. He pulled on his Winston, coughed, spat on the ground. "Sure, if you get off on poking through ashes trying to make out which is human and which is . . . something else."

The young trainee caught the older deputy's hesitation and looked at him quickly. Roy studied the glowing tip of his cigarette and stopped talking.

Milo Fernandez looked off toward the south as though trying to see the burned-out village through five miles of forest. "What do you think was going on there, Roy? At Drago? Before the fire?"

"Who knows? Cult of some kind. Los Angeles types. The people living there never went much outside their own village."

"There were stories."

"Yeah, I heard the stories. Bunch of crap."

"Not human, people said."

"Crap."

"There was howling, they say. In the woods. At night."

"So what? There's lots of funny noises in the woods at night."

"People still heard things out here after the fire. After everybody in Drago was burned up."

"Look, amigo, some other time we'll sit around a campfire and scare the shit out of each other with ghost stories. I'm not in the mood now, okay?"

"Sure, Roy. I'm just curious."

Something rustled the bushes up ahead. The two deputies

8

raised their heads, listening. They looked at each other, then back toward the sound.

"Who's there?" Roy Nevins called.

Silence.

Another rustle of brush.

"Craddock . . . ? Vane . . . ?"

No answer. A flash of movement. A head rose above a clump of brush twenty feet ahead of the two deputies. A face looked at them. A pale face streaked with mud. Dark, matted hair. Eyes wild, with lots of white showing.

"Hey!"

The face ducked out of sight. Squishy sound of running feet on the wet ground.

"Son of a bitch." Roy mashed the Winston out under his shoe and took off. Milo was already ahead of him, chasing the fleeing figure, who ducked and weaved among the trees.

The runner left the trail and fought through the undergrowth. The two deputies followed. Roy Nevins swore as the thorns clutched at him and mud seeped over the tops of his shoes.

"Halt!" Milo Fernandez called out. "Sheriff's officers!"

Roy pounded on, the breath wheezing through his open mouth. He fumbled at the leather strap that snapped to the holster over the butt of his .38 police positive. Regulation. Never could free the damn thing in a hurry. The hell with it. Firing your piece only meant trouble these days. You had to account for every fucking bullet. Nothing in sight to shoot at anyway. He could only catch glimpses of Milo's back as the young deputy charged after the fleeing figure.

There was a thump of colliding bodies up ahead and a damp thud as they hit the ground. Roy floundered through the brush and almost fell over Milo. The young deputy was applying an armlock to the fugitive, who lay prone on the damp pine needles.

"I got him, Roy."

9

"So I see. Suppose you flip him over so we can see what we got."

Milo warily eased his hold. When the figure on the ground did not move, he grasped a shoulder and turned him over.

"A kid," Roy said disgustedly.

The face that looked up at the deputies was pale and frightened. Oddly, he seemed not to be breathing hard.

"What'd you take off for?" Deputy Nevins said.

The large, frightened eyes flicked from one of the deputies to the other. The boy made no attempt to answer.

"Get up."

The boy rose to a crouch.

"And don't think about running anymore. We're taking a ride into town."

Nevins took the boy's arm and raised him to a standing position. The muscles were firm under the smooth flesh. He gestured with his head for Milo to get going. The younger deputy was staring at the boy's face.

"Let's go," Nevins said. "I want to get him back to the car before it gets dark. What's the matter?"

Milo Fernandez hesitated. "Take a look. There's something funny about his teeth."

Chapter 2

The room on the second floor of La Reina County Hospital was pleasant and bright. Outside the window of the small private room a night bird sang. The boy sat propped in the bed in a half-sitting position. His green eyes skipped around the room as though searching for an escape.

Holly Lang stood at the foot of the bed and smiled down at him. She was tall and supple, with short dark hair and hazel eyes. Her smile was good, and it usually made other people smile in response. But the boy's expression did not change.

"Well, you look a little better now that you're all cleaned up," she said.

The boy's eyes flicked over her and away.

"How are you feeling?" she asked.

No answer.

"A little scared, I guess." Holly kept her tone soft and conversational. "I don't blame you. Hospitals can be scary. My name's Holly. Do you want to tell me yours? It's all right if you don't. There's no hurry."

The boy's fingers moved restlessly on the edge of the sheet.

11

"I'm a kind of a doctor."

The green eyes met hers for an instant.

"Not the kind that sticks people with needles," she said quickly. "Mostly, I just talk. And I listen, too, if you want to talk to me."

The boy turned away and stared through the window at the dark trees. His expression told Holly nothing.

Holly waited, watching his face. "What happened to you out there?" she said, more to herself than to the boy. "What's haunting you now?"

La Reina County Hospital had more the look of an expensive mountain resort than an institution. It was tucked into the picturesque wooded hillside overlooking the town of Pinyon. Behind it the Tehachapi Mountains rose from gently sloping foothills. The facilities and the equipment at La Reina were excellent, courtesy of the California taxpayers. The same could not be said of the staff.

Somehow La Reina County Hospital had become caught in the backwash of bureaucracy and was known as a haven for medical misfits. Med school graduates from the lower third of their class found a home there. Doctors with a questionable past, nurses with borderline records . . . these made up the staff at La Reina County.

There were always more beds than patients in residence. The administration lived in fear that during one of the periodic budget battles in Sacramento someone would ask why the hell they needed a hospital down there at all. The funds would be cut off and a lot of people would be out of work. Somehow, the budget checkers in Sacramento kept missing it.

Dr. Hollanda Lang, known to everyone as Holly, did not belong with the staff misfits. She had passed up a lucrative private practice as a clinical psychologist to work for the state Social Services Department. When people asked her why, she told them she was absolving her liberal guilt.

12

Holly found it embarrassing to admit how deeply she cared about helping people.

And La Reina appealed to her precisely because of its quirky reputation. Her opinion of the medical establishment was not high, and here among the outcasts she found some original thinkers she could relate to. Her one disappointment had been in the lack of challenge in her cases. Until they brought in the boy from the woods.

Holly looked down at the pale boy now, wondering what it would take to communicate with him. In the two hours since he'd been brought in, the boy had not spoken. She had finally gotten the curious onlookers cleared out of the room and felt the boy was at least beginning to relax with her.

There was a sound at the door behind her. She turned, annoyed at the interruption.

Sheriff Gavin Ramsay stuck his head into the room.

"All right if I come in?"

"Could I stop you?"

"Sure. Just say go away."

Holly felt the muscles tighten at the back of her neck. She knew her aversion to police was an unreasonable throwback to her campus protest days, but she couldn't help it. "Come on in," she said.

Ramsay nodded to her. "Thanks, Miss Lang. I'll make this as short as I can."

"It's Doctor."

"Oh, right. Dr. Lang. Sorry."

She made herself relax. "That sounded pompous, didn't it? Shall we try first names? I'm Holly."

"Gavin," he said.

Not a bad-looking man, Holly decided, if you liked the macho type. Sort of a younger Marlboro Man. She had seen him around Pinyon and thought it was a pity that he had to be a policeman.

"How's the kid?" he asked.

"Doing well enough."

13

"Has he said anything yet?"

Holly looked quickly at the young patient. The green eyes regarded the sheriff warily.

"We're just getting acquainted," she said. "So far I've done all the talking."

"I'd like to ask him a few questions."

The boy seemed to shrink a little in the bed.

"Suppose we step out into the hall," Holly said.

"Sure."

She followed Ramsay out through the door and looked up at him when he turned. Holly was five-eight in her stocking feet, and well built. Not many men could make her feel small. Gavin Ramsay could, and she resented it.

"I wish you'd give me some warning before you barge into the room."

"Sorry. The door was ajar."

"Well . . . no harm done, I suppose."

"I'm relieved to hear that."

"You must understand it's part of my job to keep my patient from being disturbed."

"Fair enough," Ramsay said, "but you've got your job and I've got mine."

"I'm not sure I understand."

"I've got a couple of hunters missing and a dead man downstairs in the pathology lab."

"What has that to do with this boy?"

"I don't know that there's any connection, but I want to find out. From the looks of the kid when they brought him in, he was out in the woods for at least three days. That's about how long our man downstairs has been a corpse."

"You're not suggesting that this boy has anything to do with it?"

Ramsay's eyes flashed blue fire. "Why not, because he's a minor? Last week a twelve-year-old in East Los Angeles set his mother on fire because she found his heroin stash. A seven-year-old girl in Beverly Hills drowned her baby

14

brother in the swimming pool because he got too much attention. Two boys in Glendale hung a baby girl from a swing set. The boys were six. Want to hear more?''

''No, thank you. I'll concede that there is no age limit on criminal behavior, but I won't jump to the conclusion that this boy is guilty of anything.''

''Holly . . . Dr. Lang . . . all I want to do is talk to him.'' Gavin raised his arms. ''See, I didn't even bring any handcuffs.''

''Well, he isn't talking yet. He's had a frightening experience, and it may take a while. Shouldn't you be trying to find out who he is?''

''I should and I am. I've put his description out on the wire. So far he doesn't fit any missing-boy report.'' Gavin looked back over her shoulder into the room. ''You will let me know if he says anything?''

''Certainly, Sheriff.''

He started to go, then turned back. ''Is there any chance we can get back to using first names?''

She held a stern expression for a moment longer, then relaxed. ''What the hell. . . . See you, Gavin.''

''See you, Holly.''

The boy's eyes followed her as she came back and sat in the chair next to the bed. She smiled at him, studying his face. The two deputies who brought him in had said there was something ''weird'' in the way he looked. Probably a trick of twilight and their imaginations. Holly saw only a frightened boy of perhaps fourteen. High forehead, straight nose, firm mouth. The eyes were a deep, lustrous green. Certainly nothing there that could be considered ''weird.''

''Getting sleepy?'' she said.

The boy's head rolled from side to side on the pillow.

A response. The first sign he had given that he understood. Holly kept her voice gentle. ''I'll just sit here for a while, then. If you feel like talking, fine. If not, that's fine, too.''

The boy's eyes never left her. Holly thought she could see his body relax, just a little, under hospital sheet and blanket. She picked up a magazine from the bedside table and pretended to read. She did not leave until she was sure the boy was asleep.

Chapter 3

During the next three days Holly spent many hours at the boy's bedside. She could not coax him to speak, but his face brightened when she came into the room, and she was cheered by the small sign of recognition. They watched television together and listened to music. Holly talked about whatever came into her mind, and read to the boy from the books and magazines in the hospital library.

On the morning of the third day the administrative chief of staff met her outside the boy's room. Dr. Dennis Qualen was a soft-faced man with steely gray hair. He was always careful about his diction, as though he were being recorded.

"So, Dr. Lang, how is it going?"

"We're making progress."

"Really?"

"That sounds like you have doubts."

"No, no, perhaps our definitions of progress differ. I've read the reports and can find no indication that there is anything wrong with the boy."

"Nothing physical."

"Exactly. Which leaves us with mental illness."

"Let's say psychological trauma."

"Terminology aside, have you considered turning the boy's case over to someone better equipped than we to handle him?"

"Who did you have in mind?"

"The State Youth Authority, for instance."

"That's for juvenile criminals."

"I understand from Sheriff Ramsay that there is a very good chance this boy might fit into that category."

"There is no evidence of that."

"Perhaps not, but I must consider the best course for the hospital."

"And I have to consider the patient. Listen, Doctor, I've seen cases like this before—loss of the power of speech due to some psychic trauma. If you give me another week, I'm sure I can show you marked improvement."

"A week is out of the question."

"Doctor, believe me, I can help this boy if I'm just given the time."

Dr. Qualen fingered the medical school emblem on his tie clasp. "You may have two days."

"I could do much more in a week."

"Two days. After that the boy will be turned over to the Youth Authority. I cannot take a chance on him becoming violent."

Without waiting for further discussion, Dr. Qualen spun and marched away down the hallway. Holly suppressed an urge to give him the finger. She went into the boy's room.

He was sitting up waiting for her.

"Hi," she said. "Sleep well?" She looked over at the vertical window. It was cranked open three inches to the tough mesh screen outside. "Fresh air always helps me sleep. But then, I guess you've had all the fresh air you want for a while."

Holly pulled her chair over to the bed and sat down. "I want you to do something for me today. I want you to think about the time you spent out there. No, don't turn away from me. It's important now that you think about it. Then maybe we can talk.''

Before she could go any further, Dr. Wayne Pastory sailed into the room. He wore his white jacket over a pale yellow Izod Lacoste shirt. He touched the glossy black hair he was so proud of, which he wore combed straight back in a style of the past.

''Well, well, well, so this is the wild boy I've been hearing about. How are we doing, fella?''

Holly glared at him. She did not like anything about Wayne Pastory. With his sharp features and bright little eyes and the quick way he moved, he reminded her of a weasel. She didn't like his reputation either. He had been kicked out of a genetic research project at Stanford for faking the results of an experiment. No charges had been made, but Pastory's name had gone on an informal medical blacklist.

He walked over to the bed and reached down. The boy shied away from his hand.

''What's the matter, son? I just want to check your pulse.''

''His pulse is normal, Doctor,'' Holly said, trying to keep the irritation out of her voice. ''So are his temperature and blood pressure. It's all on the chart.''

''Good. If you'll stand by, I'd like to look him over.''

''I am not a nurse,'' Holly said, spacing her words carefully.

Pastory studied her, his mouth quirked in a private smile. ''Sorry, Doctor. I meant that you and I would make the examination together, of course.''

''The examination has been completed.''

Pastory stroked the end of the gold Cross pen that peeked out of his jacket pocket. ''Aren't you being overprotective of this patient, Doctor?''

''I don't think so.''

''Have you given any thought to what we have here?''

"What we have is a boy who's been through a terrifying experience. A boy who could use some rest and quiet."

"What we have," Pastory went on, ignoring her, "just might be the first survivor from Drago."

"There's no reason to assume he's from Drago," Holly said. But over Pastory's shoulder she saw the little muscles tighten around the boy's mouth.

"But the possibility does exist," Pastory said. "And think what this could mean to us if he is one of the Drago people. No one really knows what happened there. If we were to produce a flesh-and-blood survivor . . . the opportunities would be limitless."

"You're thinking of taking him on the Johnny Carson show?"

"Of course not. I'm speaking strictly of the importance to medical research."

"Doctor, this is just a lost, frightened boy."

"Maybe, but I read the report of the deputies who brought him in. They mentioned some facial peculiarities."

"Take a look at him," Holly said. "Do you see anything peculiar?"

They both looked down at the boy in the bed.

Holly felt a sudden chill. Did the hair grow a fraction lower on the boy's forehead than a moment ago? And his eyebrows . . . she did not remember them being so heavy. And was there a new hardening around his mouth? She looked away for an instant, then back at the boy. The impressions faded. She must not let Pastory plant suggestions in her mind.

Pastory leaned down over the bed. "I don't know," he said slowly. "There's . . . something."

"He's tired," Holly said. "I think you'd better leave us."

"Are you in charge here, Doctor?"

"Until I'm told differently."

For a moment the two faced each other. Pastory was the first to look away. "I'll be back," he said.

With a last searching look at the boy, he left the room.

Holly turned back to the bed. What was it she had found strange about his face a moment ago? He looked normal enough now. Just a poor confused boy.

The hopeful mood in which Holly had begun the day was dissipated by the encounters with Qualen and Pastory. The boy had withdrawn once again, and she was sitting at his bedside feeling discouraged when Gavin Ramsay stopped by.

"Got time to talk?"

Holly glanced at the boy, who had fallen into a light sleep. "Aren't you supposed to read me my rights or something?"

"Hey, I'm just trying to be sociable."

"Were you being sociable when you told Dennis Qualen we had a dangerous criminal here?"

"He's the chief of staff; he's entitled to know what I'm doing here. However, that's not quite the way I put it to him."

Holly drew in a breath and let it out slowly. "Sorry. This day hasn't begun well for me. Not your fault." She got out of the chair. "There's a patients' lounge at the end of the hall with a coffee machine. I'll buy."

They walked to the lounge, which was brightly furnished with comfortable chairs, checkerboards, card tables, and a pinball machine. An old man in a wheelchair stared at the television set, where a game show was silently in progress. The old man did not seem to miss the sound.

Holly dropped coins into the machine. It spilled a stream of brackish-looking coffee into two plastic cups. They carried the cups over to a table and sat down.

"Any word yet on who he is?" Holly asked.

"Nope. As far as I know, he might have stepped off a flying saucer."

"That's not very funny."

"You're right, it isn't."

They sat for a minute sipping at the hot brew, not saying anything. Holly watched him over the rim of her plastic cup. Finally she said, "Can I ask you a question?"

"Ask," he said.

"What are you doing here, anyway?"

"Waiting for your kid to snap out of his trauma so I can ask him what he was doing out in the woods."

"No, I mean what are you doing here in Pinyon?"

"Everybody's got to be somewhere."

"Are you happy being sheriff of a county with a population that could fit into a high school gym?"

"Sure. Why not?"

"There was talk a while back about you running for governor."

"Any such talk was strictly the fantasy of my ex-wife and my ex-father-in-law.

"Forrest Ingraham."

Ramsay gave her a long look. "That's the man. What else do you know about me?"

"Oh, a little. You went to Willamette University, enlisted, of all things, in the army, fought in Viet Nam, won some medals, came home, went to law school, married Forrest Ingraham's daughter, were elected sheriff, got a divorce."

"That sure covers the high spots. Don't I have any secrets?"

"Lots, I'll bet. They're none of my business. I just wonder why you stay here."

"I like it. Oh, I've had other offers. From the police departments in Cleveland, Buffalo, and Jersey City. Would you leave La Reina County for any of those?"

"I suppose not," she said, laughing softly.

"Well, then."

"Why do you have to be a policeman? Do you get some kind of kick out of it?"

His expression hardened. "Sure. I get off on clubbing down peace-marching college kids and locking up widows who can't pay their rent."

"Oh-oh, did I touch a nerve?"

"You're damn right. You ACLU types who spit out *policeman* like something that tastes bad give me a pain in the ass." He paused for a deep breath. "Sorry. We'd better get off this before I go into one of Jack Webb's old *Dragnet* speeches."

"I guess we aren't ready for a personal conversation."

"I guess not," he said.

They got up and dropped their cups into a trash container near the door.

"Just one thing," she said. "I don't belong to the ACLU."

"Nobody's perfect," he said.

Holly's breakthrough with the boy came that night while she sat in the chair next to his bed. She snapped off the television set after *The Love Boat*.

"I don't know about you," she said, "but I'm tired." She tucked the sheets in around the boy and smiled down at him. "See you in the morning." She paused in the doorway and looked back. In a talking-to-herself voice she said, "Damn, I wish I knew what to call you."

"I'm Malcolm." It was a dry croak, barely more than a whisper, but to Holly it was like a shout.

"Malcolm?" she repeated, trying not to sound too excited.

He nodded.

"That's a good name. Do you remember mine?"

The green eyes watched her.

"It's Holly," she said. "Holly Lang."

"Holly," the boy said in the same dry whisper.

"That's right. Do you have a last name, Malcolm?"

The boy looked confused.

"Well, that doesn't matter now. We have one name. That's enough to start with. Do you want to talk some more?"

The boy's eyes drifted off to a corner of the ceiling.

"That's all right," she said. "You get some sleep, and tomorrow we'll start fresh."

Malcolm looked back at her and nodded again. Holly left the room, elated.

She was in early the next day, eager to begin with Malcolm, but as she passed the reception desk the young woman there called her over.

"Dr. Qualen said for you to come to his office as soon as you got in."

Holly frowned. "Did he say what for?"

"Not to me."

Dr. Qualen stood up behind his rich mahogany desk and greeted Holly formally. "Ah, Dr. Lang. Good of you to stop by. I won't take much of your time."

She hid her impatience, waiting for him to get to the point.

"How are things going with the boy?"

"I've learned that his name is Malcolm."

"I see. Not what we'd call a significant breakthrough."

"That depends. I still have today."

"I wonder if perhaps another approach might speed things up."

"Apparently Dr. Pastory has talked to you."

"As a matter of fact, he has. He tells me you were rather abrupt with him yesterday."

"I was ticked off. He was upsetting my patient."

24

"The very point I wanted to make. The boy is not officially anyone's patient. As I told you, I am not convinced that the case falls under our jurisdiction."

"I remember. You mentioned the Youth Authority."

"That remains an option; however, Dr. Pastory has some thoughts of his own on the boy."

"What does he want to do, dissect him?"

"That's not very professional, Doctor."

"No, I suppose it isn't. I'm sorry. Is the case still mine, at least through today?"

"Yes, of course. I hope there won't be any more friction between you and Dr. Pastory."

"I'll do my best."

"Fine, fine. I'm glad we had this little talk."

Holly swallowed her opinion of their little talk and left the office.

The boy was waiting for her.

"Good morning, Malcolm."

The boy turned away from Aquaman on television and looked at her. "Good morning, Holly."

"You remembered my name."

"I always knew it."

"Well, good." She came over and sat down. "Today let's see what else you can remember."

A tiny frown line creased the boy's brow.

"Don't worry. I'm not going to hook you up to a machine or give you shots or anything like that. We're just going to relax and talk."

Gavin Ramsay stuck his head in the door. "Is it safe to say good morning?"

"Hi, Gavin," Holly said. "Come on in and meet Malcolm."

Ramsay gave her a brief questioning look, then came into the room and walked to the foot of the bed.

"Hi," he said to the boy.

Holly said, "Malcolm, this is Sheriff Ramsay."

The boy looked to Holly for reassurance, then back at Gavin. "Hello, Sheriff."

Ramsay stuck out a hand. The boy took it and they shook hands gravely.

"Glad to see you're talking again, son."

"We were just about to find out what else Malcolm can remember."

"Oh?"

"I thought we might try hypnotism. Do you know what hypnotism is, Malcolm?"

"You put somebody to sleep."

"Not exactly. It's just a way to relax and let things come back that we misplaced somewhere."

"Does it hurt?"

"Not a bit. In fact, a lot of people say it makes them feel better. Do you want to try it?"

The boy looked at Ramsay. "Is he going to stay?"

"Not if you don't want him to."

Malcolm considered for a moment. "It's all right; he can stay."

Ramsay pulled a chair back against the far wall and sat down out of the way.

"Now, Malcolm," Holly began, "I want you to take three deep, deep breaths. All the way in and all the way out. That's good." She breathed in and out with him. So did Ramsay. "I bet you're feeling more relaxed and comfortable already. I know I am." She spoke in a low, soothing tone.

"We're going to start our relaxing way down there with the tips of your toes. Think about your toes. Do you have a picture of them in your mind? Now if you try, you can feel them start to tingle and relax, one at a time. Little toe first, then the next, and the next, and the next, and now the big toe. Doesn't that feel good? Nice and comfortable. Now

26

your feet, Malcolm. Relax your feet and let that nice warm feeling flow slowly up your ankles. It's like easing your legs into a tub of nice warm water. So comfortable . . . so relaxed . . ."

Ramsay was leaning back, enjoying the relaxed, comfortable feeling in his legs, when Milo Fernandez stuck his head through the door and hissed at him.

"Sheriff . . . hey, Sheriff."

Holly looked over and put a finger to her lips. Ramsay got up and stepped out into the hall. In a moment he returned and spoke softly to Holly.

"I've got to go."

"Trouble?"

"It could be. I'll talk to you later."

When he was gone Holly turned back to Malcolm, who sat propped against the pillows, a dreamy expression on his face.

"All right, Malcolm, let's go back now into the forest. There are trees all around. Tall and cool. A soft wind is blowing, making the branches sway and rustle. Let's go back there and remember, Malcolm. Listen to the sounds. Sniff the air. Remember the forest. . . ."

Chapter 4

Memories of the forest came back to him in fragments.
The cushiony feel of pine needles under his feet.
A whisper of rain in the high branches of the trees.
Dappled sunlight filtering down on a summer afternoon.
Fresh smells of evergreen and of flowers.
Nightsounds: monotonous song of a tree frog, the hoot of
an owl, the cry of some small creature caught in its talons.

A childhood in the forest village of Drago, with carefree
days, deep, dark nights, surrounded by people whose faces
were blurred now in memory but who loved him and cared
for him.

Then, without any warning, childhood ended. The years
that followed were a jumble of strange schools, narrow
beds, cold faces of people who were paid to teach him and
feed him and give him a place to sleep. The memories were
jagged, like pieces of a broken mirror. A face, a school-
book, a forbidding house in a strange town. Nothing fit together. It was a lost time.

Then the lost time was over and he was back. Back in the
forest. Back in Drago. But it was not the same. The days
were troubled, and the nights full of danger. Malcolm was

apart from the others of the village. They possessed some secret knowledge that had been withheld from him. Knowledge wondrous and terrible, knowledge he must have. This much he learned when he was brought before Derak, the leader of the village.

Malcolm could not even guess at the age of Derak. Not old, certainly. Not in years. Yet it seemed he had always been there. Derak was strong and vigorous, but there was in his eyes something older than time.

The house where Derak lived was small. It was his alone. The other people of Drago lived in groups—four or six or eight of them to a house. Derak lived alone because he was the leader.

Sometimes a woman stayed there with him. Malcolm seemed to remember a woman from before. When he was little. The woman was dark and lithe and smelled of warm wildflowers. Her eyes were the same deep shade of green as Malcolm's. She was gone now. He wondered about her, but he was too timid to ask.

Malcolm felt ill at ease sitting alone with Derak on a sofa in the small house. He perspired, and he did not know what to do with his hands. Derak smiled. When he spoke, his voice was soft, but Malcolm could sense the strength within the man. A strength that could have broken Malcolm like a dry twig, had he wanted to do so.

"Relax, boy," said Derak, as though he had read Malcolm's thoughts. "I'm not going to hurt you. No one here will hurt you. This is your home. Do you understand that?"

"Y-yes."

"Good. I suppose you want to know why you have been brought back."

"I don't even know why I was sent away."

"It is the way of our life. You have seen, I suppose, that there are no children in Drago, except the very young."

"Yes."

"You, too, were here when you were very young."

29

"I remember. A little bit."

"A child reaches an age where he asks questions. Questions with answers he is not ready for. When that time comes we have to send him away. To the outside, where he can learn about the world out there. When he is ready to know about us and about Drago, we bring him back."

"Am I ready now to know those things?"

Derak smiled at him. A strange, sad smile. "You are more than ready, Malcolm."

"I don't understand."

"Have things been happening to you? To your body? Things you can't explain?"

"Y-yes. Sometimes . . . in the night."

"It is usually in the night at first. Or when you are afraid. Or hurt. Or very angry. We always try to bring the child back and explain these things to him before the changes occur. Because of troubles here, we could not bring you back at your proper time. So you are late, Malcolm, through no fault of your own. You have already experienced some of the things that will happen to you, things that you cannot understand."

"Will there be more?"

"Oh, yes. Much, much more."

The boy's throat constricted with a rush of emotions. Finally he got out, "Why?"

"It will all be explained to you, Malcolm. Who you are, what you are. What we all are, and what our lives must be."

"When?"

"Tomorrow. There is a ceremony. Nothing big, just our people—your people—gathering around you to show you our secrets and teach you our ways. You will spend tonight alone. After tomorrow, you will know who you are, and you will never be alone again."

"Why do I have to wait? Why can't we do it now?"

Derak looked out the window at the deepening shadows. "Tonight there is something else we have to do. After tomorrow all of our lives will be changed. You will join us then.''

There was a finality in Derak's tone that would permit no further discussion. Malcolm was taken to a small cabin at the edge of the village. There was a low cot of wood and canvas with a woolen blanket, a single candle for illumination, and nothing more. The door closed behind Malcolm, and he was alone.

He could hear them outside, the people of Drago, as they walked toward the big building at the center of the village. The big building was sometimes a barn and sometimes a meeting hall. And there were times of celebration when the people danced and the music was something to hear. Tonight there was no music. The voices of the people as they walked were somber and subdued. Malcolm lay awake, shivering, on the stretched canvas of the cot and waited.

Inside the building Derak stood in the center of the wooden floor. The others entered and took their places in a circle around the leader. The quiet talk among them faded and finally died as they waited for Derak to speak.

''My friends . . . my family. We have lived in Drago without trouble for many years. Longer than our people might have hoped when first they settled here. Our history is not one of places, it is one of movement. From the Carpathians to the Urals to the Andes. From the icy lands of the far north to the steaming jungles of the equator. Always there comes a time when we are forced to move on. Here in Drago we have lived well, but it is over. Now we must move again. There are people, outsiders, who suspect what we are. They fear us, and in their fear they will try to destroy us. As always before, that means we must go.''

Derak turned slowly and looked at the people ranged around him in a circle. Shadows from the flickering lanterns danced and skittered over their faces.

''But before we go,'' Derak said, ''we will give them something to remember.''

31

And he began to change.

Derak tore the shirt from his back and flexed the powerful muscles of his shoulders. His chest swelled and cracked as the bony structure within reshaped itself. His lips drew back to show the strong yellow teeth. The killing teeth.

Around him the others followed the lead of Derak. They threw off their clothes while their bodies twisted and stretched in a jerking dance of metamorphosis. The faces, human a moment before, thinned and lengthened. The ears grew, the noses pushed forward into muzzles. Short, coarse hair sprouted on their bodies. The hair spread, thickened into fur. The human voices became low, muttering growls. And there was the howling.

Malcolm sat suddenly upright on his cot in the small cabin. The candle flame guttered and died in a whisper of the night wind that seeped through cracks in the walls. The voices howling in the night were strange and frightening, yet they touched something deep within the boy. They spoke to him in a language he did not know. They called him. He longed to go to them.

Then there were other sounds. The scrape of heavy booted feet, a crunch of brush, muttered curses. Malcolm began to sweat. He stared into the darkness, fearful of something he could not define.

Inside the barn of a building, they heard the other sounds too late. There was a heavy scrape and a thud as the door was barred from the outside. Those within froze for a moment in wild attitudes of change . . . half-human, half-beast. They sniffed the air and caught the scent of men outside, then the biting odor of raw gasoline. An instant later in a blast of heat and light, the barn was afire.

Panic.

Three ways a werewolf can die. By a weapon of silver. By fire. And a third way that was never spoken of. The fire was all around them, and the fire was death.

Inside the barn was hell. Humans, wolves, creatures in all

32

stages between, stumbled into the beams and crashed the blistering walls, searching for an escape. Their voices mingled in an outcry of agony and rage. Twisted muzzles pushed through the boards of the walls for air but were seared and sizzled by the flames outside. Claws scratched frantically at the wood. The men with the torches had done their work well. The building was surrounded by a wall of flame.

Some of the creatures in the barn broke through to the outside, their misshapen bodies afire, and ran till they dropped in a blazing, screaming heap. The men with the torches watched grimly as they died.

Most stayed inside the building. They huddled together as the flames leaped up the walls and across the roof. Their terrible jaws gaped in helpless rage. The blazing roof fell, and the screaming stopped.

But not all of them died. A few got away. A few always get away.

At the sound of the agonized howling and the furnace blast of the burning barn, Malcolm bolted from his cot and stumbled out into the inferno that had been his village. Men ran from house to house with cans of gasoline and blazing torches. One after another they were set afire.

For long minutes Malcolm stood in frozen horror. The shrieks of the dying were all around him. The smell of the dead made him retch. His body twitched and jumped of its own volition. The smells around him were keener, his night vision sharper than ever in his life. The message was clear in his mind.

Run!

And Malcolm ran. Away from the carnage of Drago. He was faster and stronger than ever he dreamed he could be. The forest was his as he loped through the brush, darting among the trees, leaping easily over any obstruction. Faster and faster he ran, putting the night and the forest between him and the blazing ruin of Drago. He ran in a deep crouch, his hands sometimes clutching at the ground, helping to pull him along. In the midst of his grief at the loss of his village and his people, Malcolm felt something else. Freedom. Freedom and power.

On the other side of the burned-out village, on the crest of hill, a huge, wolflike figure looked down on the dying flames. Its fur was singed, and a ragged gash from a splintered board ran the length of the animal's side. The wound would soon heal. The anger would remain.

If he had escaped, there would be others. To help them survive, he must find them and bring them together. He was the leader.

Derak pointed his muzzle to the sky. The cruel teeth gleamed in the moonlight. He tested the air. There was the acrid smell of burning flesh and fur. The bite of gasoline. The sweat stink of the men. And there was the familiar scent of the others, those who had escaped . . . and somewhere in the night forest . . . his son.

Miles away, moving swiftly in the other direction, Malcolm paused and raised his head to listen to the howling.

Chapter 5

The forest took him in. It sheltered him from the night and hid him from the men who shouted and cursed as they crashed through the brush, searching out the few survivors of Drago. In the morning the shouts were farther away. The smell of smoke still hung in the air. The sun was a pale disk behind a curtain of cloud. Malcolm rested and realized he was terribly thirsty. His instinct was to cry, but he did not. Instead he set out to find water, and the forest showed him where to look. There were shallow pools from the last rain, hollowed-out stumps that held enough to drink, and half-hidden streams that a man could miss if he did not stop to look.

Food was easier. Pine nuts were plentiful, and there were wild blackberries and grapes. The leaves and stalks of goosefoot and the fleshy green purslane were tough and chewy, but they gave him nourishment. Sometimes he ate things that cramped his stomach and doubled him up in pain, but soon he learned which foods to avoid and which would give him the strength to go on.

But to go where? Everything that he had known was behind him, burned. Destroyed. Gone. He had no destination.

35

The days passed. And the nights. He stopped counting. Sometimes Malcolm could hear the men in the woods. They were still out there stalking him. And he could smell them. Smell the acrid sweat of the hunter. The men were clumsy in the woods, and slow-moving compared to the boy. Still, he could not risk discovery. The men had guns. Malcolm well remembered what the men had done to his village. To his people.

By night he moved, restlessly and without destination, sustained only by the conviction that he must keep moving. During the day, when he would be more easily seen by the searchers, he rested under a simple lean-to constructed of boughs. It was an aimless existence, and a gnawing ache grew in Malcolm's heart. Somewhere, he felt, there was a place for him, could he but find it.

The growing ache was not only in his heart. For the first time in his life Malcolm knew hunger. Real hunger. The edible plants he found in the forest—the berries, the roots, the bark stripped from tender saplings—these were enough to keep him alive, but he was never completely free from hunger. Hunger for meat. It was a pain that never left him. A pain that grew worse every day.

Then one morning in desperation he snatched at a squirrel that sat on a stump regarding him curiously. Malcolm was surprised at the ease with which he had caught the little creature. He killed it quickly, tore away the fur as best he could with his hands, and devoured it. He ripped the raw flesh from the tiny bones with his teeth. The meat was rank and tough, but it was better than bark.

Soon Malcolm discovered he was quick enough to run down and catch other small animals with his hands. Opossums, raccoons, once even a small deer. The streams were not deep enough to provide fish, but there were frogs to be taken. Malcolm's muscles grew lean and hard in his hunting exertions, his teeth white, his jaw strong enough to crack a bone.

There was no question of making a fire to cook the meat once he had caught it. Malcolm carried no matches, and a fire would surely attract the men. At first he had to force himself to gag down the raw meat, still warm from the living blood, but he learned. Before long, to his surprise, he liked it best that way.

The days stretched out, one indistinguishable from the next. During the nights he continued his aimless travels. Once he circled back to where the village of Drago had been. Nothing was left but ashes. Everything gone. Everyone dead. Malcolm never went back again.

And yet Malcolm sensed he was not alone. They were out there somewhere, others of his kind, running and hiding just as he was. He longed to find them, join them, but he did not know how. Sometimes in the night he could hear the howling. And he cried.

The nights grew colder. During the days it rained often. Malcolm learned to make a more sturdy shelter of evergreen boughs, overlapping them so the needles pointed downward and formed a runoff for the rainwater. He sat cramped for long, cold hours in his shelters, hugging his knees and shivering.

There were fewer men in the forest hunting him now. The danger was not as great, but it was still there. As the scent of the men grew fainter, Malcolm grew careless.

His misstep came on a stormy evening as he searched along the trail for the makings of a shelter. He was hurrying, hunched against the rain. Still, had Malcolm been alert as he normally was, it would never have happened. Before him on the trail was a patch of ground covered with leaves. He should have seen that the leaves lay in an unnatural pattern. But this time he did not look before he stepped.

For a moment he did not know what had happened to him. There was a frightful crunching sound and searing pain shot up through his right leg. He fell heavily to the ground. The pain tore at him like fiery claws. On sheer instinct he tried to

37

scramble to his feet, but the leg would not bear his weight. And something was holding it. Something heavy.

When he looked down, there below the tattered end of his pant leg he saw the steel jaws gripping his ankle. The flesh of his lower leg was shredded, and pinkish-white shards of bone jabbed out through skin. Blood seeped into the cracked leather of his shoe. He tried to move his foot. The grinding sound was almost worse than the new flash of pain. He fainted.

The night was an endless agony with long, dark periods of tortured dreams and stretches of consciousness during which he tried to rip his foot free of the steel trap. Clouds rolled down from the mountains and opened in great torrents of icy rain. Thunder boomed and echoed in the hills. Lightning streaked the sky where it was visible through the treetops.

Malcolm thrashed about on the ground in delirium. While his mind whirled, strange things happened to his body. Once he brought his hands to his face and in a blaze of lightning he saw the pads and claws of an animal. Or did he dream that? Reality blurred as the pain took possession of him.

The storm thundered and crashed through the night, then faded. The dawn was bleak and damp. A steady rain continued to fall. Malcolm awoke slowly in a fever, and for an instant he did not know where he was nor how he had come there. He should be in a warm bed, not out freezing in the forest. Then the pain hit him again, clearing his mind, and the memory of the terrible night came back. He shifted his position and the steel jaws ripped his flesh. The trap. He remembered the trap. But he forgot everything else when he looked up and saw the giant.

Well, maybe not a giant, but a big, big man. From Malcolm's point of view, lying there on the trail, the man loomed like a mountain. The wild beard and the hair that hung to his shoulders were a dark, fierce shade of red. One of his hands could have covered both of the boy's. His chest and shoulders were massive as granite. He wore tough, ragged jeans and a buckskin jacket. Even through his pain Malcolm felt fear, sensing the immense power in the big man's body. Then he saw the giant's eyes. They were brown and bright and immeasurably kind.

The giant knelt beside him. Malcolm saw the brown eyes narrow with reflected pain when he looked at the ruined ankle. When Malcolm tried to sit up, the giant pressed a strong, gentle hand on his forehead and eased him back down.

"You sure got yourself into a fix, son." The bass voice rumbled up from the deep caverns of the giant's chest. "You'd best lie still while I have a look."

He moved with uncommon grace for a man of his great size. He was careful to shield the ankle from Malcolm's eyes with his body as he examined it.

"Son of a bitch," the big man rumbled. "Steel teeth, double-spring. These mothers are illegal."

Malcolm winced as the big man's hand touched his foot.

"Easy, pardner. I know it hurts, but the first thing we've got to do is get this thing off you. It's going to hurt even more in a minute when I pry it loose, but there's no easy way to do it." He turned his head and the kind brown eyes looked down into Malcolm's. "How about it? Can you stand a little more hurt right now?"

Malcolm nodded.

"Good boy. Close your eyes for a minute. Close 'em real tight. Think about the happiest time you ever had."

Malcolm closed his eyes. He tried very hard to think of a happy time, as the big man had told him. But no thoughts would come. Only a blackness with fire and screams of the dying.

There was a loud metallic crack and another fiery shot of pain in his ankle. Malcolm's eyes snapped open. The big man knelt beside him now, holding the cruel steel trap in both hands.

"This is what grabbed you, son," he said. "Damned foul contraption." Then, as the muscles in his arms and shoulders bulged, he twisted the trap like the jaws of a shark until the end of a spring popped loose with a loud twang. He tossed the broken trap into the brush and returned his attention to the boy.

"You okay?"

Malcolm nodded, blinking back the tears. He was afraid to trust his voice, not wanting to show weakness before the big man.

"Ready to take a walk?"

Malcolm looked down helplessly at the mangled ankle. It was free now of the steel jaws, but the torn flesh had turned a puffy blue-black shade. The foot pointed down and back at an impossible angle.

The big man again shifted his body to cut off Malcolm's view of the ruined ankle. "Oh, I'll do the walking," he said. "It's going to jostle you a little bit, but we've got to get you out of here." He slipped his powerful arms beneath the boy and scooped him up as easily as though he'd been stuffed with feathers. The big man rose effortlessly to his feet and started along the trail.

"Feel like talking?" he said.

Malcolm tried, but the best he could do was a small whimpering sound.

"Don't blame you," said the man. "I'll do the talking, then. I'm accustomed to that. And you can listen. That'll be a rare treat for me. Have to talk to myself most of the time."

The big man strode easily through the brush, carrying Malcolm in such a way as to minimize movement of his ruined ankle. The rhythm of the man's pace lulled the boy into a semidoze. When he spoke, the big man's rumbling voice was comforting.

"My name is Jones," he said. "There used to be more to it, but I figure that doesn't matter, seeing as I'm the only one living out here, and not likely to be confused with anybody

40

else. The folks in town know who Jones is. The crazy hermit, some say. The last of the hippies. Nature Boy. I couldn't care less what they call me, just so they leave me alone.

"And they do. I been living out here almost twenty years. Never have trouble with people. If you never see them, you can't have trouble with them."

They continued for several minutes in silence before Jones spoke again. "Well, I do see a few people now and again. Hikers. Bird watchers. Lost kids sometimes. Hunters I have nothing to do with. When the animals start shooting back, then maybe I'll talk to hunters. Mostly I meet youngsters out backpacking. They remind me a little of myself back in the sixties. They're not as serious about things as my generation, maybe. More interested in getting a good job than banning the bomb, but I guess you can't blame them. It was a lot easier to get angry about a war if they were liable to draft you to go fight it.

"But there's nothing wrong with today's kids. Different values, that's all. Hell, most of the kids I went on protest marches with are working for IBM now, or somebody like that. Not Jones. I'm forty years old, ought to know better, but I still believe that if the world's going to be made better, it won't be the big corporations that do it. That's why they call me the crazy hermit."

Jones shouldered his way through a dense growth of scrub pine, and suddenly they were in a clearing. There was a neatly tended patch of grass, dotted with wildflowers. A smooth dirt path lead to a solid little cabin of rough logs. A wisp of blue smoke trailed from the chimney. A homey touch was added by soft curtains at the window.

"Be it ever so humble," Jones said, "this is it. There was a girl with me a few years back. Woman, I should say. She's responsible for the curtains. And the flowers. Used to be more of them, but I'm not so great at flower gardening. Veggies yes, flowers no. Her name was Beverly. Blond

41

hair, the longest legs you ever saw. Dedicated, too. Peace Corps. Save the whales. All that. Beverly thought she wanted to try the natural life. I was glad to oblige.''

"What happened to her?'' Malcolm's voice was weak and quavery. He had not used it in a long time.

"She moved out.'' Jones answered casually, as though they had been enjoying a two-way conversation all along. "Turned out the natural life wasn't quite what she thought it would be. The rain got to her, for one thing. She was a San Diego girl. Never in her life saw it rain more than two days running. Up here sometimes it'll rain for a month, more or less. Doesn't bother me, but Beverly about went crazy. Then there was the baby.''

"You had a baby?''

"We did. Little boy. Beverly wanted to name him Star Child, but I wouldn't go for that. I'm not that spacy. Held out for John. Honest name. Solid. Biblical, if you're into that. He'd be a couple years younger than you now. You got a name?''

"I . . .'' Malcolm's mind was suddenly empty, as though sucked clean by a giant vacuum. He was frightened. "I don't know.''

"Doesn't matter. With only the two of us, there won't be any confusion about who I'm talking to. Back in town they'll want to know, but maybe you'll remember by then.''

Jones carried the boy across the clearing to the door of the cabin. He pushed it open with his foot. Inside there were rough-hewn, comfortable-looking chairs, a table rescued from some thrift shop, sanded down and painted apple green, and a pair of army-style cots with stretched canvas on wooden frames. There was a cast-iron sink with a hand pump for water. On one wall was a stone fireplace with a great iron kettle simmering over the coals of a log fire. Whatever was in the kettle smelled wonderful.

"Beverly hadn't considered that living natural was going to mean no disposable diapers for John. No television to keep him occupied. No baby-sitter. She had to go all the way into Pinyon for the obstetrician. One day she just took him and left. Can't blame her. At least I did the kid one favor. I saved him from a life of being called Star Child.''

Jones carried Malcolm into the cabin and kicked the door shut behind him. It was warm inside. The aroma from the simmering kettle wrapped around them.

"Stew," Jones said. "Turnips, zucchini, tomatoes, wild onion, plantain. Care to try some?"

Malcolm bobbed his head, then winced in sudden pain.

"First we'd better see what we can do about that ankle. I'll clean it up for you now. By tomorrow morning this rain will stop and we'll hike into Pinyon and get it fixed up properly."

Jones eased the boy down onto one of the cots. He brought over a basin of water and a soft cloth. Very gently he sponged the wounded ankle, keeping up a running chatter about nothing in particular.

He held the boy's leg in his strong, gentle hands and studied the torn flesh. "Looks like you've got a little infection going there," he said. "I'm going to put some stuff on it now that will sting a little. I boil it down from pine bark and a few other things. It'll clean out the infection fast. Better than iodine for sure."

From a shelf over the sink Jones took down a tightly corked bottle. He poured out a thick brown liquid onto a wadded cloth. The concoction smelled of pitch. He sponged it generously on the boy's wounded ankle. And it did sting like fury, but Malcolm never let on that it hurt.

"That ought to get it," Jones said. He wrapped a length of clean white cloth around Malcolm's ankle and foot. He ripped one end to make long strips and tied them in a knot.

"Too tight?"

Malcolm shook his head.

"Okay. Now how about some stew?"

"I am pretty hungry."

43

"I'll bet you are."

Jones served up the hot stew in wooden bowls along with chunks of coarse bread. To drink there was a steaming, bitter herb tea. Malcolm ate until he could hold no more. The tea, once it was down, warmed him and made him drowsy. The big man helped him ease his shattered ankle up onto the cot and brought a fresh khaki blanket to cover him.

"Get some sleep now, son. We've got to be up early tomorrow."

The pain in Malcolm's foot eased and gradually drained away. He relaxed, enjoying the feeling of a full belly for the first time in many days. The warmth of the cabin and the deep shadows from the dying fire, the soft splash of rain above him on the roof, all combined to lull the boy into a long, deep, untroubled sleep.

Chapter 6

For long hours after the boy had fallen asleep Jones sat in one of the chairs in the cabin and watched the dying coals. The chair of wood and woven reeds creaked and settled comfortably under his weight. Outside the rainfall softened. It would be clear in the morning. Jones frowned, thinking about the boy he had found in the trap.

In the years he had spent alone in the woods he had brushed the lives of many people with many different backgrounds. This boy was not like the others. Something strange about him. Despite the boy's reticence, Jones could sense a danger that lurked somewhere deep inside him. Something to be feared. Something not quite natural.

The big man dug out an old corncob pipe, stuck it in his mouth unlit, and chewed meditatively on the stem. He had not smoked anything since his teen-age years, but it calmed him to chew on the old pipe. It helped him sort out his thoughts.

Tragic fact: the boy's foot was destroyed. No doctor living could save it. When he awoke Jones would give him another draft of the herb tea to keep him drowsy during the long trip they had to make into Pinyon. Jones was not worried about carrying the boy that far. He was confident of his own strength. But a certain amount of jostling would be unavoidable. His strength could not ease the boy's pain.

The kid had been exceedingly brave so far, but he was probably still in partial shock. When he fully realized the damage to his body, he would need a friend close by.

Jones eyes narrowed and his great shoulders bunched as he thought of the men who had set the deadly trap. He had not struck another human being in anger for more years than he could recall, but at that moment Jones would have happily ripped the trappers' limbs from their bodies.

The boy stirred in his sleep and mumbled something unintelligible. Jones got up and walked over to the cot. He laid his big hand on the boy's forehead. There was a fever, but less than it had been. Jones pulled the blanket up snug around the boy's shoulders and walked back to his chair.

The presence of the boy in his cabin brought back thoughts to Jones of his own son. Sometimes, not often, the big man let himself think about John. What he would look like now. What kind of a young man he would become.

John would now be, let's see, going on fourteen. That would put him in high school. Jesus, it was hard to think of that tiny, helpless human as a gawky teenager. Probably the boy would be living with his mother in some comfortable California suburb, if Jones correctly read the direction Beverly was going. He would have an upwardly mobile step-father who wore a three-piece suit to work and fired up the backyard barbecue on weekends. Well, what was wrong with that? What if John had stayed here? What kind of a life would he have had with a ragged hermit for a father, living in the woods?

"A damn good life, that's what," Jones muttered aloud. As he had many times in the past, Jones regretted that he had not fought to keep his son. Probably he would have lost, but at least he would have tried. He grunted and bit down hard on the pipestem, consigning the doubts to their place in the closed-off attic of his mind.

He got up again and laid a big chunk of fir on the coals. In a moment little flames licked tentatively up the bark. The log was still moist, and it would burn slowly. It would probably last till morning. Jones went back to his chair and sat down, listening to the sizzle and pop as the fire probed at the pitch pockets in the log. He closed his eyes and let himself dream.

As always, his dreams were of Beverly. In his heart he had known from the start that she was not for him. Living off the land had sounded to her like an adventure. Like the six months she spent in the Peace Corps, teaching the Tanzanians things they had no desire to know. She never really saw it as a true life-style.

She was happy enough in the commune, where there were other people around to sing folk songs with while they held hands in a big circle around a campfire. Having a shopping center with a big Safeway nearby didn't hurt, either. Jones tried it for a while, but that scene was not for him. Living in one of those hippie communes was like using somebody else's bathwater.

Then as now, Jones was his own man. He did not join movements or march for causes because it was trendy. He did it because he believed. And if he stopped believing, he stopped marching. Why lock yourself into something that no longer made sense?

Beverly, now, she had grabbed on to every hip liberal cause that came around. But if her beliefs did not run as deep as his, Jones didn't give a damn. She was so achingly beautiful it still brought a lump to his throat. He had loved her blindly and uncritically from the moment he had seen her sitting naked under the sun, her shining yellow hair spread like a veil down over those wonderful breasts.

Sexually, she had been everything a man could ask. Something out of an adolescent's erotic dreams. She knew

47

instinctively where he wanted to be touched and how. She could carry him to dizzying heights of desire, then, when he thought he must surely lose his mind, she would bring on his climax, prolonging it to a point where he lay drained, spent, helpless, and happier than a man should be.

Maybe once a month now Jones would go down to the bars around Saugus and Newhall and find a willing woman. There were always a few strays hanging around the bars. He stayed away from Pinyon. Too many people knew him there. He did not want a relationship; he wanted sex. And that was what the women he met in the bars provided. But even in those momentary bursts of passion he could never stop thinking of Beverly. Most of the time he figured it was just too much trouble to hike all the way to Saugus. Then he let his right hand be his woman.

Gradually his massive head fell forward, cushioned by the mat of red beard, and the giant slept.

He awoke at dawn, startled with the sense that something was not as it should be. Instantly he was on his feet. His eyes darted around the gloomy interior of the cabin until he spied the blanket-covered form on one of the cots. Then he re-membered. The boy.

While Jones watched, the boy stirred as though he could feel eyes upon him. He came fully awake all at once, like an animal sensing danger. From the boy's expression, Jones thought for a moment he would try to run out the door.

"Hey, easy, son. It's me, Jones, remember? You're safe here."

For the first time since he had found the boy in the trap Jones saw the semblance of a smile on the young face. Thin, and not firmly in place, but undeniably a smile.

"I forgot where I was," the boy said.

"Can't blame you. I wake up the same place damn near every morning, and I still forget sometimes."

The boy started to sit up. Jones said, "You'd better not move around too much with that ankle."

The boy looked down at the hump where the blanket covered his right foot. "Ankle?"

"Don't tell me you forgot about that, too! Maybe it's just as well. At least you got some sleep."

"Was my ankle hurt?"

"I'm afraid it was. Hurt pretty bad. I'd better have a look at it."

While the boy watched curiously, Jones peeled back the blanket, exposing the foot, still tightly wrapped in the bandage he had fashioned. Very gently the big man untied the torn strips and unwound the clean white cloth.

"Holy shit!"

"What's the matter?" The boy struggled to sit up while Jones held his right foot up off the cot, examining it.

"I don't believe what I'm seeing."

He had expected the swollen and discolored skin, torn by the steel teeth, the shattered bits of bone, snapped tendons, ligaments, blood, pus. What he saw was fresh, unbroken skin on a foot that moved this way and that with no apparent discomfort to the boy. The only sign of his terrible wound was a faint patch of shiny pink scar tissue where the trap had bitten through the flesh.

"I flat don't believe it," Jones said again.

The boy sat up, bracing himself with his hands, and looked curiously from his foot to the face of the big man.

"Doesn't it hurt?" Jones said.

The boy shook his head.

"Not at all?"

"Nope."

"Can you stand on it?"

Still handling the foot gingerly, Jones put it back on the canvas of the cot. The boy swung his feet out to the wooden floor and stood up. He took several steps away from Jones, then back. He jumped up and down. He did a little impromptu dance step.

"Well, I'll be damned."

49

"Feels fine," the boy said.

Jones sat on the edge of the cot, staring down at the boy's feet. "Either you are the fastest-healing son of a gun the world has ever seen, or we've just witnessed a miracle."

"Maybe it wasn't hurt as bad as you thought."

Oh, yes, it was hurt all right, Jones thought. Nothing in the world of medicine was going to save that leg much below the knee. He was not likely to make a mistake like that. He opened his mouth to say as much, then saw the strangely pleading look on the boy's face. The boy did not want to hear just now that there was something very strange about him.

"Maybe you're right," Jones said. "Anyway, you appear to be in fine shape this morning. You ought to be able to walk into Pinyon with me. Save me a load."

The boy looked up. "Do we have to go?"

"Course we do. Somebody's going to be looking for you."

"I doubt it."

"Sure they will. You've got folks, haven't you?"

"I-I don't remember."

"Well, they'll remember. And they'll be damn worried about you."

"I could stay here with you."

"No way. That's all I'd need is to have a big-ass search party come crashing in here and find me with a runaway boy. So far the local people haven't called me a kidnapper or a pervert, but all they'd need is something to put the thought in their heads. I'm taking you back, boy, and that's final."

The boy was silent for a moment. Then he said, "Does it have to be today?"

"Well . . ." And immediately Jones cursed himself for weakening. The boy's face lit up with a smile, a real one this time.

"I don't eat much, Jones. And I can help around here. I

can cut firewood. I can help with your garden. You've got a leak right over the door. I'll bet I could fix that.''

''I could fix it myself if it bothered me that much,'' Jones said grumpily.

The boy looked at him sideways. ''My foot's still a little tender.''

Jones ran his fingers through his wiry red beard. ''Well, I suppose it wouldn't hurt to give it a day's rest.''

The boy's happiness was so obvious that Jones was embarrassed and turned away. What kind of life must this kid have been living to want so much to stay in a broken-down forest cabin with a burnt-out hermit?

''But tomorrow, bright and early, rain or shine, we head for Pinyon, hear?''

''Whatever you say, Jones.'' The boy sat on the bed and began happily lacing the blood-caked shoe onto the foot that by all rights should have been a mangled stump.

''Tomorrow,'' Jones repeated in his deepest no-nonsense voice. ''Tomorrow we hike.''

It was four days before they started for Pinyon. During that time the boy had not only repaired the stubborn leak over the door that had plagued Jones for a year; he had cleaned out the weeds from what remained of Beverly's flower gardens and helped Jones straighten up his vegetable plot. He had chopped and stacked a month's worth of firewood and brought back pails of wild blackberries and pine nuts from the nearby woods.

More than all that, he gave Jones somebody to talk to. The big man had forgotten how good was the sound of another human voice. Even better, another ear to listen, for in fact the boy talked very little, while Jones almost never stopped. Jones talked about how it was living off the land. He talked about his own memories as a boy. He talked about the turbulent time of his young manhood. He talked about Beverly. And he talked about John.

The boy listened. He listened, and whether he fully understood or not, he nodded at the right places, asked the right questions, and agreed when it was important to agree. He still claimed to have no memory of his own past, and Jones did not press him. If it was true, there was nothing Jones could do about it, and if the boy was concealing something, that was none of Jones's business.

On the morning of the fifth day, Jones was wearing his heavy boots and buckling up his backpack when the boy awoke. When the boy started to speak the big man held up a massive hand to silence him.

"Before you say a word, forget it. Today's the day."

"Aw, Jones . . ."

"No. I set out a pair of boots there that might fit you if you put on three or four pairs of socks. Don't worry. I've got plenty. You wash up and I'll get some breakfast going."

They ate hot biscuits with butter and blackberry jam and washed them down with some of Jones's powerful coffee. The boy made no more protests, but as they left the cabin and were halfway across the clearing he stopped to look back.

"It was a good time, Jones."

The big man waited until the boy was ready, then they turned and walked together into the heavy forest. "Yes," he said. "It was a good time."

Abe Craddock and Curly Vane were mad as hell. They had caught something in their trap almost a week ago and some son of a bitch had let it out. No animal would ever get itself out of one of those traps. It could very well have been one of those things from Drago. There were still a few of them in the woods. They had heard the howling.

What made it even worse, whoever had freed the animal had deliberately ruined the trap. Those babies didn't come cheap. You couldn't get them at a regular sporting goods store. So as they tramped through the woods for the fifth straight day of looking for the trap robber, Craddock and Vane were mad as hell.

Moreover, they were drunk. Each of them had put away enough Jim Beam to knock out a normal man. But Craddock and Vane were experienced drinkers. Over the years they had built up a tolerance for the stuff as they tore up their livers.

Abe Craddock was a beefy man with a perpetually red face and an ass that stretched the seat of his jeans. Curly Vane was thinner, less talkative, and if anything, meaner than his companion. The two of them, when they got to drinking, were as welcome around La Reina County as the Mexican fruit fly.

It was Curly who heard the sounds in the woods off to their left. He held up a hand to warn Craddock, and the two of them stood there holding their breath, listening.

Something was definitely moving through the brush. Something big.

"Bear?" Craddock said in a hoarse whisper.

"Maybe." Both men brought their guns up to ready.

Curly Vane carried a heavy old Winchester deer rifle that could put a copper-jacketed slug through a brick wall. Craddock, whose marksmanship was poor, favored a twelve-gauge shotgun that he loaded with 00 buckshot. Anything he came close to with that cannon was as good as dead.

They waited. The sound of their own heavy breathing muffled the noise of whatever was approaching through the brush. They had never encountered anything bigger or more dangerous than a deer in these woods. Whatever was coming toward them now, they convinced themselves, was no deer.

The brush parted twenty yards away with a suddenness that made both men jump. A fierce, hairy head rose above the low chaparral and glared.

"Bear!" shouted Craddock.

Curly Vane squeezed off three shots.

53

Craddock's shotgun thundered.

The rifle slugs pounded into Jones's chest like three rapid hammer blows. For a second all he felt was the impact, then came the pain as the cold air hit the tunnels the bullets had bored into his lungs. He roared and started for the hunters. His only thought through the pain was to get his hands on the rotten bastards. Then the load of Craddock's buckshot blew away most of his head, and Jones's pain was over.

"Oh, fuck me, it was a man!" Curly moaned.

"What'd you shoot for?" Craddock said. "I wouldn't'f shot if you didn't."

"Shut up, you stupid fuck. We got to get out of here."

Craddock seized him by the arm. "Hold it! There's another one."

"Oooh, shit!"

They turned back and saw that there was, sure enough, a companion with the man they had killed. More of a boy than a man. He knelt over the bloody remains of the big man, sobbing. Then he raised his head and looked straight at Craddock and Vane. Curly Vane brought up the Winchester.

"What are you doing?" Craddock said.

"We've got to kill him, you dumb fuck. He seen us."

Vane's rifle cracked. A branch snapped off inches from the boy's face. For one frozen instant the boy stared at the hunters. His lips spread in a snarl unlike anything the men had seen on a human face. Then he was up and running.

Curly fired again, but the boy was already lost in the brush. They could hear his feet pounding the carpet of fir needles. He was fast.

"Come on," Curly urged. "We've got to catch him."

The two hunters crashed through the brush, heedless of the branches that whipped their faces and tore at their clothing. Ahead they caught glimpses of the fleeing boy. Their only thought was to kill.

* * *

There was yet another witness to the killing of Jones. After many weeks of searching out the scattered survivors of Drago, Derak, the leader, had finally found Malcolm. He saw him leave the cabin with the big man and start for the town. Derak had paced them silently, awaiting his chance to move in and take the boy. He knew of Jones and had no wish to harm the big man. But Malcolm had to be brought back to his own kind.

Then the other two had approached. The drunken men with their guns. The scent of them alone, their sweat, the whiskey on their breath, had been enough to start the change in Derak. He felt the bones shift and crack and reshape themselves under his skin. He stripped away the restraining clothes and dropped silently to all fours. His jaw worked silently as the teeth grew to their terrible length, strong, yellow, and sharp as knives.

Without warning the men had fired and Jones fell. Malcolm dropped beside him, and for a moment Derak thought the boy was going to go through the full change for the first time in his life. If it happened before he was prepared, it could be devastating. But the boy's body was not quite ready. He rose and fled.

The men fired at him and gave chase.

The ancient rage of his kind welled up in Derek. He flexed the powerful muscles under the thick coat of coarse fur and bounded after them.

The men were far too clumsy to elude him. Derak broke from the bushes with a roar and fell upon the one nearest to him, the one with the thin body and the head of tight black curls. He bore the man screaming to the forest floor and tore out his throat. The other threw down his useless gun and ran.

As his rage ebbed, Derak's hunger grew. He pushed his muzzle into the raw open flesh of the man's chest and fed.

Chapter 7

Abe Craddock was a mess.

On his best days Abe Craddock did not look like anything a man would want to take home to dinner, but when Gavin Ramsay entered his office with young Milo Fernandez, Craddock was in worse shape than the sheriff had ever seen him.

He was sitting stiffly in one of the office chairs with both hands clamped around a Styrofoam cup of coffee. He tried with little success to hold the cup steady. Much of the coffee had spilled down the front of his denim jacket, adding to other stains that crusted the man's clothing.

Deputy Roy Nevins leaned against the far wall of the office, well away from Craddock, who smelled like a sewer. The fat deputy turned gratefully when the sheriff and Milo entered.

"Hi, Gavin," he said. "One of the lost sheep is found."

"So I see. Is he hurt?"

"Doesn't appear to be."

"Then what's the matter with him?"

"Damned if I know. He stumbled in here half an hour ago babbling about lions and tigers and bears, or some damn thing. I couldn't make heads or tails out of what he was saying, so I sent Milo down to the hospital to get you."

"Has Mrs. Craddock been notified?"

"Yep, I called right away. Betty Craddock says as far as she's concerned we can lock the so—" He glanced over at the shivering hunter. "Lock the guy up and throw away the key."

"Have we got anything to lock him up for?"

"Damned if I know. Defacing the local scenery, maybe."

"I'll talk to him," Gavin said. "You can go get some lunch if you want to."

"Thanks, but the smell of our friend here ruined my appetite. I wouldn't mind some fresh coffee, though." He nodded at the Styrofoam cup gripped by Craddock. "That was the last of the office pot."

"Go ahead," Gavin told him. "I'll give a yell if I need you."

"I'll be at the inn," Nevins said with obvious relief. He shrugged into a jacket and hurried out the door before the sheriff could change his mind.

"Is it all right if I stay?" Milo asked.

"Sure. I need a second officer here for interrogation anyway."

Abe Craddock swiveled his head toward Gavin. Fear glittered in his small, red-rimmed eyes. "Interrogation?" he croaked.

"That means I want to ask you some questions, Abe."

"I t-told the fat guy everything."

"Sometimes Roy doesn't get all the details straight," Gavin said in a soothing tone. "You don't mind telling me again, do you?"

"I-I guess not." Craddock carried the cup to his mouth and sipped noisily. A brown trickle ran down his unshaven chin. He wiped it away negligently with the back of a scabbed hand.

57

Gavin walked over and perched with one buttock on his desk. The sour smell of Abe Craddock was sharp in his nostrils.

"Okay, Abe, any time you're ready."

"It was a bear," Craddock said. His eyes darted nervously about the room. "We shot a bear."

"You said 'we'?"

"Yeah."

"Is that you and Curly Vane?"

A spasm shook Abe Craddock, spilling most of the coffee left in the cup. "Yeah. Me and Curly. We was out together. Hunting. It was a bear."

"You are telling me that you and Curly Vane saw a bear?"

"Shot it. Shot at it."

"Right up here in our own Tehachapi Mountains?"

"Yeah. Bear." The big man in the chair seemed to try to pull his head down into his shoulders.

Ramsay took a kitchen match from his shirt pocket and stuck the end of it between his teeth. He did that sometimes when he wanted to look rustic and relaxed. He also did it to keep himself from losing his temper and yelling at a citizen.

"Abe," he said very quietly, "there has not been a bear reported in La Reina County or anywhere within a hundred miles of here since the 1930s." Ramsay had no idea if his figures were correct, but they were close enough to make the point of what he thought of Abe Craddock's bear sighting.

"It was a bear," Craddock insisted. "A big one."

"Where's Curly, Abe?"

The sudden question seemed to jolt the big man, as it was supposed to.

"It . . . it got him."

"The bear got Curly?" Ramsay fought down his rising impatience.

"Not the bear. Worse."

Craddock began to shake. He raised the Styrofoam cup

58

and swallowed the dregs of the coffee, gagging as he did so. Ramsay moved over and took the cup from his hand. He shook the few remaining drops of coffee into the metal trash can.

To Milo Fernandez he said, "Get me Roy's office bottle."

The young officer looked doubtful. "Gee, Sheriff, I don't—"

"It's in the center drawer of his desk. Behind the Mexican travel brochures."

Milo sat down and pulled open the desk drawer with obvious reluctance.

"Don't worry," Ramsay told him. "I know it's there and Roy knows I know. I don't give a damn if he has an occasional shooter. Right now I'm appropriating the bottle for official use."

Milo pulled out a bottle of Seagram's Seven Crown and handed it to Ramsay. The sheriff poured a generous slug into the coffee cup and gave it back to Abe Craddock.

"Here, Abe, this will do you more good than coffee. Steady you down."

Craddock seized the cup and drank greedily, swallowing the entire contents in two gulps. He held out the cup for more.

"That's enough for now, Abe. We don't want you to get *too* steady. Now do you want to tell me once more about you and Curly and this . . . bear?"

Craddock slumped in the chair. The shaking in his hands lessened as the whiskey took hold. He spoke in a hoarse monotone. "It looked like a bear. We thought it was a bear. No shit."

"And you shot at it."

"Curly did."

"He was the only one who fired?"

"Well, I guess I did, too."

"Did you hit it? The . . . bear?"

Craddock's head dropped. He frowned down at his hands as though they had betrayed him. In a voice barely audible he said, "We hit it."

"It wasn't a bear, was it, Abe?"

"No." The words were wrenched out of him. "It was a man." He looked up beseechingly at Ramsay. "It looked like a bear, though. Anybody would of thought so. All hairy the way he was, and he jumped up so fast. How was we to know?"

Ramsay drew a deep sigh and walked back over to sit on the edge of his desk again. It was Milo Fernandez who finally broke the silence.

"Is it the guy over in the hospital freezer?"

Ramsay nodded. "I picked up the pathologist's report this morning. Three thirty-oh-six slugs in the chest, face blown away by a shotgun blast. Nibbled on by small animals." From the corner of his eye he saw Abe Craddock flinch. "Name's Jones. Kind of a local character. Been living up in the woods since before I got here. Came to town once in a while to do odd jobs. Harmless. Kind of likable, matter of fact."

"We didn't know it was no man." Craddock's voice took on an unpleasant whine.

Ramsay turned back and gave him a hard look. "Tell me about Curly Vane."

Craddock began to tremble again. "Something got him."

"Not another bear?"

"No." Craddock shook his head emphatically. "It was real. Like a wolf, kind of."

"Come off it, Abe," Ramsay said. "I didn't buy your bear, and I sure as hell don't buy your wolf. What happened to Curly? Did you shoot him, too?"

"No, Gavin, I swear to God!" Craddock braced his hands on the arms of the chair and strained forward. "It was like a wolf, but it wasn't a wolf. Bigger. Bigger than a man,

60

even. And it kind of . . . stood up." His voice faded, as though he knew his words lacked conviction.

"What did you do then? Did you try to help him?"

"There wasn't nobody could help Curly when this thing hit him."

In spite of himself, Ramsay felt a chill between his shoulder blades. "Do you have any idea what it was, Abe?"

Craddock nodded, his eyes shifting toward the door. "It was one of them things from up at Drago. Some of them got away, you know."

"Give it a name, Abe."

"All right, damn it, call me crazy if you want to. It was . . . a werewolf."

For half a dozen ticks there was dead silence. Then Ramsay said, "Keep an eye on the office, Milo. Abe and I are going for a ride."

There were about two hours of daylight remaining when Gavin Ramsay brought Craddock to the spot where the two young hikers had stumbled across Jones's body. Although he paid little attention to the fantastic stories about Drago, the sheriff had no desire to be caught in these woods after nightfall.

He gestured at the patch of ground where they stood. There were dark stains visible on the carpet of fir needles.

"This is where we found him, Abe," Ramsay said. "Remember the spot?"

Craddock looked at the ground, then quickly away. "Yeah. You can see the bush here where he kind of reared up. We had no way of knowin' if it was a man or what."

"So you blasted away."

"Honest, Gavin, I'm tryin' to tell you how it happened."

"Okay, okay. After you shot and he fell, what did you do?"

"Then we saw the other one and we—"

"The other one?" Ramsay snapped.

61

"Oh, yeah, didn't I say?"

"No, Abe, you didn't."

"Well, when we came closer we seen there was another guy. Smaller. Like a kid, maybe."

"A kid," Gavin repeated.

"Yeah. Well, he saw us coming and he took off running. We went after him."

"Why, Abe?"

"Well, we, uh, thought he'd be scared and might hurt himself or something."

"You weren't going to shoot him, too, were you, Abe?"

"Jesus, Gavin, shooting the hermit was an accident. What do you think I am?"

I know damn well what you are, Ramsay thought. I know what Curly Vane is, too. Or was, as the case may be. He said, "Which way did you go?"

Craddock looked around, seeming to sniff the air. He was on surer ground now. He pointed off at an angle. "That way. The kid left the trail and took off through the brush. Curly and me went after him."

"Show me."

"I am showin' you." Craddock jabbed with his forefinger. "Off that way."

"Let's go."

"You don't want to go in there, Gavin."

The muscles tightened around Ramsay's jaw. "I said let's go. I'm not playing games with you, Abe."

Craddock met the sheriff's hard gaze for a moment, then turned and led the way through the brush in the direction he had pointed.

"I want you to show me where this 'wolf' or whatever it was jumped Curly," Ramsay said.

Some fifty yards into the brush Craddock stopped. He pointed. "It was up there at the base of that leaning fir tree. I was just about here when it hit him. He never had a chance. Nobody would of had a chance with that thing."

Ramsay walked in careful steps to the tree Craddock had pointed out. He hunkered down at the base of the trunk and examined the ground. The dead needles were stained dark and crusted. He pulled out one of the plastic Ziplock bags he had brought from the office and carefully scraped a few of the needles into it. There was also a whitish powder and bits of what might have been bone. Ramsay took some of that too.

A flash of color beyond the tree caught his eye. He walked over and prodded the brush aside with his foot. A bright red cap with a Budweiser logo on the front lay there upside down. There were shredded bits of a jacket, tough denim pants, a boot, part of another boot. All of it was stiff and black with clotted blood.

Ramsay turned and beckoned. "Come here, Abe."

Craddock approached reluctantly, taking care not to step where the ground was stained dark.

"Recognize these?" Ramsay said.

"Oh, shit." Craddock turned away. He clapped a hand to his mouth too late. The coffee and whiskey he had taken in sputtered out between his fingers. He bent over and retched until nothing more would come.

Ramsay stood quietly and waited for him to finish.

Finally Craddock stood up. His normally ruddy face was pale and bloodless. He nodded. "That's Curly's hat. The other stuff, that's his, too, as best as I can tell."

Ramsay scanned the area. "It sort of looks like that's all that's left of him."

From off toward the mountains came a sound that froze the two men where they stood. A long, wild, ululating howl.

In the sudden deeper silence that followed, Abe Craddock turned a stricken face to Ramsay.

"Sheriff, do whatever you got to do to me, but in the name of God, let's get the fuck out of here."

Ramsay hesitated only a moment, then he nodded and they started back toward the trail.

Chapter 8

"I am going to count up to five, Malcolm," said Holly Lang. "At the count of one you will begin to awaken. When I reach five you will be wide awake, and you will feel rested and refreshed."

The boy sat propped comfortably in the hospital bed. His eyes were closed, the lashes moist and dark against his pale skin. He smiled gently and nodded.

"You will remember everything you have told me," Holly continued, "and you will not be frightened. I am going to begin now. *One.* You are beginning to wake up."

The boy on the bed stirred. His slim fingers flexed, testing the texture of the hospital blanket.

"*Two.* You are feeling good, feeling rested, a little more awake now."

The boy sighed. A soft, contented sound from his chest.

"*Three.* Waking up now, feeling refreshed and rested."

His eyelids fluttered. His lips parted slightly.

"*Four.* You can open your eyes now, Malcolm, and look around if you want to. You can hear the birds outside in the trees, feel the breeze coming through the window."

The boy opened his eyes. He blinked. His eyes moved comfortably about the room, settling on Holly.

"*Five.* Wide awake now. Wide awake and feeling fine." Holly smiled at the boy. "Hi, Malcolm."

The boy pulled in a deep breath, stretched his arms, and returned the smile. "Hi, Holly."

"That was pretty easy, wasn't it?" she said.

"I didn't really go to sleep, you know."

"I told you it wasn't like that. None of this trance stuff. That's only in comic books."

"I knew what was happening all the time. I could hear you asking me questions, and I felt myself answer you. It was just that all of a sudden I could . . . remember." A shadow crossed the boy's face.

"And now you remember everything that you told me, don't you?"

"Yes. I remember the fire. And living in the woods. Running, always running, because men were trying to catch me. I remember the trap. And . . . oh, I remember Jones." Malcolm stopped, a look of pain on his face.

"It's all right, Malcolm," Holly said gently.

"He's dead, isn't he?" the boy said.

"I don't know that for sure."

The boy nodded. "He's dead. Jones was the best person I ever knew. And they killed him. Those two men. But I told you all about that, didn't I?"

"Talk about it all you want to," Holly said. "Sometimes talking helps take away the hurt."

"They killed him. With guns."

Holly watched closely as the boy's gaze drifted off somewhere beyond the walls of the hospital room. She leaned forward in the chair where she sat beside the bed. Was there a change in the color of his eyes? Or was it a trick of the late-afternoon sun slanting in through the window?

"Something happened after that and I can't remember. Did I tell you what it was?"

Holly shook her head silently. There were still empty patches in his memory that the hypnosis had not penetrated. She did not want to break into the boy's train of thought now. He did look different. She was sure of it. The shadows were deeper under his cheekbones. And there was something strange about his nose and his upper lip.

"I don't know why the men didn't kill me, too," Malcolm went on. His voice had grown deeper and had a rasp to it.

His throat must be dry from all the talking, Holly told herself. But his eyebrows . . . weren't they heavier now than a moment ago? And she did not remember them growing all the way across the bridge of his nose.

"The next thing I remember I was running again. I didn't know if the men were chasing me or not. I just knew I had to get away. I was afraid again, only this time it was even worse than before. It was worse because Jones was dead. He was my friend, and I lost him."

"It's all right to grieve for a friend," Holly said softly. "It hurts to lose someone, but at one time or another it must happen to all of us. There will be other friends."

Malcolm was silent for a minute. Then he spoke again. "I was so tired of running. When the other two men saw me, the ones who brought me here, I didn't try very hard to get away. I knew they were different from the first two, the ones who killed Jones."

"How did you know that, Malcolm?"

"I could tell by the way they smelled. You know you can smell it when somebody wants to kill you. Or when they're afraid of you."

Holly nodded. She knew the sweat glands emitted a different chemical under the stress of fear, but few humans were equipped with a sense of smell keen enough to recognize it.

"Excuse me, Malcolm," she said, standing up. "We don't need those curtains drawn anymore. Let's catch what we can of the last of the sunlight."

She spread the curtains all the way open, brightening the room with an orange glow from the setting sun. With a reluctance she could not explain, Holly turned to look at the boy in the bed.

He smiled at her. Just a normal, somewhat thin fourteen-year-old boy. His eyes were a warm green. There were no unusual shadows under the cheekbones. Straight nose, well-formed upper lip. Rather fine, arched eyebrows. Nothing strange here at all. As she had thought, it was a trick of the lighting.

"The funny thing is," Malcolm said, "it seems like only a few minutes ago you were going to hypnotize me. But that was morning, and now the sun's going down."

"Sometimes hypnotism plays tricks with time," Holly said. "A few seconds can stretch into hours. Or the other way around. How do you feel otherwise?"

"Fine. Tired, though. I feel like I did all that running all over again."

"You'll get a good night's sleep tonight," she said. "I'll have your dinner sent up right away."

"Thank you."

Holly gave an unnecessary tuck to the blanket on Malcolm's bed. She smiled at him and started out of the room.

"Holly?"

"Yes?"

"About Jones. You said it hurt to lose a friend, and it does. And you said there'd be other friends. I wonder . . . will you be my friend?"

"I'd like that," Holly said. "I'd like that a lot. See you."

She slipped out of the room into the corridor and stood for a moment with her back against the wall. She swallowed hard to get rid of the lump in her throat. Right now she should be feeling quite pleased with herself. In a remarkably short time she had brought the boy out of an apparent catatonic state and restored at least a portion of his memory. Why, then, did she feel this chill of apprehension? There was more to Malcolm's story. Much more. Holly Lang was not sure she wanted to know it all.

Enough of that kind of thinking. She had work to do. She turned to start down the corridor and gasped as she almost ran into Gavin Ramsay. The tall sheriff caught her to avoid a collision. He held her for a moment with his strong hands on her shoulders, then released her.

"I was just on my way to call you," she said.

"And I was looking for you."

"After you left this morning, Malcolm talked almost non-stop. He told me all about your dead man in the woods."

Ramsay nodded. "Jones."

"You know?"

"Your pathologist caught me on the way out of here this morning with my deputy. He told me who the dead man was and how he died."

"Then Malcolm isn't in trouble anymore?"

"Not with me, he isn't. But we still don't know who he is. Did you find out?"

"Not really." She hesitated. "I think he's from Drago."

"No kidding."

"His memory begins with a fire that destroyed his town."

"If he is from Drago, he'll be the first survivor to turn up," Ramsay said.

"You understand I'm not sure. I'll want to work with him a lot more."

"No problem. The Drago business is none of my affair, anyway."

"One thing will probably interest you—he remembers the two men who shot Jones."

"I know who they are, too, but the boy's testimony will be important."

"Could it wait until tomorrow? He's pretty tired."

"I don't suppose a day will make any difference." Gavin

68

rubbed his jaw, bringing a rasp from the stubble of beard. "You have any plans for tonight?"

Holly turned brisk. "I always have plans. Tonight I'm going to write up my reports, go home, take a long bath, grill myself a steak, and watch an old Bogart movie on television."

"Let me rephrase the question," he said. "Will you have dinner with me?"

"A date? Why, Sheriff, I had no idea . . ."

"I hate it when they get cute," he muttered.

Holly laughed. "Dinner sounds like fun. But considering the quality of restaurants hereabouts, why don't you come to my place? I've got two of those steaks."

"That is an offer I can't refuse. What kind of wine do you like?"

"Something dark red and dry. You pick it out. Is eight o'clock all right?"

"Fine. Where do I show up?"

"I have a little house in Darnay. Seventy-one Garden Street. I'll leave the porch light on."

"I'll find you."

He winked at her and swung off down the corridor. Holly looked after him for a moment, feeling foolishly light-headed about the date. She shook herself back into a serious mood and headed for the tiny office where she could type up her notes on today's session with Malcolm.

Dr. Wayne Pastory stepped quickly back into an alcove when he saw Holly Lang approaching. He had done a good deal of research during the day and had decided on a course of action. Right now the lady doctor was the last person he wanted to see.

When Holly was safely around a corner in the hallway, Pastory stepped out of the alcove and headed for the stairs. He climbed to the second floor, passed through the glass doors into the administrative wing, and stopped at the reception desk before the office of Dr. Dennis Qualen. After the

69

obligatory banter with Qualen's matronly receptionist, he was allowed to enter.

"Ah, Wayne, you caught me on the way out," said the chief administrator. "I hope this isn't anything that will take a long time."

"No, no, just a few words," Pastory said. "About the boy in one-oh-eight."

Qualen pushed papers around on the polished mahogany desk. "That one. Malcolm Something-or-other, his name seems to be. Our sheriff was just in here talking to me about him."

"Oh?" Pastory tensed, hoping his plan had not been derailed.

"Apparently we are not harboring a juvenile murderer. According to Ramsay, someone else was responsible for the dead man in our basement."

"But no one has claimed the boy?"

"Unfortunately, no. Nor has anyone come forward with an offer to pay his bill. Certain members of our staff seem to be under the impression that we are a charitable institution."

"I think I know who you mean," Pastory said. "My reason for wanting to see you is to suggest a way to get us off the hook."

"Oh?" Qualen was interested but noncommittal.

"As you know, I operate a modest clinic of my own north of here."

"Ah, yes, I believe you have spoken of it. I forget— where, exactly, is it located?"

"My suggestion," Pastory said, passing quickly over the question, "is that the boy be transferred there. I am quite well equipped to take care of him, and I think the boy will be useful in some important research I'm conducting."

"What sort of research?"

"I'm not really prepared to discuss it at this stage. You understand, sir."

Dr. Qualen drew a finger along the aristocratic line of his nose. "What you suggest is not normal procedure."

"I realize that, sir," said Pastory. "But I think in this case it might pay to bend the procedures a bit. For one thing, this will relieve the hospital of additional expense, and I understand the budget is under some scrutiny at Sacramento."

"I don't see how all the necessary arrangements could be made without going through channels."

"These things can be expedited, as we both know. The thing is, time is short. I'd like the boy transferred to my place tomorrow."

"Tomorrow? Nothing can possibly be accomplished that quickly."

Pastory produced a manila folder with a flourish of a magician making a rabbit appear. "To speed things along I went ahead and did the necessary paperwork."

"You *are* in something of a hurry to get on with this, aren't you?"

Pastory leaned confidentially forward across the desk. "I'll be frank with you, sir. If my theories about this boy prove out, there will be considerable recognition, acclaim even, that will go beyond the medical community. More than enough recognition for one man."

Qualen stiffened. "That sounds unpleasantly like a bribe, Doctor."

"Nothing of the sort, sir. But it doesn't hurt to remember that quite a few of our friends in high places got where they are by finding a way around the normal procedures."

Qualen glanced over the multicolored forms. "I'm still not at all sure I can go along with this. It's highly irregular."

"You'll notice," Pastory put in, "that I have entered my own name in every case where there is a question of responsibility. Not that I expect any trouble about a routine transfer, but if there should be, it's on my head."

"I see." Dr. Qualen slipped on a pair of reading glasses. "Give me a few minutes to look these over. If, as you say,

71

everything is in order, I see no reason why I should delay the transfer of this patient into your care.''

Pastory smiled. ''A good decision, sir. I'm sure it's in the best interests of everyone concerned.'' He leaned back in the chair and waited with a confident smile.

Chapter 9

The beast moved silently through the darkening forest. Small creatures of the night skittered from its path or froze into attitudes of self-protection. The beast padded forward in a balloon of silence as the smaller creatures ceased all sound and movement at its approach.

But tonight the smaller animals had nothing to fear from the beast. It was intent on other matters. Every few yards the beast would pause and rise manlike on its hind legs, lifting its muzzle to the sky. It would sniff the air—testing, searching. And then, finding the one scent among many, it would drop again to all fours and move on.

At the crest of the final hill the beast stopped. The coarse fur bristled at the base of its powerful neck. Below lay the sprinkling of lights that were the town of Pinyon. Directly at the bottom of the hill was a large rectangular building with many lights. From the building came a profusion of scents. Some sharp and medicinal, others heavy with death and decay. The scent of humans was powerful. Humans in their sickness. Yet among the confusion of the many odors the beast again picked out the one it sought.

Moving stealthily on great padded paws, the beast crept down the wooded hillside toward the hospital.

Gavin Ramsay leaned close to the mirror over his bathroom sink and gave his face a critical look. Unsatisfied, he buzzed the electric shaver over his chin for the third time. He had a chin cleft that Elise had always said was cute but that sheltered a tiny ridge of whiskers that were hell to shave off. He tested the area with his fingers and decided it was as smooth as it was ever going to be. He blew out the shaver, splashed on some English Leather, and walked back into his combined living room/bedroom/kitchenette in the Pinyon Inn.

Gavin's was the only room at the inn with cooking facilities. He seldom lit the stove, and he used the half-size refrigerator for little more than keeping beer cold. Most of his meals were eaten downstairs in the coffee shop or brought home from one of the fast-food places down the road in Darnay. Still, having a kitchen, however inadequate, made the room seem a little more like home.

He and Elise had lived in a spacious California ranch house in Darnay until the divorce. The house, like the Camaro, and damn near everything else, had gone to Elise. Gavin had been stunned to find how suddenly cold and calculating his loving bride had turned when she decided the marriage wasn't going where she wanted it to. While he had stumbled through the proceedings with a nice-guy lawyer whose heart was back in Iowa, she had latched on to a high-powered firm from Los Angeles with half a dozen names on the letterhead. It was no contest.

But what the hell, it was over now. The last he heard, Elise was in New York dating some hotshot political columnist for the *Times*. That would suit her. Her father, too. Gavin had been a great disappointment to both of them.

He pushed open the accordion door on his closet and surveyed the meager wardrobe therein. Two khaki uniforms of

74

the La Reina County Sheriff's Department. One suit, blue. Two sport coats gray tweed and camel hair. Three pairs of slacks, gray, blue, and brown. Two neckties, one with stripes, one with little fleurs-de-lis. Assorted shoes.

These, except for the uniforms, were the clothes he hardly ever wore. His real clothes were in the dresser drawers. Jeans, corduroys, soft cotton shirts, sweaters.

During the marriage Elise had outfitted him like the rising young politician she hoped he would be. He had had two full closets then of suits, jackets, and pants from the best tailors in Southern California. Gone now, all gone. No, Elise had not taken his clothing, but Gavin had wasted no time giving most of it away when he moved out. It was one thing from his marriage he definitely did not miss.

For tonight, however, jeans and a sweater simply would not do. Holly Lang was not just another date. His dates had been few since the divorce. Generally, they consisted of a few drinks in a quiet bar, dinner maybe, then off to bed. Neither he nor the women involved had any stake in the relationship beyond an evening's entertainment. That was the way he wanted it. For some reason he felt differently about Holly.

He chose the camel hair jacket and gray slacks. Briefly he considered wearing a necktie, but he decided that was too much and settled for a soft blue sport shirt.

"You look terrific," he told his image in the mirror. "All ready for the prom."

Downstairs he climbed into the old Dodge wagon, shoving the accumulated debris off the seats. He frowned at the coating of dust and wished he had washed it more recently. He would have to remember to park in the shadows.

He drove the ten miles along the dark highway to Darnay, listening to a golden-oldies rock station from Los Angeles. He had no idea what songs were played, nor did he care. The music was company, that was all.

Entering Darnay, Gavin stopped at a liquor store and

bought a bottle of California cabernet sauvignon. He found Holly Lang's address with no trouble. It was a yellow clapboard bungalow with white shutters, set well back from the quiet street. The lawn was neatly mowed. A row of flowers before the house looked like somebody cared about them. As promised, Holly had left the porch light on.

She met him at the door, wearing a colorful silk blouse with a soft, dark skirt that followed the smooth curve of her hips. Gavin realized it was the first time he had seen her out of the more severe lady-doctor outfits she wore while working. He decided she looked pretty damn good, and told her so.

"Thank you," she said. "I like your jacket."

He held up the bottle of wine for her inspection. "Is this okay?"

"Perfect. If you want to pull the cork we'll let it breathe for a while before dinner."

They entered through a small living room that she had furnished in shades of brown, gold, and rust. In a dining alcove a table was covered with a white linen spread and set for two, complete with candles and long-stemmed wineglasses.

He followed her into a sparkling kitchen and managed the corkscrew while Holly bustled about, straightening things that did not need straightening.

"I don't exactly know what that 'letting it breathe' business is all about," she said, "but it seems to be part of the ritual."

"Like rolling the cork between your fingers and sniffing at it," he added.

"And what's the difference between the aroma and the bouquet?"

"I didn't know there was one."

At the same time they stopped and looked at each other.

"We're babbling, aren't we?" she said.

"Uh-huh."

"We're both adults; we've been in the company of the

opposite sex before. There's no excuse for mindless social chatter, is there?''

''None at all.''

''Whew. With that out of the way, would you like a drink before I throw on the steaks?''

''I'd love one.''

''I have vodka, Scotch, bourbon, and gin. I can make a pretty good martini.''

''Scotch will be fine.''

''Do you like anything in it?''

''Ice.''

She made his drink and a vodka and tonic for herself. They carried them into the living room and sat on the sofa with the drinks before them on a hatch-cover coffee table. Some easy cocktail jazz was playing on the stereo unit. Gavin could not tell if it was a record or the radio.

''Do you ever hear from your wife?'' she asked suddenly.

For a moment he was startled into silence, then laughed. ''*Ex*-wife,'' he amended. ''You sure know how to break the ice.''

''If we're going to start dating, we ought to know about each other, don't you think?''

''Are we going to start dating?''

''I think we have, don't you?''

''Apparently.'' He sipped at the Scotch. It was good, heavy stuff, not one of the lightweights with pretty labels and no flavor. ''No, I never hear from Elise. Ours was not one of those friendly divorces you hear about. Now and then I hear *about* her from mutual friends. They mean well, but I'd just as soon they wouldn't bother.''

''You sound bitter.''

He considered for a moment. ''If I do, that's something I've got to fix. Bitter people are no fun to have around, and I certainly don't want to be one. They pollute the atmosphere like sour meat. I don't hate Elise. I am not down on humanity or women, or even the institution of marriage. I got gouged in the divorce, but I guess that was mostly to soothe my wife's pride. Elise never lost anything in her life, and if I was going to get away, she was going to be sure I didn't take much with me.''

"I saw her several times when you both lived in Darnay. She's a beautiful woman.''

"There's no denying that,'' he said. "She's also intelligent and witty. And ambitious. Who invited her tonight, anyway?''

Holly colored, then smiled at him. "I have been asking a lot of questions, haven't I? It's only fair that you have a turn. Is there anything you want to know about me?''

"Plenty, but I'll let it come out in the normal course of events.''

"I've never been married,'' she volunteered. "That's not the stigma for a woman in her late twenties that it used to be. Still, there were three whole years that it was always on my mind.''

"Not anymore?''

"Not the way it was. I had this *relationship*, you see. He was a doctor. Psychoanalyst, actually. Beautifully handsome, clever, and always in command. He was the only man I saw for those three years.''

"But no marriage?''

"There was a small hitch. Bob already had a wife. He was going to leave her, though, just as soon as the time was right. Sure he was. I wasn't really so naive that I believed that, but I wanted it to be true so bad that I hung around three years.''

"All over now?''

"Yup. It just about killed me the first time I refused to see him. The second time was easier, and the third. After that he didn't try anymore. I understand he now has a lady lawyer from San Francisco waiting for him to leave the missus.''

"Bob's loss is the world's gain.''

"Thanks. I wasn't fishing, but a compliment is always welcome."

Gavin pulled in a deep breath and let it out. "I hope the therapy session is over now so we can get on with acting silly."

"Right. Do you want another drink, or should I start throwing dinner together?"

Gavin rattled the ice cubes in his glass. "I'm still working on this one. I hope you're not going to ask for help. Pulling corks and opening cans is the extent of my kitchen talent."

"Mister Macho," she said. "I'll bet you're good at moving furniture."

"Want to feel my biceps?"

"Maybe later. You can come out with me and watch if you want to."

"Sure. I might even learn something."

Gavin found a spot to stand where he was out of the way and watched with honest admiration as Holly moved efficiently about the kitchen. She tossed together a salad of fresh greens, checked the broccoli she had steaming, and switched the oven on to BROIL. She sprinkled some kind of seasoning on a pair of thick New York steaks.

"How do you like yours?" she asked.

"Rare."

"Good. Me, too."

Miraculously, she got everything on the table at the same time. Gavin poured the wine and they sat down.

The salad was crisp and not overdressed, the steak was beautifully rare, and even the broccoli, not Gavin's favorite vegetable, was tender and tasty in a light cheese sauce. Conversation ranged over likes and dislikes in food, favorite television shows, the weather, local events, and came to rest finally on the boy who lay in room 108 at La Reina County Hospital.

"He's a strange one," Holly said. "I don't think he even knows everything about himself."

"Are you talking about the Drago business?"

"Partly that." She studied Gavin's face in the candle-light. "You don't believe the stories they tell about Drago, do you?"

"Werewolves? You've got to be kidding."

"You might be a little more open-minded."

"Okay, I'll try. Let's see, when the moon is full they sprout hair and fangs and go around biting people." He pretended to concentrate. "It's no use. I keep seeing Little Red Riding Hood."

Holly sighed. "The all-American skeptic. Where do you think the story of Little Red Riding Hood came from?"

"The Brothers Grimm?"

"It is based on old legends. Lots of fairy tales are. Ever hear of Peter Stump? Clauda Jamprost? Jacques Bocquet?"

"No, no, and no."

"They were documented werewolves of the sixteenth century."

"Documented, eh? By who, Walt Disney?"

Holly's eyes flashed a danger signal. "If you don't mind, this isn't something I feel like kidding about."

"I'm sorry. You've been doing some homework, haven't you?"

"Yes, I have, and I'd like to be able to talk to somebody about it without a lot of cheap jokes."

Gavin held up his hands. "Okay. No more wisecracks. If this is important to you, I'd like to understand and talk about it with some intelligence. But it will take a little time. Let me do some homework of my own, okay?"

"Okay." After a moment Holly relaxed and sipped at her wine.

"Just one question before we drop it for the night," he said.

"Ask away."

"Do you think our boy Malcolm is a werewolf?"

She frowned. "I'm not ready to go that far. I think he may

be afflicted with some form of lycanthropy. I want to know more about him.''

''I'll do what I can to help if you want me on the team,'' Gavin said.

She held up her wineglass in silent assent. They clinked in a toast and drank to the partnership.

It was past midnight when Gavin set his coffee cup gently down on the table. He cleared his throat and rubbed his hands together.

''I'd better be pushing off,'' he said. ''Work day tomorrow.''

''Right,'' she said. ''Me, too.''

He stood up.

She stood up.

''Dinner was terrific.''

''Glad you liked it.''

''Next time my treat.''

''You got it.''

They stood facing each other for a long moment, their weight shifting from foot to foot as though they were mirror images.

''I'd better tell you this,'' he said. ''I would really like to go to bed with you. I mean it's been on my mind from the minute I walked in. No, from the minute I put on my best sport coat to impress you.''

She watched him, her head tilted slightly to one side.

''And if we don't mess up somehow, I'm almost sure you and I are going to do it.''

She opened her mouth to speak, and he went on quickly. ''But I have the feeling neither of us is ready for it right now.''

Holly let out a long-held breath. ''You know, Sheriff, you're a more perceptive man than you let on sometimes.''

''I just didn't want you to think I was gay.''

"I detected that," she said. "Those pants of yours fit quite well."

"Why, you saucy little minx."

"That's me."

Their good-night kiss was long and warm and deep, and filled with promise.

Gavin drove back toward the Pinyon Inn, grinning foolishly in the dim glow of the instrument lights. He had to remind himself that there was still a whole lot he did not know about Dr. Holly Lang. Her preoccupation with the occult was one thing that disturbed him. His grin faded as he thought about the boy who lay in room 108. Gavin thought about him and about the tales of Drago, and he wondered. . . .

Malcolm's eyes snapped open and he sat suddenly upright in bed. He sniffed the air and turned toward the window to stare at the darkness outside.

Someone was there. Someone or something. Calling to him. The boy's thin body tensed. His nerves tightened with a crazy desire to run out there and join whatever waited for him in the night. Beads of perspiration broke out along his hairline.

It was as though he belonged out there, in the night, not here in a comfortable bed. That was his place. And yet . . . and yet things were different now. He had a friend. He was no longer alone, running, always running. He thought of Holly. Made a picture of her face in his mind. The picture held him where he was. Still, the silent voice called to him from outside.

Another sound intruded. The barely audible pad of the night nurse's rubber-soled shoes out in the corridor. Malcolm lay back quickly and closed his eyes, feigning sleep. The door opened. The night nurse looked in, listened to his regular breathing, and backed out again.

Malcolm did not rise. The call from the night was still there, but weaker now. He could block it out if he tried. By and by he fell into a shallow sleep that was troubled by strange urges and wild dreams.

Out on the hillside, yellow-green eyes glaring across at the many windows of the hospital building, the beast growled from deep in its massive chest. The one it sought was inside, that much the beast knew, but there were too many conflicting scents to tell which of the windows was the right one.

The beast made a complete circuit of the building, staying in the deepest shadows, going to a low, loping run when it had to cross the paved parking area. Instinct cried out for it to smash through the glass doors at the entrance and savage any human that crossed its path until the boy was found. Reason told the beast that this was not the way. It was a time for cunning. The killing would come later.

Effortlessly the beast climbed the hill behind the building and slipped down into the shallow valley beyond. There beneath a bush it found a neatly folded pile of clothing. The beast sniffed the air, judged it safe, then lay down next to the clothing and curled its powerful body in on itself as the painful transformation began.

Chapter 10

Malcolm awoke sweating.

The gray rectangle of the window told him it was early morning. The sensations of last night jolted back into his consciousness. He remembered the terrible certainty that something out there in the woods had called to him. His own wild urge to answer that call. Then the quieting mind picture of Dr. Holly Lang, and the troubled dreams that followed.

He strained his senses now, and he could still feel the presence of something out there. It was much fainter now, but not completely gone. Malcolm was frightened, yet his blood surged with a strange exhilaration. He resolved to tell Holly all about it. She would understand. She would know how to help him.

A few minutes later the door opened and a nurse entered. She had orange hair and a lumpy potato nose. She was not one of the nurses Malcolm had seen before. She carried a small tray that was covered with a white cloth. When she set the tray down on the table across the room from his bed it made a little clinking sound.

"Well, already awake, are we?" the nurse said in that

fake-cheerful voice they use. "And my, how chipper we look. Did we have a good sleep?"

Malcolm did not bother to answer. He knew the nurse wouldn't pay any attention to what he said anyway.

"Are we ready for a surprise this morning?"

Malcolm turned his head away.

"Malcolm's going on a little trip."

He turned back to the nurse. She had a mole on the side of her neck with a single orange hair growing out of it.

"I thought that might interest you," she said brightly.

"A trip where?"

"That's going to be the surprise. I don't want to spoil it for you."

An oily-haired man in a white doctor's coat came through the door. Malcolm remembered him. He was the nasty one who had given Holly a hard time when Malcolm was first brought in.

"This is Dr. Pastory," the nurse said as if she were giving him a great big present. "He's going to be *your* doctor now."

"I don't want a new doctor."

"You don't know how lucky you are," Potato Nose told him. "A lot of people in your position don't have any doctor at all."

"Where's Holly?" Malcolm said.

Pastory spoke for the first time. "Dr. Lang has other patients to attend to." His voice was as oily as his hair.

"I'd rather have her."

"You will find, Malcolm, that in this life we don't always get what we want." He turned to the orange-haired nurse and said in a low voice, as though Malcolm could not hear, "Give him fifty cc's."

The nurse lifted one edge of the white cloth and took something from the tray she had brought in with her. She held it down low, shielded by her body so Malcolm wouldn't see it. He knew what it was, though.

85

"How about rolling over for me, big fella?" she said, all palsy again.

"What for?"

"We've got to poke a little medicine into you, that's all. A tiny pinprick in the bottom. You've had them before."

"But what is it?"

"It will make you feel better."

"I feel fine."

Dr. Pastory moved over closer to the bed and frowned down at Malcolm. His eyes were small and bright, and there was something in them Malcolm didn't like.

"Do as the nurse says, Malcolm. We have some strong young fellows working here who can come in and flip you over if you won't cooperate. Do you want me to call them?"

Malcolm looked at the nurse and saw he would get no help from her. Feeling trapped, he rolled over on his side, facing away from them. The nurse yanked the blanket and sheet down and pulled the short hospital gown up to expose his buttock. He felt the sharp sting of the needle and a tightening of the flesh down there as something was pumped into him.

He felt the needle slide out and smelled the tang of alcohol as the nurse swabbed him off. She gave him a familiar little pat and pulled the gown back into place. Malcolm rolled onto his back and looked up at the two of them.

"That wasn't so bad now, was it?" the nurse recited.

"I want to see Holly," Malcolm said. "Dr. Lang."

Pastory showed his small, even teeth. "*I'm* your doctor now, Malcolm. You'd better get used to that."

Malcolm felt a tingling sensation spread over his body. He braced his hands and tried to sit up but found he was dizzy and lay back down.

"Just relax," Pastory told him. "Don't try to fight the medicine. You can't win, you know." The words had a funny echoing sound.

"I don't want to relax. I don't want you for my doctor."

86

That was what Malcolm tried to say, but it came out all mush-mouth. His tongue felt thick and foreign, like a hunk of strange meat.

''The more you fight it, the more trouble it makes for everybody.'' Pastory's oily little face swam in and out of focus.

With a great effort Malcolm sat up. The doctor reached for him and Malcolm batted his hands away. ''You're not my doctor,'' he mumbled.

Pastory bared his teeth, and for a moment Malcolm thought the doctor was going to strike him. But he got control of himself and turned to the nurse.

''Better give him another fifty cc's.''

''But doctor, for a boy his age, that's—''

Pastory's little eyes flashed, though his voice remained calm. ''Please do what I ask, Nurse.''

With her cheeks reddening, the nurse turned her back and did something with the things on the cloth-covered tray. Pastory stared impassively down at Malcolm.

''Don' wan' any more shots.'' Malcolm had trouble getting the words out past the tongue that did not belong to him. ''Wan' see Holly.''

''Will you please hurry?'' Pastory snapped at the nurse, who was still fumbling at the tray.

''No more shots,'' Malcolm said feebly.

The orange-haired nurse turned toward him, making no attempt this time to conceal the hypodermic needle. She reached down with one hand and flipped Malcolm onto his side. His body would not respond to the messages sent by his brain.

He barely felt the second needle prick. The nurse eased him over on his back and he watched as she and Dr. Pastory floated side by side in some murky void. The room grew warm, then hot. Malcolm could feel the sweat rolling off him, but he could not move a hand up to clear his eyes. His power of speech was gone. All he could manage were soft grunting noises. The light grew dim. And dimmer.

"That's done it." Dr. Pastory's voice floated to him through a long tunnel, distorted and barely audible. "I won't be needing you anymore, Nurse."

The shadow shape that was the nurse floated back away from him and disappeared. Dr. Pastory went away, too, but just for a moment. Then he was back with somebody else. Another man. The features were only a blur to Malcolm, but he sensed that the newcomer was not a doctor or a hospital employee. He smelled wrong. There was none of the astringent tang of surgical soap, medicine, and alcohol that clung to the hospital people. This one smelled of tobacco, stale sweat, and urine.

Malcolm felt himself lifted roughly from the bed and placed on another flat, yielding surface. He sensed the door to his room being opened, and he was floating out through it into the corridor. No, not floating, rolling on soft rubber wheels. Rolling, rolling. The fluorescent lights passed overhead in dim, wavery images, as though seen from underwater.

Suddenly the air was cool on his face. There was a breeze with the scent of pine in it. He was outside. A dim recollection of a voice that called him from out here fought for a space in his consciousness, but the drug was too strong.

Malcolm was lifted again, placed inside some sort of metallic box. A van. Dr. Pastory got in beside him. He gave an order. An engine fired and Malcolm sensed movement. Then the fever returned and consciousness slipped away.

At ten o'clock Dr. Dennis Qualen strolled in through the entrance of La Reina County Hospital. He was, as always, impeccably turned out. Today he had chosen a dark blue worsted with muted pinstripe and a tie of pale yellow. He acknowledged the greetings of staff and employees with a nod and half smile. Dr. Qualen did not believe in becoming too familiar with the people under him. Particularly since he did not intend to spend one day longer than necessary at La Reina. He had feelers out to bigger institutions in San Francisco, Houston, and Miami. Once he had straightened out the budgetary problems here, and had the figures to show it, he would surely be hearing from them.

He rode the elevator to the second floor, passing an encouraging word to a small boy in a wheelchair. The boy stared at him dully. He watched as the nurse wheeled the boy toward the orthopedic ward, then he turned and walked briskly toward the glass doors to Administration. Once beyond them he felt a tangible relief. Those doors represented a barrier to Dr. Qualen that kept the sordidness of disease and death separate from the nice clean business of running a hospital.

He barely noticed a neatly dressed young man with sandy hair who sat in one of the chairs across from the reception desk. A salesman, the doctor surmised. Some new wonder drug, or a piece of expensive equipment that no modern hospital should be without. La Reina was not in a buying cycle at present, but Qualen tolerated salesmen for the gossip they carried of the outside medical community.

The doctor smiled coolly at Mrs. Thayer as he went by. For his own taste he would have preferred a receptionist with a bit more style, and better tits. However, he knew that the matronly Mrs. Thayer gave his office a solid, business-like appearance. And she was excellent at guarding his door from patients and other unwanted visitors.

As soon as he settled himself in the burgundy leather chair behind the mahogany desk, the intercom buzzed. With a sigh he reached over and flipped the switch.

"Yes, Mrs. Thayer."

"A gentleman out here to see you, Doctor."

"Who is he with?"

"Apparently he is not representing any firm."

"Then what does he want with me?"

"He says it's about the boy they brought in from the woods. The boy in one-oh-eight."

Qualen frowned. He glanced over at the transfer papers for Malcolm, riffled through them, and saw that Dr. Pastory's name had been correctly entered, making him the responsible party.

He said, "Did you tell him I am not concerned with patients' affairs?"

"The gentleman was quite adamant about wanting to see the man in charge. He's been here since I came in, at eight o'clock."

Damn. Qualen hated to start the day with some petty annoyance. "Does he have a name?"

"Yes, Doctor. Mr. Derak."

It meant nothing to Dr. Qualen. Had an unpleasant foreign sound. He sighed. Might as well get it over with.

"Ask Mr. Derak to come in."

The doctor assumed a businesslike pose and watched as his visitor entered. He was not as young as he had appeared at first glance. It was difficult to guess his age. Something about the eyes, an odd shade of green, seemed very, very old. Nevertheless, he was presentable enough. His sandy hair was cut short and neatly brushed. The jacket and slacks were not top quality, but good. He had a nice smile. Strong.

"Good morning, Mr. Derak," said Qualen with just the right mixture of cordiality and restraint. "What can I do for you?"

"You have a boy here. I understand he was found wandering in the forest and was brought in by deputy sheriffs."

"Ah, yes," Qualen said after a pause to indicate he was trying to remember the case.

"I'd like to see him."

"Mr. Derak, visits with patients are handled through the desk in the main lobby. You must have passed it when you came in."

"I talked to the woman there, and I talked to her supervisor. I could not get satisfactory answers from them. They suggested I see you." A rather unpleasant note crept into Derak's voice.

Qualen resolved to have a talk with that woman and her supervisor at the first opportunity. He said. "You are a relative of . . ." He made a show of looking through the papers on his desk. ". . . Malcolm."

"In a way."

The doctor looked up, expecting a further explanation. Derak offered none. His green-eyed gaze was uncomfortably direct.

"As it happens," Qualen said, "that patient has been transferred."

"Transferred?" Derak took a step closer to the desk. "He was here last night."

"That's true. The transfer was effected early this morning."

The sandy-haired man became agitated. One hand pulled loose the knot of his necktie. "Where was he taken?" His voice sounded different. Coarser.

"I'm really not at liberty to say. If you will leave your name and address with my—"

"You will tell me now," said Derak. The voice had roughened into a growl.

Dr. Qualen stared at the man in astonishment. He had thrown off his jacket and was actually tearing at his shirt. And his face, my God, it was twisting into something quite inhuman.

The doctor reached for the intercom box. Derak's hand clamped onto his wrist with a grip that crackled the bones. Qualen stared at the hand. Before his bulging eyes it changed. Grew into a terrible mutant paw. Thick, wiry hair sprouted from the back. The nails thickened and pushed out into claws. Qualen looked up at the face.

Even as he began to scream, the doctor knew the acoustic

walls would let no more than a murmur escape to Mrs. Thayer outside.

With a strength born of terror, Qualen wrenched his wrist free of the terrible grip. He ran around his desk and tried to make it to the door. Derak, or whatever this thing was that Derak had become, was faster. He threw himself past the doctor and used that misshapen, hairy paw to roll the dead bolt home, locking them in.

The only other way out was the window of reinforced glass, and that gave on a sheer drop of twenty feet to the concrete parking lot. Qualen backed away, watching in horrified fascination the transformation taking place before him.

The man's body twisted and swelled and grew to a height that towered over the six-foot doctor. There was a terrible cracking as the skeleton reshaped itself inside the creature. The face . . . the face was all muzzle and teeth and burning eyes of green hellfire.

In a movement too swift for him to follow, Qualen felt himself seized under the arms and lifted clear of the floor. His shrieks echoed dully off the soundproofed walls. He felt the hot breath of the creature as the great jaws opened; he smelled the stench of it. There was a moment of searing agony as the teeth sank into his throat. A hot gush of his life's blood. A last roar in his ears. Then blackness and oblivion.

It was the faint but unmistakable crash of glass from inside Dr. Qualen's office that roused Mrs. Thayer. The only thing in there that could make a crash like that was the window. She buzzed the intercom, got no answer. With mounting unease, Mrs. Thayer rose from her chair, walked to the door of Dr. Qualen's office, tried the knob. Locked. She rapped lightly, then again, louder. There was no response. Something was wrong. Dreadfully wrong.

Mrs. Thayer snatched the telephone from her desk and

punched out the internal emergency code. In less than a minute two burly orderlies came running in from the corridor outside.

"There's trouble in Dr. Qualen's office," she cried. "The door's locked and he won't answer me."

The orderlies hesitated only a moment, then attacked the door while Mrs. Thayer stood back out of the way. The door soon splintered under their combined assault. The men rushed inside, stopping as though they had hit a wall when they saw the bloody thing sprawled over the desk of the administrative chief. Behind them Mrs. Thayer started into the room, then gave a little cry and backed away, her hand covering her mouth.

At the same moment the men turned toward the broken window. They crossed the room together and looked out, scanning the parking lot below. Nothing.

One of them pointed up at the hillside. "Look!"

The other followed his pointing finger. "What is it? I don't see anything."

"I thought . . . for a minute it looked like something up there. Running."

"A man? What?"

"I don't know. I can't see it now. It was more like a big dog. Or . . . Christ, I don't know. Let's get help."

Later, of all the ghastly events of that morning the two men would remember the sound they heard from somewhere up on the wooded hill. They would remember the howling.

Chapter 11

The people at the hospital provided Ramsay with a small unused office at the rear of the first floor, next to the kitchen, to use for his interviews with the staff and employees. It had only a desk, two chairs, a file cabinet that would not open, and a hastily installed telephone. There was also a pervasive smell of bland hospital cooking coming in through the single window.

One of the chairs was occupied by a stenographer on loan from Ventura County. She took rapid, silent notes as Mrs. Audrey Thayer, secretary and receptionist for the late Dr. Qualen, answered the sheriff's questions.

Through the window Ramsay could see search parties laboring up the thickly wooded hillside, where the suspect might or might not have been seen running by one of the orderlies who found the body. Overhead was the persistent thrum of helicopters. There was one from the Ventura County Sheriff's office and several from television news departments.

The media had appeared miraculously less than two hours after Ramsay had received the report of Dr. Qualen's murder. So far he had been able to avoid them with the help of deputies Nevins and Fernandez, who stood out in the hallway looking as mean as they could manage.

Sooner or later he would have to talk to them, but Ramsay was determined to get as much as he could of his real work done first. Like most lawmen, he had a healthy distrust of reporters, a distrust he knew was mutual.

"Is there anything more you can tell me about this Mr. Derak?" Ramsay asked the woman across from him. "Any little thing, no matter how unimportant it seemed at the time, might be helpful."

Mrs. Thayer frowned thoughtfully and shook her head. Her hands were busy twisting a flowered hankie into a snake. "I'm sorry, Sheriff, but there really isn't anything more than what I've already told you. He was just an ordinary-looking man. Rather pleasant, he seemed at the time. Very insistent, though, about seeing Dr. Qualen."

At the mention of her late employer, Mrs. Thayer's ample chest convulsed in a sob. She unwound the hankie and dabbed at her eyes. Ramsay waited for the spasm to pass before he went on.

"And he said nothing to you about what business he had with the doctor?"

"Only that he was sent up there by Eleanor Chung. She supervises the admission desk in the lobby."

Ramsay nodded. He had already talked to Miss Chung and the woman who was on duty when Derak came in. They said he insisted on seeing the patient known as Malcolm in room 108. Since he could show no evidence that he was related, they explained he would have to wait until regular visiting hours, then clear it with the doctor assigned to Malcolm's case. They declined to give him any more information, and when the man refused to leave, referred him to Dr. Qualen.

"How long was he in the office with Dr. Qualen before you heard the crash of the window breaking?"

95

"Not long. Not more than fifteen minutes. I don't see how he could have . . . could have . . ."

Ramsay spoke up quickly to head off another outburst of sobs. "And you heard nothing before that because of the soundproof construction of the walls. Is that correct?"

"Nothing. Once, very faint, I thought I heard a voice, but I couldn't be sure."

Milo Fernandez entered, glanced at Mrs. Thayer, and spoke to Ramsay. "Dr. Underwood is outside with his report."

"Good. Thank you very much, Mrs. Thayer. That'll be all for now."

"You'll catch the . . . the terrible person who did this, won't you, Sheriff?"

"Yes, we will," Ramsay said with a lot more conviction than he felt. "He won't get away."

Reassured, Mrs. Thayer gave him a teary smile and left the office. Ramsay told the stenographer to take a break, and sat back to wait for the pathologist.

Neal Underwood was a man happy in his work. He was plump and pleasant and had thinning blond hair that still had a curl to it. His biggest satisfaction in recent years had been the cancellation of *Quincy*, the farfetched television show that had a choleric pathologist rushing around shouting at everyone, solving crimes, making fools out of doctors and police alike. Dr. Underwood did his job in a quiet and efficient manner and had far more friends than enemies. He could make small jokes about how his patients never complained, and he did not even mind being referred to around the hospital as Dr. Underground.

He took the chair across from Ramsay and laid a folder on the desk between them.

"As savage a killing as I've seen in some time," the pathologist said pleasantly.

"What was the cause of death?"

"My preliminary findings show it to be loss of blood

96

from a severed jugular. The lower face, throat, and upper chest were severely lacerated. Many of the wounds, I'm relieved to say, probably occurred after the victim was already dead. He died very quickly.''

''Any guess as to the weapon?''

''You're not going to like it.''

''Try me.''

''Teeth.''

Ramsay let several seconds go by while he held the pathologist's mild gaze. *''Teeth?''*

''I told you you wouldn't like it.''

''Human teeth?''

''Not likely. The human jaw is not constructed for attack. To kill with its teeth, an animal needs a protruding muzzle. That allows the jaws to open like this.'' Underwood demonstrated with his two hands, touching at the heel, making teeth of his fingers.

''What kind of an animal might that be?''

''Oh, lots of them. Shark, alligator, tiger, hyena . . .''

Ramsay saw him hesitate. ''And?''

''And a wolf.''

''Uh-huh. Would you say it's possible to construct a weapon that would make wounds like that, resembling teeth?''

''I suppose it would be possible, but it would make a damned inefficient weapon. It would be an awkward thing to carry around, too. Impossible to conceal.''

Ramsay pinched the bridge of his nose. He felt a headache coming on, but the next question had to be asked. ''Have you seen a killing like this before, Doctor?''

Underwood nodded slowly. He was no more eager to answer than Ramsay was to ask. ''Similar. Several of them.''

''Like to tell me where and when?''

''Right here. Last year. During the business at Drago.''

Ramsay groaned inwardly. The damned dead village of

Drago was destined to haunt him. "What do you think killed those people?"

"Wolves," Dr. Underwood said without hesitation. "Yes, I know there hasn't been a wolf sighted around here since the turn of the century, and I know none was ever found, but that's my story and I'm sticking to it. Wolves. Where they came from, where they went, that's not my problem."

"You heard the stories?"

"Werewolves? Sure, I heard them. Who didn't? But if you think I am going to write werewolves and witches and fairies into my reports . . . well, forget it."

"It was no wolf that walked into Dr. Qualen's office," Ramsay said quietly. "A man walked in there. One man. He carried no visible weapon."

"Sheriff, I don't envy you your job." Underwood slapped the folder he had laid on the desk. "There's my preliminary report. Make out of it what you will. Beyond the medical facts and observations contained therein, I have nothing to offer."

"Easy," Ramsay said. "Believe me, Doctor, I don't want werewolves any more than you do. I've just got to come up with some answer as to how a single man could do that kind of damage in a short space of time, then jump through a reinforced plate-glass window to a concrete slab twenty feet down, then run off up into the woods and somehow elude a professional ground and air search party."

Underwood gave him a sympathetic smile. "Sheriff, I'll bet nobody told you it was going to be easy. Are you through with me?"

Ramsay waved him away. "Yeah, thanks, Doctor. I'll be down to talk to you later. Try not to mention you-know-what to our reporter friends, will you?"

"Are you kidding? I walked past a bunch of them in the lobby, and all they're talking about is werewolves. I even saw a couple of them sharpening wooden stakes."

Ramsay could not resist a smile. "That shows how much they know. Stakes are for vampires."

Dr. Underwood nodded sagely and left the office.

It was past two o'clock and Ramsay had not eaten since his coffee and donut early that morning. His stomach rumbled, reminding him of the omission. He got up and went to the door where the deputies stood guard. To Fernandez he said, "How about seeing if you can scrounge something to eat? I'm not ready to run the gauntlet in the lobby yet."

Before the young deputy could answer, Holly Lang appeared, wheeling one of the hospital food carts.

"I thought you men might be getting hungry," she said.

"You're magic," Ramsay told her.

She gave a tray to each of the deputies and wheeled the cart into the office. Ramsay closed the door behind her.

On covered plates there was cole slaw, roast beef, hot rolls, mashed potatoes, and peas. There was Jell-O for dessert and a thermal carafe of coffee.

"Not exactly cordon bleu, but nutritious, or so they tell me in the cafeteria."

"It looks great. And I promised the next meal was going to be on me."

"I'll catch up with you," Holly said. "Dig in while it's hot."

Ramsay began to eat. He could feel Holly watching him. "Go ahead and ask," he said.

"All right. How are you doing?"

"Just swell. It appears that a nice-mannered fellow named Mr. Derak walked into Dr. Qualen's office, bit him to death, jumped out the window, and disappeared. It's a piece of cake."

"You know Malcolm is gone, don't you?"

"Yes, of course."

"The nurse, Rita Keneally, says Dr. Pastory came in early this morning, had Malcolm sedated, and took him away."

"So?"

"Don't you think there's a connection? This man Derak came here wanting to see Malcolm."

"If there is a connection, I'm sure it will come out when we talk to Dr. Pastory."

"But I've asked, and nobody knows where he is."

Ramsay swallowed a mouthful of roast beef. "Holly, I am investigating a murder. I have two capable deputies and more help than I really want from the sheriffs of Ventura and Los Angeles counties. Suppose you stick to curing the sick and leave crime to me."

"God, I hate it when they get condescending."

"If by 'they' you mean me, I'm sorry that's the way it sounded to you, but I do have an awful lot on my mind."

"Isn't kidnapping a big enough crime to get some attention?"

"Kidnapping? You're talking about Malcolm?"

"Who else?"

"As I understand it, that was a fairly routine transfer of a patient from one facility to another."

"Bullshit!"

Ramsey lowered a forkful of mashed potatoes back to the plate. From a desk drawer he drew a clear plastic folder with several sheets of a printed form inside. The sheets were spattered with a brownish stain.

"I have here," Ramsay said, "what they tell me are the official and correct forms for transfer of our patient Malcolm from La Reina County Hospital to some clinic. They are a bit messy, because they were found on the desk of the late Dr. Qualen, who was more or less lying on top of them."

"Have you read them?"

"Well, no, but—"

"I have," Holly snapped. "And there are some glaring irregularities."

"How did you get hold of these reports before I did?" Ramsay asked.

"I have friends here. The point is that although Dr. Wayne Pastory's name is all over those forms transferring Malcolm to his own clinic, nowhere is the location of that clinic spelled out."

"So?"

"So I want to know where Malcolm was taken."

"When Dr. Pastory shows up we'll ask him. How about that?"

"Fine, but what makes you think he's going to show up?"

"What happened here this morning won't exactly be a secret by the time the six o'clock news hits the air," he said. "Unless Pastory is a damn fool, he'll show up here voluntarily and give us his version of what happened."

"Pastory is no fool," Holly said tightly, "but he may be something much worse."

"What does that mean?"

"It means Malcolm could be in real danger. While you sit here waiting for Pastory to stroll in and chat, he could be harming that boy in some dreadful way."

"Now listen to me, Holly. I know you have a special feeling for Malcolm, but it seems to me you're letting it get in the way of your professional judgment. I will want to question Dr. Pastory as a witness, but as far as I know, he has committed no crime. This man called Derak is a bona fide murder suspect. That is my number-one priority, and it's going to stay that way until I have reason to change my thinking. Is that understood?"

She glared at him. "Oh, absolutely, Mr. Sheriff, sir. You just go ahead and play Dirty Harry and hunt down your phantom murderer. I trust you won't mind too much if I do what little I can to try to find a boy who may be in trouble like you've never imagined."

"Do whatever you want to, Holly," Gavin said, making

an effort to soften his tone. "But I'll appreciate it if you'll try not to interfere with the investigation."

She sprang to her feet and glared, fists clenched at her sides. "Don't worry, Sheriff. I won't come within shouting distance of your precious investigation."

Without giving him a chance to reply, she spun on her heel and marched out of the office, startling Nevins and Fernandez, who were finishing up their lunches out in the corridor. By the time Ramsay got to the door she was not in sight.

"What did you do to the lady doctor, Sheriff?" Roy Nevins asked. "She came out of there like her tail feathers was on fire."

"I asked her to please stay out of my way."

"Oh. Well." The deputy nodded as though that explained everything.

When he could postpone it no longer, Ramsay made his way out through the crowded lobby of the hospital. Every third person seemed to be carrying a television Minicam on his shoulder. Those who didn't have cameras had tape recorders and phallic microphones, which they thrust at anyone who moved within range. When Ramsay appeared they surged toward him like piranha to a goldfish.

"Have you made an arrest, Sheriff?"

"Any suspects?"

"What kind of wounds did the dead man have?"

"Is it true his head was bitten off?"

"Is there a link to the killings last year at Drago?"

"What's your opinion of the werewolf theory?"

Ramsay held up a hand like a traffic cop and waited a full minute until the reporters subsided into near silence. He said, "There have been no arrests. We are following up on several possible suspects. I cannot describe the fatal wounds at this time for fear of jeopardizing the investigation. The victim's head was not bitten off. No connection has been found to any other crimes. In my opinion werewolves exist only in cheap horror movies. Thank you all very much."

As he started toward the door the reporters crowded in around him, thrusting their ball-headed microphones close to his face, gabbling questions all at the same time.

"Excuse me. I'm sorry. I have a very important meeting that could be vital to the investigation. No, I cannot give you any more information. Excuse me."

Ramsay's progress through the crowd slowed to a near standstill as the mass of bodies around him pressed closer. As he was about to be pushed backward, a thick-shouldered man with forearms like Popeye shoved his way through the crowd, ignoring the complaints and curses from the reporters.

"Right this way, Sheriff. The car's outside."

The man was vaguely familiar, but Ramsay could not immediately place him. However, this was no time to ask for ID. He fell in behind the man like a running back behind his pulling guard, and together they plowed a furrow through the gaggle of reporters, out the door, and down the wide walkway to a beat-up Volkswagen Beetle. Ramsay jumped into the passenger's side and the other man wedged himself behind the wheel. He slammed the little car into gear and they took off, barely missing a camera crew from the Los Angeles ABC affiliate.

By the time the reporters had collected themselves and dashed for their own vehicles, the Beetle had roared around the corner and turned off the road onto an all but invisible wagon track that led out of sight behind a row of eucalyptus trees. There the driver stopped and cut the engine.

When the caravan of media cars had roared past on the highway, Ramsay turned for a better look at his driver. "Thanks for the rescue," he said. "You've got a handy way with crowds."

"I played a little football years ago at Stanford."

"Do I know you?" Ramsay asked.

"You might have seen me around. Name's Ken Dowd. I own a little shop in Darnay. Heard about what happened at the hospital this morning and thought maybe I could help you out."

"That so? In what way, Mr. Dowd?"

"Call me Ken. Well, I heard how they're saying this killing was like the ones they had over at Drago before the town burned down. Werewolves, you know."

"I know," Ramsay said wearily.

"Well, back then I had occasion to help a fellow out. Came up from L.A. Had to go into Drago after a woman or something. He came to my shop."

"What do you call your shop, Ken?"

The broad-shouldered man looked embarrassed. "The Spirit World. My wife's idea. I told her it sounded like a liquor store, but that's what she wanted, and half the money to set it up was hers. We sell occult books, Ouija boards, powders, potions, charms, chants. You name it."

"That's interesting, Ken, but I don't see how it's going to help me."

Dowd reached behind the seat and brought up a cardboard box the size of a double deck of playing cards. He handed it to Ramsay. The box was surprisingly heavy for its size.

"What is it?"

"Take a look."

Ramsay raised the flap and looked inside. It took a moment for him to recognize the contents.

"Silver bullets?"

"Caliber thirty-eight. I figured they ought to fit your police revolver."

"You're not joking with me, are you, Ken?"

"I am not. And I won't waste a lot of time arguing with you about whether there's such things as ghosts and vampires and werewolves. I have my own beliefs, but I'm not interested in convincing anybody else. I saw the way some of those people died in Drago, and I don't want to see any more. You can take these bullets or not, whatever you want. I happen to think they might save your life, and maybe some others, too."

Ramsay looked closely at the man and decided he was not drunk or crazy or a fool. He hefted the box of bullets and dropped it into a side pocket of his uniform jacket.

"Thanks, Ken. I'll take them."

Dowd nodded soberly. "I don't think you'll be sorry, Sheriff." He fired the Volkswagen engine and drove back to the road.

Chapter 12

It was impossible for Malcolm to tell how long he rode inside the van. There were moments when he was almost awake and he could see Dr. Pastory sitting close by, watching him. There were heavy curtains across the rear window, and the only illumination came from up front in the cab, where the other man was driving. Malcolm did not have the strength to turn and look up there, and he soon lapsed back into unconsciousness.

He had only vague sensations of when the ride ended. First the vibration of the engine stopped, then there were the metallic sounds of doors opening and closing and the voices of the two men. The chill of outdoor air was on his face briefly, then it was warm again. He felt the familiar touch of sheets on his body and the slight give of a mattress under him. To his drugged brain that meant he was back in the hospital. Safe. Holly would be here soon. He slept.

When finally his brain cleared and he came fully awake, Malcolm saw at once he was not in the hospital. The bed was similar, and the room had the same kind of medicinal smell, but there was a coldness here. Not in the temperature, for the room was quite warm, but in the atmosphere. Malcolm had no idea where he was; he only knew it was a bad place.

The room was very plain. There was his narrow bed, a four-drawer bureau, a little nightstand, and a straight wooden chair. The room had one door, no window. In a corner was a white enameled sink with a mirrored cabinet above it. On one wall hung a picture of a dog on a hillock overlooking a flock of grazing sheep. The picture showed storm clouds building on the horizon.

Malcolm peeled back the covers and swung his feet out of the bed onto the floor. He was dizzy for a moment and had to shut his eyes. When he opened them he felt a little better. He looked down and saw that he was still wearing the foolish little garment they had given him at the hospital.

He stood up, walked carefully the few steps to the door. He tried the knob. Locked. Malcolm was not surprised. He prowled around the room touching things, feeling their surfaces.

He ran some water over his hands at the sink and splashed it on his face. He looked at himself in the mirror. The young face that looked back at him was very sad. Dark half-moons shadowed the eyes.

The bureau was unfinished wood of some kind. Malcolm pulled out the drawers one by one. Three of them were empty, but the top drawer contained clothes. There was underwear, jeans, T-shirts, sweaters, socks, tennis shoes.

"Well, hello, Malcolm. How are you feeling?"

The voice startled him so that he spun away from the bureau and almost lost his balance. Dr. Pastory stood in the doorway. He had opened it without making a sound.

"I see you found the clothes. It's all right; they're for you. I hope they fit. I'm not used to buying clothes for a boy. Young man, I should say."

Malcolm shrugged.

"I thought you'd be tired of wearing that hospital gown. I don't blame you."

Pastory was trying hard to make his voice friendly, but it was still oily and cold to Malcolm. The doctor came over and took his arm to guide him back to the bed. His touch was as unpleasant as his voice. He had an antiseptic smell to him. Malcolm sat down on the bed. Pastory took the chair and hitched it over close.

"Now then, how do you feel?" he said again.

"Sick to my stomach," Malcolm told him.

"Well, that's not unusual. The drug does that sometimes. It's nothing to worry about. We'll get some food into you and you'll feel tip-top again."

"Where are we?"

"It's a little place of mine where we can get you all well again."

"I'm not sick."

"That's a matter of opinion, Malcolm. Definitely a matter of opinion."

Dr. Pastory was looking at him in a strange, piercing way, but then he put on the fake oily smile again. "Why don't you put on some of your new clothes? Are they what boys are wearing today?"

"They're okay."

"Good. You just get dressed now and I'll show you where we're going to work together."

"Work?"

"In a matter of speaking. You're an unusual young man, Malcolm. I'm going to give you a few tests—oh, nothing that will hurt or anything like that—and see if we can find out what makes you so unusual."

"I don't think I want to take tests."

Pastory's little eyes glittered. "I told you before, Malcolm, in this life it doesn't always matter what we want. Now will you get yourself dressed, or should I bring in somebody to do it for you?"

"I'll do it."

"Good. That's the spirit I like to hear." The doctor went

out. The door closed soundlessly behind him. There was a whispered click of the lock. Malcolm turned the knob just to be sure. It was locked, all right.

He tried on some of the clothes from the bureau. Everything was a size or so too big, but not so much that it mattered. And it did feel good to be wearing real clothes again.

When he was dressed Malcolm sat down on the bed and waited. In a few minutes Pastory came back in bringing a mug of some hot brown liquid. There was another man with him. The other man was big, with a barrel chest and thick neck and bristly black hair. His lips were thick and set in a permanent sneer. He smelled bad. Malcolm recognized the smell from the morning he was taken from the hospital. Was it only this morning? Whatever they shot him up with had messed up his sense of time.

Pastory handed him the mug. "Drink this. It's full of vitamins and other good things."

Malcolm drank. It tasted like a heavy beef broth. Not too bad.

"Later on you can have solid food, but I think for now we'd better stick to liquids."

"How long am I going to be here?"

"That depends." He pulled the door all the way open. "Come along now."

"What are you going to do?"

Pastory dropped the fake pleasant expression he'd been wearing. "I haven't time to explain every little thing to you. Kruger, bring him along."

The big man grabbed Malcolm by the shoulder and dug his thumb into a nerve there.

"Hey!" the boy protested.

"The doctor wants you to come along." Kruger had a high singsong voice that did not fit with his size. He pulled Malcolm to his feet and propelled him out the door.

He was taken along a short hallway and into another room, larger than the one where he had awakened. A skylight in the ceiling made it very bright. There were shelves on the walls holding all manner of bottles, vials, beakers, and jars. Some of them contained liquids or powders; others were empty. Along one side of the room was a counter with a stainless steel sink and a little gas burner. All along the counter there was a cluster of instruments and equipment that meant nothing to Malcolm.

In the center of the room was a high, narrow table, padded, with tough leather straps riveted to the sides. Under the table was a complicated system of gears so it could be tilted in any direction.

"This is a laboratory," Malcolm said.

"Very good," Pastory said, as though to an apt pupil. "Would you like to jump up on the table there?"

"No."

"I think, my boy, we had better understand how things are run around here. When I make a suggestion, it is not really a suggestion. It is an order. And when I give an order, you obey. That way we will all get along much better. Now get up on that table."

Malcolm felt his face growing hot. His shoulder still hurt where Kruger had dug into the nerve. He walked to the table, turned around, and gave a little jump so he was sitting on it.

"That's the idea," Pastory said. "Now lie back, please."

"What for?"

Pastory snapped his head at the big man who was standing by eagerly. "Kruger!"

Before Malcolm knew what was happening, Kruger had pushed him down flat on his back and had buckled a strap around one of his wrists. He flailed out with his free hand.

"Cut it out!" he yelled.

Kruger drew back a massive arm and cracked the back of his hand against Malcolm's cheek. Malcolm tasted blood. His eyesight blurred for a moment and there seemed to be an

110

edge of fire around everything. There was a strange growling sound in his ears, and Malcolm was surprised to realize it came from his own throat.

Pastory hurried over to the table. "Did you see that? Wonderful! Get the other hand strapped down, Kruger. And his feet. Quickly!"

As the doctor peered down on him Malcolm's flash of anger drained away, to be replaced by a numb feeling of hopelessness.

"There, he's changing back now," Pastory said. "But did you see it, Kruger? Did you see what happened to his face?"

"It looked funny there for a minute. Like his teeth were too big for his mouth, or something."

"Or something!" Pastory repeated. He leaned very close to Malcolm, took his chin in one hand, and turned his head this way and that. His breath had a minty smell.

"Are you all right now, Malcolm?" he asked.

"I want to get up."

"In time, my boy. In time. Tell me what you felt just then, when you tried to get at Kruger."

"I-I was mad. He shouldn't have hit me."

"No, you're quite right. I'll see that it doesn't happen again."

Pastory walked back to the counter and began to write furiously in a hardbound notebook. He spoke more to himself than to the others in the room. "It appears that anger triggers the change. I wonder if other powerful emotions will have the same effect. We will have to look into that."

He returned to the table. "Open your mouth, please."

Malcolm hesitated.

"It's only a thermometer. See? All I want to do is take your temperature. Now open, please."

Reluctantly Malcolm obeyed, and the doctor slipped the glass tube expertly under his tongue.

"I am going to take a sample of your blood now. A very small bit, Malcolm. You'll never miss it."

The boy watched as Pastory inserted the hollow needle into a vein on the inside of his elbow and drew crimson fluid up into the cylinder.

"There now." The doctor withdrew the needle and taped a wad of cotton over the tiny hole it left. He took the thermometer out of Malcolm's mouth and examined it. "A touch above normal. Nothing to be concerned about."

"Can I get up now?" Malcolm said.

"Very soon, my boy. There is just one more shot now, one that will relax you and make you feel good. Then we'll get you up and get you something to eat."

Pastory gave him the needle in the shoulder, then backed away, looking very pleased with himself. "You just relax for a minute or so, Malcolm. I want to go and check some references. If you need anything, just tell Kruger here. Okay?"

Malcolm rolled his head to look at the doctor, but he did not answer. A heavy feeling was spreading through his body. He did not want to do much of anything.

As soon as Pastory went out and closed the door, Kruger came over and stared down into the boy's face. The man's heavy features were twisted in open hostility.

"You'd better not do anything like that to me again," he said.

"Didn't do anything." It was an effort for Malcolm to get the words out.

"You know what I'm talking about. That thing you did with your face and your teeth. I don't care what the doctor says. You'd better behave or I'll hurt you."

The big man talked to him some more, but Malcolm floated off to a warm, cozy place where the words made no sense.

After that, time had little meaning for Malcolm. He knew he was being measured and weighed, prodded and pricked,

112

tested, retested, fed, and purged. He did not care about any of it. Sometimes he would be left alone and Kruger would be there. The big man glowered at him constantly and made threats, but Malcolm had no energy to respond.

The worst part was when he was strapped to the table. Then Pastory would do things to him that he didn't like to think about. Things with little electric wires and such. Sometimes the doctor made it very cold in the laboratory, sometimes unbearably hot. He was always writing in his book, looking very excited. With the drug in him, Malcolm couldn't care.

Then Dr. Pastory made a mistake with one of the shots he regularly gave Malcolm. The boy moved his arm just as the needle went in, and the drug squirted harmlessly onto his sleeve. So intent was Pastory on watching Malcolm's face that he did not see. When he went away Malcolm could feel himself growing steadily stronger and more alert.

Later that night—or maybe it was day, Malcolm could never be sure—Kruger came into his room. The boy saw him but pretended to be asleep.

"You awake?" Kruger demanded. "Yeah, I can see you are. Come on, it's time to get you up and get you dressed." He started toward the boy.

"Don't touch me," Malcolm said. "Keep away."

"Listen, you don't tell me what to do and what not to do. Maybe you need to be reminded of who's boss around here." Kruger lumbered over to the bed, reached down, and seized Malcolm's wrist.

A dull anger pushed its way into the boy's clearing mind, but he still did not have the strength to pull away.

Gripping Malcolm's wrist with one hand, Kruger pulled a cigarette lighter from his pocket with the other. He snapped on the flame and brought it slowly up under the boy's palm.

The sensation of heat quickly grew into pain. It brought back terrible memories of a night of flames and screaming and the stench of burning flesh. The flesh of his people.

In a sudden convulsive movement, Malcolm snapped his head to one side and clamped his teeth on the hairy wrist of the man who held him. The skin broke easily, and he worked his jaws from side to side, biting through the tougher muscle meat. His tongue felt the slick, ropy tendons through the taste of blood.

Kruger's scream shattered around his head like breaking glass. The cigarette lighter dropped to the floor. Malcolm bit down harder, finding a wild joy in the sensation of sinking his teeth into living flesh.

"Kruger!" The shout came from Dr. Pastory, who had run into the room in response to the big man's cry.

"Get him off me!" Kruger shrieked, trying to pull his arm free.

Malcolm, eyes closed in a kind of ecstasy, bit down all the harder. He felt bones grind against his teeth.

There was a short, sharp stab in the back of his neck, and Malcolm recognized it as the jab of a needle. Instantly he lost feeling in his face. His jaw muscles slackened and Kruger pulled his lacerated arm free.

"Look what that little son of a bitch did to me! Look at my arm! I'll kill the little bastard!"

"Shut up, Kruger."

Malcolm watched dully as Dr. Pastory pulled his assistant away and looked at his arm.

"He took quite a chunk out of you," Pastory said.

"Damn near bit through the bone. Will it get infected or anything?"

"I'll dress it for you in a minute. What I want to know is, what did you do to provoke him?"

"Nothing. I didn't do nothing."

Pastory stooped and picked something off the floor. "What's this?"

"My lighter. I-I must have dropped it."

"Don't lie to me, Kruger. Don't ever lie to me. You

114

know all I have to do is say the word to have you put back in the bad place."

"Please don't, Doctor. I was just fooling around. I didn't mean to do anything to him."

"Get out of here. Go to the laboratory and I'll come in and take a look at that bite. It may even turn out to be helpful to me."

Cradling his injured arm, Kruger left them alone.

Pastory came over and touched Malcolm's face. The anesthetic had left him without any feeling there, but Malcolm could see the doctor poking at the flesh and muttering to himself.

"Incredible. Absolutely incredible. Malcolm, you are going to make me a very rich and famous man. We have a lot of work to do in the next few days, but then we'll start reaping the rewards. And don't you worry, my boy. I'll take very, very good care of you."

Malcolm sank back on the narrow bed. All the anger was gone. All he felt now was an icy despair. He was ready to give up and die, except for one thing. He still held in his mouth the delicious taste of Kruger's blood.

Chapter 13

Sheriff Gavin Ramsay of La Reina County had moments during the next few days when he seriously questioned his choice of career. The investigation of Dr. Dennis Qualen's murder was not going well. It was, in fact, going very badly.

The search of the surrounding hills turned up nothing. The only flurry of excitement had come when one of the searchers shot another in the foot. After that the fun was out of the whole thing. The volunteers had gone back to their jobs. The helicopters had returned to their home counties or their TV station heliports. Only a few men from the State Forestry Service now combed the woods, doing mostly cleanup and repair of the damage to the environment done by the searchers.

The detailed pathology report had arrived from Dr. Underwood and had done nothing to lift Ramsay's spirits. The wounds that had killed Qualen were definitely identified as having been made by teeth. Unfortunately, they were not the teeth of any animal known to exist on the face of the earth. The traces of saliva were no more helpful, falling somewhere on the spectrograph between human and canine.

While the sheriff suffered, the media had a field day. Every man, woman, and reasonably articulate child in Pinyon had been interviewed at least once. Deputies Nevins and Fernandez became media heroes, the first to his delight, the latter with some embarrassment. All the old horror stories of Drago were dug up and embellished until La Reina County was presented to the rest of the nation as a sort of Southern California Transylvania, where no one walked out of doors at night.

Most galling to Ramsay was the fact that Abe Craddock had been bailed out by one of the supermarket tabloids and was being kept in seclusion while his personal eyewitness story was being ghostwritten for the paper. Rumor had Craddock collecting a comfortable five-figure price for his lurid recollections of the thing that had eaten his buddy.

And, in fact, a pall of fear had descended over the tiny mountain town. Blinds were drawn, shutters reinforced, doors double-locked at night where before no one had bothered with so much as a hook and eye. Nightly patronage at the Pinyon Inn dwindled to a few hard-core regulars who drank little and talked in guarded tones. They came and left in pairs or groups. No one wanted to be alone.

The tiny library was immediately denuded of all books touching on werewolves, vampires, witches, or anything remotely occult. Then the librarian refused to stay there alone any longer and the doors were locked.

The happiest man in the county was Ken Dowd, whose Darnay occult shop, The Spirit World, emptied its shelves of all manner of charms and talismans that might protect the bearer from whatever evil lurked in the woods.

Nor was the occult dealer the only beneficiary of the werewolf boom. The Light of the World Christian Store, also in Darnay, had a run on crucifixes from customers who did not know Calvary from the Seventh Cavalry. The Light of the World people had to reorder crosses on a rush basis from a religious supply firm in Los Angeles, and still they could barely meet the demand.

Bibles were also a hot item in La Reina County, with King James topping the list, but even the updated versions were outselling the newest Garfield book. Enterprising roadside peddlers appeared with pictures and statuettes representing Jesus, Mary, and a variety of saints and were doing fine business until local authorities clamped down. From outward appearances, La Reina County was the scene of the greatest Christian revival since Billy Graham filled the L.A. Coliseum.

As if all this were not enough to add gray hairs to the head of Sheriff Ramsay, Holly Lang was after him continually to devote more of his efforts to locating the missing boy, Malcolm. The sheriff was trying to maintain an expression of gentle concern on an early morning several days after the killing as Holly stood across the desk from him, gesticulating angrily.

"Damn it, Gavin, that weasel Pastory is keeping him somewhere," she insisted. For a moment Ramsay thought she was going to pound on the desk, but she brought herself under control. "Why aren't you doing something? Why aren't you looking for him? You're supposed to be the sheriff."

"Comments from the public are always welcome," Ramsay said. "Maybe you will be kind enough to suggest where I might look."

"That's just it. I've talked to everybody at the hospital, and nobody knows where this mysterious clinic of Pastory's is, or if it even exists."

"Ah, then you see part of my problem."

"Problem, hell. I want to hear solutions from you."

"I am doing the best I can, Holly," Gavin said with all the patience he could muster. "I have a want out on Pastory as a material witness. His relatives, of which there seem to be very few, deny all knowledge of his whereabouts." He pulled a sheet of paper from an overflowing basket on his desk. "To quote his brother Kyle in Boise, Idaho, 'I don't know where the s.o.b. is and I don't give a damn.' His clinic is not listed with the California Medical Association or any other group that I've been able to turn up."

"So what are you doing now?"

"Right now I am doing what I can to find the killer of Dr. Dennis Qualen."

"So, are you making any progress?"

"I have before me reports of all killings in the western United States during the past five years that were in any way similar to that of Dr. Qualen."

"And?"

"And you'd be surprised how many people are ripped to pieces. When I eliminate the chain saws and the axes and the certified mad dogs and the circus maulings and one farmer in Oregon who seems to have been eaten by his pigs, do you know what's left?"

"Please tell me," Holly said.

"Drago."

"Oh, Jesus!" she said in exasperation.

"Amen," he added piously.

"I trust, Sheriff, that you won't mind if I do what I can on my own to locate Dr. Pastory and Malcolm."

"Holly, I hope you are not going to get a gun and go rushing off like a crazed vigilante."

"I do not believe in guns," she said.

"I am relieved to hear that. As long as you stay within the law, I can do nothing to stop you. I have to insist, however, that you will in no way interfere with the actions of legitimate police officers."

"That sounds like something you memorized," she said.

"It is," he admitted, "but I mean it."

"Good enough, Sheriff. You go your way and I'll go mine."

She turned smartly and marched out of the office, giving him no chance for a reply.

What reply could he make, anyway? Everything she said was essentially correct. He was the sheriff, and he was doing a lousy job. Moreover, this business had split him and Holly apart just when he was thinking something good might develop there. It was with an honest feeling of loss that Ramsay watched her climb into the little Volkswagen Rabbit with the Greenpeace emblem and drive off, scattering as much gravel as she could manage with the underpowered car.

Holly was so angry when she left Gavin Ramsay that she had to exert a force of will to pull her foot up off the accelerator. She felt like the fabled knight who leaped on his horse and rode madly off in all directions. This was not like her. She was a calm, reasonable woman, always in control of her emotions. What right did that Gavin Ramsay have, anyway, keeping her awake nights thinking about the way they had kissed at her door?

All right. She would handle it. She got the Rabbit down to an acceptable speed and headed west on Highway 126, which ran along the Santa Clara River. She kept the window on her side rolled down to let the moist morning air flow in and cool her feverish face.

She drove through Fillmore and on toward Santa Paula, taking deep breaths, feeling the muscles at the back of her neck and along her shoulders gradually relax as she ordered her mind, putting everything into its proper compartment.

Number One. She was worried about Malcolm. The boy had special qualities that she had only begun to discover. In time she would have found out who he was and what he was and helped him to live with it. That time had been stolen from her.

It hurt to know that she had been gaining the boy's trust. It was she he had first spoken to. She for whom he had called when he was hurting. What must he think of his new friend now?

Number Two. She was mad as hell at Gavin Ramsay. He brushed off her suggestions and her requests like some hysterical woman. Well, maybe that was overstating the case. Nevertheless, he *was* a whole lot more interested in catching his Werewolf Killer, as the media were now calling it, than he was in locating a missing boy. But wait, she cautioned herself, isn't Gavin doing his job the very best way he can? Was she being unfair? Maybe so, but what the hell, life was unfair. If he was going to treat her like some addled, helpless female, then to hell with him.

By the time she pulled into Ventura and parked on a bluff overlooking the Pacific Ocean and the Holiday Inn, she was under control and feeling better. She had a plan.

The foremost supplier of medical equipment in the area, Landrud & Co., was located in Ventura. If Wayne Pastory had ordered anything medical for this phantom clinic of his, it would have been from Landrud.

Holly restarted the engine and drove until she found a Texaco station with public telephones. She riffled through the Yellow Pages and located the number for Landrud & Co. She dropped a coin into the slot, punched out the number, and asked the switchboard operator to connect her with the Sales Department.

"Hello," she said, making her voice brusque and businesslike when she was put through. "This is Dr. Hollanda Lang of La Reina County Hospital. I wonder if I might see someone there about an order for new laboratory equipment."

"Of course, Dr. Lang," came the answer. "We'll be glad to talk to you. Would you like to come in this afternoon, or any time tomorrow, at your convenience?"

"As a matter of fact, I'm rather pressed for time, and if

possible I'd like to make it sooner. I'm only about ten minutes away from your building right now.''

She could almost hear the salesman calculating the probable commission on the other end. "Well, yes, I'm sure that would be possible. I can reschedule one of my own appointments and see you right away.''

"Thank you, I appreciate that. Your name is . . . ?''

"Schaeffer. Olan Schaeffer. I'll leave word with the receptionist to expect you.''

"Very good. I'll see you in a few minutes, then, Mr. Schaeffer.''

Holly replaced the receiver and drew a deep breath. She had managed a couple of white lies there without even flinching. And Gavin Ramsay thought she would get in the way of his police work. Hah!

Damn, why did she keep thinking about the loose-jointed sheriff with whose hard blue eyes that could soften like anything sometimes? So what if he was one hell of a kisser? Nuts to him.

Landrud & Co. was in a low, unimaginative cinder-block building with lots of glass around the entrance and some fake-looking greenery in front to soften the antiseptic effect. Holly parked brazenly in a slot marked CUSTOMER and entered the chrome-modern reception area.

She handed her business card to a lacquered-haired receptionist and said, "I believe Mr. Schaeffer is expecting me.''

"Oh, yes, Dr. Lang. He asked me to tell him at once when you got here.'' The receptionist smiled with several thousand dollars' worth of porcelain and touched a button on her telephone panel. Maintaining the smile for Holly, she said into the mouthpiece, "Dr. Lang is here, Mr. Schaeffer.'' A moment's pause. "He'll be right out, Doctor.''

Olan Schaeffer was a short, ruddy-faced man with thinning hair and cigar breath, which he disguised inadequately with Tic-Tacs. His suit was a muted sharkskin as befitted the serious nature of the product he sold, but he allowed himself a touch of playfulness in the orange and blue figured tie.

"Well, Dr. Lang," he said after seating her in his compact office, "I believe you said you were interested in laboratory equipment. I have our catalog here, and several brochures you might want to glance through."

"Actually, that won't be necessary," Holly said, wishing she had better prepared her story. "I'd like to talk to you about equipment ordered by a colleague of mine, Dr. Wayne Pastory."

Schaeffer's smile slipped a notch, as though he felt his commission shrinking. "Uh, was that order placed for La Reina County?"

"No. Dr. Pastory is associated with us, but the equipment I'm interested in was ordered for his own private clinic."

"I see," Schaeffer said, not seeing at all. "May I ask specifically what it is you want to know?"

"We've had excellent reports at La Reina County," Holly improvised, "about the quality of Dr. Pastory's equipment. And the price offered by you people, of course."

They exchanged little insider smiles.

"Our board of directors is interested in making a similar purchase for a new wing we have under construction."

"Ah, yes, I see. Excellent." The commission light returned to the salesman's eyes. "Well, we'll just punch it up on the old computer here and see what we shall see."

He swiveled his chair around and lifted the dust cover from a computer terminal as though unveiling a prized objet d'art. "Everything's done on the computer nowadays. Sometimes I kind of miss poking through the old filing cabinets, but I guess that's progress."

Holly forced herself to sit quietly and smile while Schaeffer flipped on the terminal and waited for the screen to come to life. She crossed her legs to give the man something to look at other than her smile, which was becoming strained.

The computer beeped politely and prompted him in pale green characters to get on with it.

"Would you spell the doctor's name for me?" he asked.

Holly wrote it out for him on a desk pad. Stiff-fingered, he punched the proper command keys, then spelled out WAYNE PASTORY, M.D. The computer beeped and buzzed and Holly began rehearsing her exit in case no information came up on Pastory. She needn't have worried, for after a final buzz and beep the screen was filled with pale green readout that listed dates, medical apparatus, prices, and other coded information.

"Dr. Pastory has been quite a good customer," Schaeffer said. "Especially in the last month."

"Ah, yes, that's what I understand," Holly said, leaning forward, trying to decipher the computer language on the screen.

"Can you tell me specifically what pieces of equipment you're interested in? Or I could run a printout of the whole file, if that would help."

"Yes, yes, I'm sure it would, but I want to be certain this is not material the doctor ordered for La Reina. It's his own clinic that I'm interested in."

"Of course. The computer knows all, tells all." Schaeffer tapped several additional keys. "No, all this was shipped to his clinic up near Bear Paw. Is that the place?"

Holly almost laughed with relief. "Yes, Bear Paw. A funny name that I can never remember. That's the place."

"Not much of a town, from what I hear," said the helpful Schaeffer. "Get a few skiers in the winter is about it. Anyway, they've got a post office and your Dr. Pastory's clinic."

Holly stood up. "Thank you so much, Mr. Schaeffer. I can't tell you how helpful you've been."

The salesman scrambled to his feet. "But the equipment. Didn't you want to go over the list?"

"Why don't you run off that printout and send it to me in

care of La Reina County Hospital? I look forward to doing business with you.''

Holly made her second hasty exit of the morning, leaving a befuddled Olan Schaeffer wondering whether his commission had just sailed out the door.

Chapter 14

While Holly Lang took hasty leave of the offices of Landrud & Co. in Ventura, Abe Craddock was draining a can of Coors in the old Whitaker place. It was a falling-down cabin set well back in the trees at the south end of Pinyon, and had not been used since old George Whitaker's Dodge had slipped off a jack while he was under it down at Art Moore's Exxon station.

The cabin had been rented from old George Whitaker's widow by a smart-talking writer fella from Los Angeles who was doing a story for one of the scandal sheets they sold where you paid for your groceries, over at the Safeway. This so-called writer had bailed Abe Craddock out of jail and promised him a cool thousand dollars just for telling him the story of what happened in the woods that day with Curly Vane and the wolf thing. The catch was that Craddock would tell his story to no one else.

Abe figured he flat had it made. Not only was he living fairly comfortable in the cabin with Betty out of his hair; he was taking this smartass L.A. writer for all the booze he could drink, and figured he could probably up the dollar price on him, too. As for the manslaughter charge against him for blowing up Jones, that was no sweat anymore. With the kid gone and Curly nothing but raw meat, there were no witnesses. It was an accident, pure and simple. Yes, things were surely going old Abe Craddock's way for a change.

The L.A. writer, Louis Zeno by name, was hammering away at the old typewriter he'd brought with him like he was trying to set the thing on fire. Abe had never in his life seen a man who could type so fast.

Zeno ripped out the page he was working on and handed it over to Craddock. "All right, Abe, I want you to take a look at this and see if it sounds all right. Remember, this is supposed to be you telling the story, and I want to be sure the facts are reasonably close to what really happened."

Craddock took the page, set aside the Coors can, wiped his mouth, cleared his throat. He began to read in a labored schoolboy manner:

"When Curly Vane and I entered the dense, dripping forest outside Pinyon on that fateful afternoon, perhaps we should have sensed . . ."

Abe stopped reading and looked up, frowning.

"Something the matter?" Zeno said impatiently.

"It's that dripping forest business. The forest don't drip. Least, I don't remember no dripping that particular day."

"That's alliteration for effect," Zeno told him.

"Huh?"

"Don't worry about it. Read the rest."

Craddock went through his preliminary mouth-wiping and throat-clearing again and continued:

". . . should have sensed a certain foreboding, an ominous presence lurking unseen in the shadows. But in our innocent good spirits, neither of us could fore-

127

see the unspeakable fate that would befall one of us before we would see the sun again. . . ."

Abe stopped again, shaking his head.

"What now?" the writer said wearily.

"Uh, I ain't sure I get that business about the sun. I mean, it was up there all the time. We weren't in no cave, you know."

"Never mind that," Zeno told him. "That's just for atmosphere. All I want you to do is make sure that what I say you say happened is more or less what happened. So if anybody asks you about it after the story comes out you can tell them, sure, that's the way it was. Okay?"

"Yeah, okay. I get it." Craddock sucked noisily at the empty beer can. "Reading this stuff is mighty thirsty work, and damn if I don't think this is the last of the Coors."

"Jesus, Abe, it isn't even noon yet, and you've put away a whole six-pack and part of another."

"Hell, that's nothin'. You should of seen me and Curly when we really got down to some serious drinking. Hell, we wouldn't leave no bottle untapped in three counties."

"I'll bet," Zeno said unhappily.

"An' you *did* say you'd provide the drinking stuff as long as I gave my story to you and nobody else. Ain't that right?"

"That's right, Abe," Zeno said. "Let's just finish this part where you walk into the woods and first see the Wolfman."

Craddock coughed loudly. "Damn, Lou, I just don't think I can rightly concentrate anymore without something to cool down my throat."

"All *right*," the writer snapped. "I'll go get some more beer. Do you think a twelve-pack will hold you till lunchtime?"

"Might be," Craddock said. "If you get the sixteen-ounce cans, it'll go farther."

"Yeah, yeah, sixteen-ounce." Louis Zeno lowered the cover onto his precious portable Royal and stood up.

Someday, some blessed day, Louis Zeno would finish the book that was finally going to make him some real money and free him forever from writing trash for the supermarket tabloids and dealing with scum like this foul-smelling Abe Craddock. He had the outline tucked away in his apartment in West Hollywood. All he needed was a free month or so to get it down on paper and off to a publisher.

In the meantime, he would just have to keep turning out stories about mothers who stuffed their babies into microwave ovens and country girls fucked by green men from outer space and assholes like Abe Craddock and his imaginary werewolf. He could look forward to one small victory when Craddock tried to collect the imaginary thousand dollars Zeno had promised him. The writer crossed the cabin's single room to where his jacket hung from a bent nail.

"You might pick up some Fritos while you're at the store," Craddock suggested. "One of the big bags."

"Big bag. Sure."

"When you get back I'll tell you the part where I took on that wolf thing with my bare hands after I seen what he done to Curly. I mean, I was holdin' my own, too, maybe gettin' a little the best of things. If only I hadn't of caught my boot there in them bushes and tripped myself up it might of been a whole nother story."

"Yeah, Abe, swell, but let's just stick to the story we've got. I'll ask the questions and you tell me what happened in your own halting words. I'm the professional. I know how to put these things together."

"I guess that's right," Abe said slyly, "but without me you wouldn't have nothing to put together. Ain't that so?"

Fuck you, you stinking ignorant redneck bastard! is what Louis Zeno thought. What he said was, "Yeah, that's so,

129

Abe. Without you I'd be standing in the unemployment line.''

"Well, don't you worry, Lou buddy, you and me are going to make us a whole shitpot full of money with this before we're through.''

Zeno shrugged into his jacket and headed for the door.

Neither man looked toward the dusty windowpane at the side of the cabin. If they had, they might have seen the eyes that watched them. Eyes that gradually changed color until they seemed to glow an unearthly green.

Derak watched the man from the city leave the cabin and stalk down the trail to the clearing, where he had parked the little orange car. The engine fired and the city man drove off. Derak looked back through the window at the gross, murdering hunter. The smoldering hatred inside him kindled to a flame. Derak moved a short distance away from the cabin and carefully removed his clothes so they would not be shredded as the transformation began.

Abe Craddock thumbed a wad of Copenhagen into his cheek and sucked out the good tobacco flavor. He should have told the writer fella to pick up a couple of tins of that, too. The dumb prick would bring anything Abe wanted as long as he got what he called an *exclusive* on Abe's battle with the werewolf. In Abe's mind the whole thing by now had actually taken place as he told the story and retold it. He came out looking a little more heroic every time.

There was no doubt in Abe's mind that he could milk more than a thousand dollars out of this. Hell, he could probably get double that. Those papers must pay good money for a story like this, and if Zeno was going to use his name he was going to have to pay for it.

Something scratched at the door.

Abe took a look at his waterproof Timex. It was much too soon for Zeno to be back from the liquor store. He didn't want to see any of the reporters who were still hanging around Pinyon, so he'd have to drive clear to Darnay.

Something scratched again.

Could the damn fool writer have forgotten something and come back for it? No, they had a special knock that Zeno would give to show it was him. He didn't want anybody else getting close to Abe before he had the exclusive story all written and handed over to the editor. That was the whole idea of hiding up here in the Whitaker cabin where nobody had come in years.

Scratch. *Scratch.*

You don't suppose the widow Whitaker would of told somebody they were up here? Not likely, since she didn't know what the fool city man wanted with her broken-down cabin and was just glad to get the ten bucks Zeno offered her.

Thump.

There was sure as hell something outside the door. Well, it wouldn't hurt to take a tiny peek. Zeno had bored a hole in the door at eye level and stuck a patch of leather over it so he could look out in case anybody came sniffing around.

Abe went over, lifted the leather patch, and put his eye to the hole. He had a full two seconds for his brain to register the fact that he was looking into another eye of the most terrible fiery green.

Then the door splintered inward like it was dynamited.

Abe staggered backward, knocking over the card table with Zeno's typewriter on it and stumbling among the empty beer cans on the floor. The thing that came at him had to bend down to get its head through the doorway. Even inside the cabin the thing's pointed, hairy ears brushed against the ceiling. The terrible black-lipped muzzle had a wet, just-born look. And the teeth. My God, the teeth. Abe Craddock vividly recalled what those teeth had done to Curly Vane,

131

and all his heroic fantasies dissolved before the roaring reality.

"No don't, no don't, no don't!" Abe cried. He might as well have appealed to the wind.

His back thumped against the opposite wall of the cabin and he could retreat no farther. A voice he did not recognize as his own whimpered in his ear.

The beast paused before him, its mighty chest twice the girth of Abe's own. The powerful jaws worked up and down. The beast seemed to savor the helplessness of the man before it.

When the beast struck, it was faster than Abe Craddock's eye could follow. He was intent on those terrible teeth when it struck out at him with a forepaw. The razor talons ripped four parallel gashes down the front of him from sternum to pubic bone.

For an instant Abe felt nothing. He looked down, stunned at the slashes through his T-shirt, his jeans, his jockey shorts, and the fatty flesh beneath. Then the pain came. And the blood.

The blood oozed at first, then bubbled out of him, splashing the bare wooden floor where he stood. Abe clutched at himself, trying to hold his intestines in place. But they bulged and coiled out over his hands like a nest of wet red snakes.

The beast let him scream for a while as his legs gave out and he sank to the floor in a pool of his own blood, guts, and shit. Abe saw the gaping mouth come down toward him. Felt the teeth clamp on his head. Heard the crack of his skull . . .

Derak curled himself on the ground near the pile of his clothes and focused his will on the shape change. The transformation from beast back to man held none of the wild joy that was a part of becoming a wolf. Ideally, there should be a full, uninterrupted night to let the tension ease and change back gradually. When it had to be forced and speeded up, the changes to the body were painful in the extreme.

However, there was no help for it now. Derak had a mission, and it was only partly complete. He had set himself the task of returning Malcolm to his own people before the boy could do irreparable harm to himself or others of his kind. If along the way he could destroy some human garbage like Abe Craddock, it would add pleasure to his task.

Derak's body shuddered. He ground his teeth against the pain. The internal organs shifted and jumped under his skin. His skeleton cracked as the bones returned to human form. The body hair vanished as though sucked back into the hide. The ears shrank and rounded off; the muzzle pulled in; the killing teeth receded into the harmless molars and incisors of a man.

Slowly, slowly, the pain eased. Derak moved, straightening his body, testing his limbs and extremities. He shivered with the cold on his naked flesh.

As he pulled his clothes back on, Derak froze at a sound from the road below and ducked behind a bush. The little orange car chugged into the clearing and stopped. The man from the city climbed out, bringing with him a half case of beer and a crinkly bag of chips. Derak watched as the man labored up the path with his burden toward the cabin. The wise thing would be to destroy him, but the blood lust was stilled, and Derak had no wish to kill now without reason.

He waited until the city man had lumbered past the bush where he crouched, then he loped silently down the trail to the car. The door was unlocked. He tore away a fiberboard panel beneath the dash and found the ignition wires.

At the top of the trail the man from the city had seen the shattered remnants of the door. He dropped the beer and the sack of chips and walked stiff-legged toward the cabin.

Derak stripped the wires with a tough thumbnail and twisted them together.

By the time Louis Zeno staggered out of the cabin, white-faced, with his mouth agape in a silent scream, his little orange car was turning onto the road toward the town of Pinyon.

As he drove, Derak pulled tissues from a carton on the dash panel and wiped away what he could of the blood and mud from his face. He was a fastidious man, and it made him uncomfortable not to bathe after a killing. However, this time the change back had to be done so fast, there was no time.

Derak's mind had not completely reoriented, and as soon as he had a chance, he pulled the car off into a sheltered spot alongside the road next to an Exxon station. He was startled to see only then that the backs of his hands were still thickly overgrown with hair. He tucked the hands away out of sight, leaned back in the seat, closed his eyes, and let himself slip into a light doze.

He awoke sometime later, refreshed and alert. He rubbed his hands front and back to be sure that the change was now truly complete. Only then did he realize he had brought the little car to a stop almost directly across from the office of La Reina County's sheriff.

Derak immediately choked down an impulse to panic. If anyone were still looking for a man of his description after the wild werewolf tales that had clouded the killing of Dr. Qualen, they would hardly expect him to be sitting in a car parked almost in the sheriff's lap.

Using mental techniques learned from those who had traveled his road before, Derak settled into a quiet watchfulness that had protected his kind through the ages.

A small, square car pulled into the parking area before the sheriff's office. A young woman got out. The doctor. Derak had followed closely the events in Pinyon, and he knew that she, of all the people here, was the most anxious to find Malcolm. If anyone could lead him to the boy, it would be she.

Derak slid lower in the driver's seat and watched as the young woman got out and went into the office.

Chapter 15

Deputy Roy Nevins was alone in the sheriff's office when Holly entered. She barely recognized the man. Deputy Nevins's uniform was spotless and pressed, complete to the military creases in the shirt. His boots, belt, and holster were shined. He was freshly shaved, had obviously just had a haircut. He was even making an effort to hold his stomach in.

"Morning, ma'am," he said, getting to his feet. His speech seemed to have softened into more of a western drawl.

Remarkable, Holly thought, what a touch of fame will do.

"Good morning, Roy. Is Gavin around?"

"The sheriff and Deputy Fernandez are out on a call, ma'am. Left me in charge. Seems there's been some trouble down at the old Whitaker cabin."

"Will you cut out the ma'am stuff, Roy? You make me feel like Dale Evans."

The deputy grinned a little sheepishly. "I just thought we ought to be a little more businesslike around here, what with all the reporters and television people and whatnot."

"Well, I suppose it couldn't hurt. How soon do you expect Gavin back?"

"That's hard to say. Seems whoever it was made the phone call wasn't bein' very clear about what the trouble was at the cabin."

Holly chewed at her lower lip. Why was there never a cop around when you needed one?

"Anything I can help you with?"

"It was just a message I wanted to give the sheriff."

"You're welcome to sit yourself down and wait for him." Roy wheeled one of the unused swivel chairs over for her.

"No thanks, Roy, I'm in kind of a hurry. I'll leave him a note."

She tore a page from Ramsay's calendar pad and wrote:

Gavin:
I managed to find out where Dr. Pastory's clinic is without getting in the way of any of your "duly authorized police officers." I'll let you know when I've found Malcolm. Good luck with your big murder investigation.

She read it over, then crumpled the page and threw it into the wastebasket. Cheap sarcasm was not her style. On another calendar sheet she wrote:

Gavin:
Dr. Pastory's clinic is located in Bear Paw. I'm on my way up there. I'll check with you as soon as I find anything.

Take care,
Holly

She placed the note in the center of his desk blotter, anchoring it with a stapler.

"Thanks, Roy," she said. "I'll see you."

"Anytime, ma'am," he said, reaching for the brim of the hat he was not wearing, then, grinning, "Oops. I'm kinda getting into the habit, I guess."

Before leaving the office, Holly checked the big map tacked to one wall. It covered all of La Reina County and included parts of Los Angeles, Ventura, and Kern counties as well. She located the tiny community of Bear Paw just on the other side of the Tehachapi Pass, beyond Clarion. She figured it as a two-to-three-hour drive, depending on road conditions. There certainly wouldn't be much traffic between here and there.

She filled the tank of her little Rabbit across the road at Art Moore's station, then headed north. Holly's mind was filled with thoughts of what she was going to say to Wayne Pastory when she found him, and she did not pay any attention to the little orange car that pulled onto the road behind her and followed her out of town.

The roads were good all the way, although narrowing to a cramped two lanes as she left the state highway. It took her slightly less than two hours to reach the community of Bear Paw. Had she not been actively looking for it, the entire town would have been easy to miss.

There was the Bear Paw Ski Lodge, a faintly alpine A-frame building with the windows shuttered and a chain across the driveway leading to the entrance. A hand-lettered sign hanging from the chain read: CLOSED FOR THE SESON.

That was it, except for a paint-peeling frame building that was combination post office/grocery store/gas station/tavern. Out in front were parked a grimy Ford pickup and an equally grimy Plymouth some twenty years old.

Holly pulled to a stop at the old-fashioned gas pumps. When no one appeared after a minute, she got out and went into the building. Three men, none of them younger than seventy, sat around—not a potbellied stove—but an electric heater. The temperature inside was a stifling eighty. Behind a scarred wooden counter a grossly overweight woman with a mustache sat on a stool while she read a paperback novel called *Love's Raging Heart*.

The three men looked up when Holly entered. The woman continued to read. No one spoke.

"Hi," Holly said finally. "This is Bear Paw, I hope."

"Sure is, honey," said the woman. She marked her spot in the book with a forefinger and looked up. "What can we do you for?"

"I was wondering if you knew of a clinic around here. Owned by Dr. Wayne Pastory."

One of the men around the heater worked his lips noisily over toothless gums. "You a friend of his?"

"Not exactly. We sometimes work together. The clinic *is* around here somewhere?"

Another of the men spoke up. His hands were gnarled and knobbed with arthritis. He kept them lying awkwardly in his lap as though they did not really belong to him. "What you want to go up there for, anyhow?"

Holly started to tell the man it was none of his damn business, but brought herself under control. "I have to see Dr. Pastory about something," she said as courteously as she could manage.

"You sick?" said the woman.

"I'm a doctor."

"You don't look like a doctor," said the third man. He had one eye that appeared to be glass. Cheap glass.

"Well, I am." Holly began to feel more than a little irritated with these unpleasant rustics.

"If you're sick, you'd do a lot better to go to Doc Simms down in Clarion," said the man with arthritis. "Good man, Doc Simms. Been around long enough to know what he's doing. Your Doc—what's his name, Pastorini . . ."

"Pastory."

"Whatever. He don't look like he's dry behind the ears yet. Name sounds like a foreigner, besides."

"Look," Holly said, putting some authority into her voice, "I'm in something of a hurry. Could you please tell me where the clinic is?"

"No need to get snippy about it," said the toothless man. "You want to go to the doggone clinic, that's you're business. We sure ain't stoppin' you."

"Where *is* it?" Holly was surprised at the whip-crack in her own voice. The four people stared as though really seeing her for the first time.

The woman finally spoke. "Go on up the way you're headed about a mile and a half. There's a logging trail turns off to your right. It ain't easy to see if you're not watchin'. Drive up that two, maybe three miles. And there you are."

They stared at her for another long moment, but no one spoke again.

"Thank you very much," Holly said. She hurried out of the store, into the car, and headed up the road.

At approximately the time Holly was pulling out of Pinyon on her way to find his clinic, Dr. Wayne Pastory was leading Malcolm from his room to a part of the clinic where he had not been before. It was a high-ceilinged room that was bare of decoration. The furniture consisted of two plain wooden chairs. There was one door and a high-up window that showed nothing but the dark trees outside.

Inside the room was a cage of heavy-guage steel wire mesh that was backed against one wall. The cage measured about seven feet square and contained a stretched-canvas cot and a bucket for waste.

Pastory unlocked the door to the cage and guided Malcolm inside. "I'm sorry to have to lock you up like this, Malcolm, but I have to drive into Clarion for supplies. I shouldn't be gone more than three hours, and I trust you won't be too uncomfortable in that time."

"Why do I have to be locked in here?" Malcolm said.

His mind was still fuzzy from the sleeping drug he'd been given the night before.

"Security, my boy, security," said Pastory, giving him a little pat on the shoulder. "It's as much for your own safety as anything else."

The doctor backed out of the cage, closed the steel-framed door, and snapped a heavy padlock through the hasp. "If there is anything you absolutely need before I get back, Kruger will be here." He turned and called toward the open door of the room. "Kruger!"

The big man entered so quickly that he must have been standing outside listening.

"I want you to stay here with our young friend," Pastory told him. "Get him anything he wants, within reason. That is, anything that will fit through the mesh. I do not want you to unlock the door except in the gravest emergency. Is that understood?"

"Don't worry, Doctor. I'll watch him good. And I won't let him out." Kruger's thick lips twitched. His tongue slid out over them.

Pastory stood for a moment looking from one of them to the other, then nodded to himself and left the room, closing the single door behind him. A minute later the sound of an automobile engine could be heard starting outside. Tires crunched on the dried pine needles that carpeted the roadway. The sound faded as Pastory rolled down the overgrown logging trail toward the county road.

Kruger hitched one of the chairs close to the front of the wire cage and sat down facing Malcolm. He smiled. The fatty tissues around his eyes squeezed them into slits.

"It's just you and me now, freak-boy. All alone. How do you like that?"

Malcolm sat on the cot and did not answer.

"You don't care if I call you freak-boy, do you? 'Cause that's what you are, you know. A freak. A goddamn freak."

When Malcolm still did not respond, the big man's smile

141

faded. He wiped a callused hand across his lips. "The doctor treats you like some kind of a prince, but all you are's a goddamn freak. Oh, I seen what you do when the doctor has you out there on the table. Your face gets all funny and long, kinda. Your fingernails grow. Like a woman's or something. And you get hair on you where hair don't belong. What do you say about that, freak-boy?"

"I don't know what you're talking about."

"Oh, you don't, don't you? I know how to make you do it, too. I watched the doctor. You want me to make you do it, freak-boy? Want me to turn you into a goddamn freak?"

"Just leave me alone."

"Just leeeave me alone," Kruger whined in a mocking falsetto. "You know, I was number one around here until you showed up, freak-boy. The doctor used to treat me real nice before you came. He took me out of the bad place and he said I'd never have to worry about anything again. He'd take care of me. And he did, too, but then he found you, and we had to bring you here, and now he don't have time for me anymore except to tell me to go fetch this or go empty that. You're the hotshot now, freak-boy. But you know something? It ain't gonna last. One way or another I'm gonna see that it don't last."

Malcolm felt the anger start way down deep somewhere. "Why don't you shut your ugly mouth?"

Kruger hitched his chair closer, pleased that he had gotten a reaction. "Oh-oh, is he going to get mad? Is freak-boy going to get mad? Go ahead, let's see you do those things with your face. Then we'll see who's ugly, freak-boy."

Malcolm felt the heat rising within him. His hands began to twitch. He forced himself to breathe slowly and deeply. He closed his eyes and thought of the words Holly Lang had used when they put him into hypnosis. *So relaxed. So comfortable. Drifting, drifting. Farther and farther away.* Gradually the fire within him cooled. His hands lay quiet in his

142

lap. He felt the waves of relaxation wash over him. Mind and body were once again under control.

"Almost had you goin' there, didn't I, freak-boy?" Kruger said. "Oh, yes, I did, all right."

Malcolm opened his eyes. He looked through and beyond the thick, ugly man. He smiled softly to himself.

"You're not makin' fun of me, are you?" Kruger said. "They used to make fun of me in the bad place. Laughed behind my back when they thought I couldn't see. I knew, though. I knew what they were doing. I took care of them, too. That was before the doctor came and brought me here."

Malcolm breathed in and out slowly. *So relaxed. So comfortable.*

"I know how I can get that silly smile off your face," said Kruger. "I know. You just wait here." Then, as though realizing he had said something funny, he laughed. "That's right. You just wait here." He laughed again and left the room.

Malcolm tried to hold on to his state of calm relaxation, but the mood was fading. Dr. Pastory was a dangerous man, and he did some unpleasant things to Malcolm, but he was always solicitous about the boy's welfare afterward. At least that was the way he acted. And there was always the hope that when Pastory had finished with his study, whatever it was, he would return Malcolm to the hospital in Pinyon. Holly was there. He could put up with Pastory as long as there was the hope of a reunion with his friend.

But Kruger was another matter. The brute had a damaged brain and was barely kept in check by Pastory's greater strength of will. If he ever went over the edge Kruger could be dangerous. Malcolm began to worry about what the ugly big man might do.

Before he could reorder his thoughts, Kruger returned. He carried with him a wand shaped like a stubby pool cue. The thicker end was wrapped with leather at the grip. The greater length of the wand was metal. Two wires protruded from the

143

butt end and ran into a flat leather packet that Kruger had attached to his belt.

"Do you know what this is, freak-boy? It's a cattle prod, that's what. The cops use 'em sometimes. Dr. Pastory used it on me when I first come here from the bad place. Then I wised up and he didn't have to use it no more. I found out where he kept it, but I never told him."

Malcolm stared at the metal prod as Kruger waved it back and forth in front of his face.

"Want to see how it works? Watch."

Kruger thrust the metal tip of the prod to within half an inch of the wire mesh of the cage. He touched a switch on the belt pack. A blue-white spark jumped with a loud *crack*.

Malcolm flinched away from the spark.

"What's the matter, you afraid of it?" Kruger said. "The doctor's been using something like it on you in the laboratory when you're strapped down. Only difference is, the one in there is a lot smaller and it don't hurt as much as this one. Want to see?"

In a movement surprisingly swift for so big a man, Kruger thrust the prod through the cage, jabbing the tip against Malcolm's face.

The pain was like hitting the nerve of a tooth. Malcolm cried out and put a hand to his cheek. He backed against the rear of the cage, but there was no way he could get out of the reach of Kruger with the cruel cattle prod.

The big man laughed, a high-pitched, mindless giggle. "Aha, gotcha now, haven't I? Can't get away, can't get away."

He stabbed Malcolm's wrist with the tip of the wand. The pain of the shock jolted up his arm. Malcolm felt the fires grow inside him.

"See? See? There you go. I knew I could make you do it. Look at your hands, freak-boy."

Malcolm looked down at his hands. Surely, they had grown larger, the palms broadening and the fingers stretching out. Even as he watched, the nails pushed out through the skin, thick and horny, bringing a trickle of blood from the tips of his fingers. The boy clamped the horrid hands out of sight under his arms.

Kruger caught him under the chin with the prod. His facial muscles twisted and jumped in the sudden agony.

"I'll show you what you really are, freak-boy. I'll show you who's ugly." Kruger capered grotesquely around the three exposed walls of the cage, stabbing here, there, anywhere he could find a bit of exposed flesh.

Malcolm's legs bent on him in a strange way and he fell to the floor. The sound that came from his throat was half whine, half growl. Like nothing human. His mind was a jumble of images—the forest at night; flames; burning flesh; a kind, bearded giant; a beautiful woman who was his friend; a doctor who drugged him and took him away; a thick-necked, witless lump of a man who tortured him.

The hands before Malcolm's face no longer bore any resemblance to his own. They had darkened and stretched and grown patches of fine black hair.

The pain continued; the anger grew. And the fire within him burned hotter.

Chapter 16

Even watching closely, Holly missed the logging trail the first time past, and she had to drive back at ten miles an hour with her head craning out the window to find it. The old trail was no more than two faint paths through the weeds leading up the hill. Years before, logging trucks had hauled the huge Douglas fir logs down from the mountain to sawmills that had long since disappeared.

Minutes after she headed up the grade, the little orange car appeared. It stopped for a moment while the driver peered up the hill, then followed Holly up the trail.

Holly drove carefully up the grade. The second-growth timber had almost reached the density of the virgin stand that attracted the lumber companies in a previous generation. On both sides the thick brush made it difficult to see. Rocks and stumps jutted unexpectedly from the center, where the weeds grew unmashed. The Volkswagen Rabbit was not designed for off-road adventure, and Holly winced with every scrape and bump against the underside of the little car.

As she emerged from one especially thick clump of trees, Holly came suddenly and unexpectedly upon the clinic of

Dr. Pastory. It was a dark, two-story house of redwood shingle and heavy oak beams, with an overhanging roof.

The house was built in the 1920s by the owner of a Hollywood studio as a playhouse for his favorite starlet. Sadly, before she could occupy it, the starlet died from drinking bootleg gin and laudanum at a party hosted by a popular slapstick comedian. The house had remained empty since that time until the studio magnate had died, several years before. It had been put up for auction, and because of its remote location, Wayne Pastory was able to buy it cheaply.

There was no other vehicle in sight, and Holly felt a rush of disappointment at the thought that she might have made the trip for nothing. However, fresh tire tracks told her that someone *was* using the place.

She snugged the Rabbit in under a tree and walked across the cushion of pine needles to the heavy front door. There was no bell, so she reached for the heavy cast-iron knocker.

Before she could lift the knocker, Holly froze at a sound from somewhere inside the house. It was a cry of mingled fear, rage, and pain. The voice was distorted, yet something in the tone made her sure it was Malcolm. Reacting to a sudden blaze of anger, she tried the latch of the heavy door, found it open, and walked in.

The interior of the old house had been redone and modernized, if not improved, with metals and plastics. Wallboard had been added to section the large old rooms into many smaller ones. Holly kept moving, following the sound of the voice, which continued to cry out every few seconds.

She passed along a hallway with doors on both sides. Some of the doors stood open, revealing cell-like rooms with narrow beds and a minimum of simple furnishings. Most looked unoccupied. In one of them, however, the bed was rumpled and recently slept in. Holly paused to look at a crumpled bit of white fabric stuffed into a wire wastebasket. She recognized the stitched blue lettering that would spell out LA REINA COUNTY HOSPITAL. A patient's gown.

She hurried on through what appeared to be a laboratory dominated by an examination table with heavy straps riveted to the corners. Although she did not pause to look around, Holly was impressed by the quantity and variety of equipment in the lab. No wonder Olan Schaeffer at Landrud & Co. had been so eager to do business.

There was a large, well-equipped kitchen, then a short flight of steps leading down to a wing of the house that was on a lower level. It was from a room down there that she heard the agonized cries.

The door to the large room on the lower level was ajar. Holly could see it was brightly lit within. She was close enough now to hear a crackling sound along with the cries of pain. She stepped through the door and stood for a frozen moment, stunned by what she saw.

A thick-shouldered brute of a man with scrubby black hair on a bullet head turned when she entered. He held what appeared to be an electrified metal rod in one hand. He was standing in front of a steel mesh cage. Inside the cage a pitiful figure writhed on the floor. A boy, Holly thought, though she could not be sure. He lay curled on the floor, muscles twitching, his limbs bent into strange, unnatural positions. On the visible areas of skin grew uneven patches of hair.

"Malcolm!" she cried. "My good God, what have they done to you?"

The face that looked up at her from the floor of the cruel cage wrenched Holly's heart. She recognized in it the boy Malcolm, yet it was not Malcolm. The bones seemed to have shifted subtly, elongating the face. The eyes were a strange luminescent green. He said something that might have been her name, then quickly covered his mouth with a darkened, long-nailed hand.

"Who are you, girlie?"

It took a moment for Holly to realize the brutish man was talking to her. She turned toward him and fought down the rage inside her. Her impulse was to strike out blindly at him, but she knew this was a time for control.

"I am Dr. Hollanda Lang. I demand to know what you are doing to this boy."

The *Doctor* seemed to confuse the man, to draw from him a touch of respect. At least temporarily. "How did you get in?" he asked.

"I walked in. The door was open."

"You shouldn't of done that." A sly look crept into his dark little eyes.

"I want you to release this boy at once."

"I can't do that. Dr. Pastory said I was supposed to keep him in there."

"Did Dr. Pastory also give you orders to torture the boy?"

"What are you talkin' about?"

"Answer my question."

"Are you a friend of the doctor's?"

The figure in the cage had pulled itself half erect on the steel mesh. The hands were more human now, the boy more recognizable as Malcolm. He looked so terribly young and vulnerable in the oversized pajamas.

"Holly," he said, his voice hoarse but clearing.

"Malcolm, thank God I've found you. Are you badly hurt?"

The boy looked down at his hands, which still bore patches of dark hair. He let go of the screen and tried to hide the hands behind him.

"I . . . I . . ."

Holly moved quickly to the cage. She laid one hand flat against the diamond mesh. He backed away.

"Don't be afraid, Malcolm. And don't worry. I'm going to get you out of here, and I'm going to help you."

She turned at the sound of a movement behind her. The big man had taken a step toward her. He was clenching and unclenching his hands. The metal rod hung forgotten at his side.

"What's your name?" she demanded.

The authority in Holly's voice held him for a moment. "K-Kruger," he stammered. "Dr. Pastory left me in charge while he's gone."

"Well, Kruger, you just get the key to this lock and open the cage right now." She spoke with an assurance she did not feel. This Kruger was obviously unbalanced mentally. God only knew what sadistic tortures he had been subjecting Malcolm to, but Holly knew she was treading a thin line with him.

Kruger shook his bullet head slowly from side to side. "No, I don't think I'm gonna do that."

She tried softening her tone.

"It's all right, Kruger. I'll explain to Dr. Pastory that I told you to let the boy out."

A crafty smile slid over the man's thick features. "Oh, no you don't. I know who you are. You're that Holly woman. The one he"—Kruger nodded toward Malcolm—"keeps calling for. You ain't no friend of the doctor's."

"You just let him out of there. Right now, Kruger, or you're going to be in a whole lot of trouble."

"Not me, girlie. It ain't me who's going to be in trouble." Moving with surprising speed, Kruger crossed the room and placed himself between her and the door.

"Run, Holly," Malcolm said in a strangled voice. "He'll hurt you."

Sensing the menace in the big man's tensed body, Holly tried to step around him to the door. He seized her by the arm above one elbow and squeezed it painfully.

"Let go of me!" she demanded, but her voice betrayed the fear that was building within her.

Kruger felt it, too. "Your little freak friend is right," he said. "I can hurt you if I want to. So you better be nice to me. You understand?"

150

"Let go!" Holly said again.

Before she could move, she was pulled hard against Kruger's body. His thick, moist lips covered her mouth. His tongue tried to force itself past her clenched teeth.

Acting on instinct, she pumped one knee up between the big man's legs. Her knee slid off the hard muscles of his inner thigh, weakening the blow to his testicles.

Kruger grunted and pulled his head back. "Bitch!"

He balled one huge fist and hit Holly on the point of the jaw.

It seemed her head had been slammed up against the ceiling. The lights went out for Holly Lang and she fell heavily to the floor. Kruger laughed and knelt over her.

When Gavin Ramsay returned to his office, supporting an hysterical Louis Zeno, two men in neat business suits were waiting for him with Deputy Nevins. They introduced themselves as Hoyden and Placerman from the California Attorney General's office.

"We got your request," said Hoyden, the senior of the two, "to assist with the investigation you're running down here."

"I can sure use you," Ramsay said. He briefly described the scene he had found at the old Whitaker cabin. "I left my man Fernandez in charge there. He'll keep the sightseers away until we can secure the area."

"This a witness?" Hoyden said, nodding toward Zeno.

"He found the body."

The writer took this as a cue to start talking. "It was the worst thing I've ever seen in my life. I'm talking *bad*, man. Blood everywhere. Pieces of my man all over the cabin. My typewriter was ruined."

"Did you get a look at the guy who did it?" Deputy Nevins asked.

"No man did that," Zeno said.

151

"What do you mean?"

"No one man could make an unholy mess like that in the little time I was gone."

"Gang of some kind?" Placerman suggested.

"Shit if I know. That's you guys' job. You figure it out."

"Try to relax, Mr. Zeno," Ramsay said. "Deputy Nevins here will take your statement."

"Stole my car, too," said Zeno.

"What's that? Who stole your car?"

"Whoever . . . whatever tore up Abe Craddock. Drove off in my car right when I came out of the cabin."

"What kind of a car was it, Mr. Zeno?"

"Datsun. 1972. Orange."

"License number?"

"I . . . I . . . oh, shit, I *know* it . . ."

"Hey, I think I saw that car, maybe an hour ago," Nevins interrupted.

"Where, Roy?"

"I was watching Holly, Dr. Lang, drive away, and this orange Datsun pulled out right behind her and went off in the same direction."

"Holly was here? When?"

"Like I said, maybe an hour ago. She left you a note." Nevins pointed at the sheriff's desk.

Ramsay snatched up the sheet from his calendar pad and read it swiftly. As Holly had done, he glanced at the wall map to check the location of Bear Paw.

"I'm going after her," he said. "Will you be all right here, Roy?"

"I can handle it, Gavin," said Deputy Nevins, sucking in his stomach.

"Good. I'm sure Hoyden and Placerman here will give you all the help they can."

The attorney general's men nodded their agreement.

"I'll be back as soon as possible."

Ramsay started out of the office, then hesitated. He

looked thoughtfully at Louis Zeno, who was still pale and shaking from what he had found at the cabin. Ramsay himself had been shocked at the inhuman violence done to Abe Craddock. He strode back to his desk and unlocked the bottom drawer. From it he took a heavy, square box and dropped it into a jacket pocket.

"What's that, Sheriff?" Roy asked.

"Bullets," he said. "Just in case." What he did not add was that they were the special bullets given to him by Ken Dowd, the owner of the occult shop. Silver bullets.

Malcolm watched in tearful, helpless rage as Kruger fumbled with the snap at the waist of Holly Lang's jeans. His fingers clamped over the heavy steel mesh like the claws of a caged beast.

Kruger paid him no attention. He popped the snap and slid the zipper down, revealing the filmy blue bikini pants Holly wore underneath. The man's breathing grew louder. His eyes glistened.

"Leave her alone," Malcolm cried. In his voice was a strange new quality. A growl. Even Kruger, in his lust, stopped and turned toward the cage.

"Hey, look at freak-boy! Look at that face! Too bad the doctor ain't here to see this. Maybe you get off on watching, huh, freak-boy? Well, you pay attention, then, 'cause I'm gonna give you plenty to watch."

He returned his concentration to pulling the tight jeans down Holly's legs. She moaned softly but did not regain consciousness. The bluish bruise from Kruger's fist was already beginning to show on her jaw.

With some difficulty, Kruger pulled the jeans completely off, taking Holly's boots with them and exposing her long, slim legs. He reached up and touched her pubic mound through the blue nylon.

Malcolm snarled. The fires inside burned hotter than ever

153

before. The sinewy, hairy hands that now grew at the ends of his arms gripped the steel mesh and pulled. With a loud *rip* the material of his pajamas tore at the shoulders, where new muscles bulged and humped. The mesh of the cage bent and started to pull apart where he gripped it.

Kruger, his fingers now hooked under the elastic of Holly's bikini, looked over. His wet, red mouth opened in surprise.

The window high on the wall above them burst inward. A beast, lithe and muscular, dived headfirst through the shattering glass. The beast landed gracefully on all fours, his great shaggy head swiveling to take in the situation. The black lips peeled back in a snarl.

Malcolm froze where he stood. The mesh of the cage before him was ripped wide enough for him to slip through, but he could not move.

Holly moaned again. Her eyelids fluttered. She tried to raise her head.

Kruger let go of her and scrambled to his feet. He stared at the creature now advancing on him.

"Get back! Get back!"

Malcolm, from inside the torn cage, stared at the beast. It rose on hind legs to a full seven feet. The talons, the gleaming teeth, the powerful jaws, all were capable of killing a man in seconds. The eyes glowed an unholy green.

But Malcolm felt no fear. There was recognition. A kinship. As the eyes of the creature held his own, the boy sensed the message in his mind: *Flee!*

When he looked down at his hands there were again smooth, smallish, normal boy's hands. He touched his face, It was his own unmarked, beardless face.

Flee! The message sounded again in his mind. A command. Malcolm squeezed his slim body through the split he had torn in the steel mesh.

"Hey! Where d'you think you're goin'?" Kruger, remembering his orders, turned his attention for a moment from the towering beast to the boy.

The beast opened its great jaws and roared. Kruger whirled to face the menace. Malcolm, compelled by the telepathic command, slipped past Kruger and the beast to the open door. There he stopped and looked down at Holly.

Conscious now, she raised herself on an elbow. She shuddered at the sight of the beast but saw that its full attention was given to Kruger. She looked to Malcolm, who hesitated in the doorway. Unable to find her voice, she motioned with a hand for him to run. Malcolm opened his mouth as though he would speak, then turned and vanished through the doorway.

The beast roared again and advanced on Kruger.

The big man, his mouth loose and drooling with fear, backed away. He stumbled, and remembered suddenly the cattle prod hanging by the wires from his belt pack. He seized the leather-wrapped grip and switched the current to its highest level. He thrust the rod out before him like a rapier.

"Awright," he babbled, "you want some of this? Come on, I'll give you some. I'll give you all you want."

He stabbed the metallic tip of the prod at the advancing creature.

The beast swatted at the measly weapon the man brandished and felt the electric shock that coursed all the way up to the hump of shoulder muscle. The shock was no more than a tickle to the beast, but it knew now what had been done to the boy Malcolm. It understood what had driven Malcolm to change as much as he had. The tiny shock was exactly what the beast needed to rekindle the bloodlust that had been so recently satisfied in the cabin outside Pinyon.

Kruger literally did not know what hit him. One moment he was holding the cattle prod, jabbing it at the huge, hairy thing that had burst through the window. The next moment his arm, fingers still twitching on the leather grip, was lying on the floor at his feet. He stared dumbly at the empty shoulder socket, where arterial blood pumped out in rhythm with his heartbeat.

Sitting now on the floor, Holly sucked in her breath as the beast cleaved Kruger's arm from his shoulder with one swift blow. She squeezed her eyes shut and turned away, unable to watch any more. She heard, however, Kruger's mewling little cries, and the crackle of teeth on bone.

Gavin Ramsay kept the accelerator to the floor all the way from Pinyon to Bear Paw. He did not bother with red lights and siren. There was not enough traffic along the way to make any difference. By the time he hit the brakes at the faint logging trail that led up to Pastory's clinic, the three-year-old Plymouth Fury bought by the taxpayers of La Reina County was sweating and snorting like a used-up racehorse.

He jounced up the grade, swerving against the brush on both sides, finally jamming to a stop when he came suddenly upon the old high-roofed house among the pines. Louis Zeno's orange Datsun was parked at an angle out in front, one door hanging open as though the driver had abandoned it hastily. Tucked neatly under a tree was Holly's little Volkswagen.

A sound came from inside the house that raised the short hairs at the back of Ramsay's neck. A snarling growl that reminded him of nothing so much as the feeding of big, dangerous animals at the zoo.

A door banged at the rear of the house. Ramsay galloped around the side of the building in time to see a figure running swiftly away, darting between the trees.

"Halt!" he called, unholstering his revolver.

The running figure never slowed down, vanishing as Ramsay watched. A shot would be fruitless at that range and with all the trees between him and the target. Anyway,

Ramsay never fired his piece without knowing what he was shooting at. Another growl came from inside the house, and he abandoned any thought of giving chase.

He started in through the open back door, then came to a stop. He thumbed the catch and rolled out the cylinder of his revolver, ejecting the copper-jacketed .38 cartridges onto the ground. Sweating with concentration, he jammed a hand into his jacket pocket and dug out six of the silver bullets. He slipped them into the cylinder, locked it in place, and ran into the house.

Ramsay almost fell down several steps into a semisunken room but caught his balance in time to stumble upright through the door. He took in the scene with a fast, sweeping glance. Against one wall stood a ruined cage. Rising shakily from the floor, clad in a sweater and bikini underpants, was Holly Lang. But dominating the room was a huge, wolflike beast that stood upright holding the armless, headless body of a man.

''Holly!'' he called.

She looked up at him, dazed and unbelieving for a moment, then scrambled toward him.

The beast, still holding the dismembered body, glared at him with bright green eyes. Ramsay raised the pistol.

At the moment he fired, Holly Lang stumbled into him, throwing off his aim. The soft silver bullet smacked into the far wall. Where an ordinary slug would have bitten out a chunk of concrete, the silver bullet flattened on impact and bounced to the floor.

The beast looked down at the bright blob of metal, then back at Gavin. A flash of understanding passed between them. The beast let the mangled body fall, dropped to all fours, and bounded past Ramsay and out the door before he could bring the revolver back into play.

Ramsay did not try to go after the thing. He stood where he was and wrapped both arms around Holly. He held her close to him until she finally stopped shivering. Then, supporting her with one arm, he picked up her jeans and her boots and led her gently out into the clear air.

Several minutes later they sat together in the front seat of the sheriff's car, which was still parked before the peaceful-looking house that was Dr. Pastory's clinic. As Holly calmed down she told him all that had happened to her since she had left his office early that morning.

"Then that was Malcolm I saw running into the woods," he said.

"Yes. We've got to find him, Gavin, and help him."

"I'm not sure we can."

"We've got to try. If you won't help me, I'll go after him alone."

"No, you won't," Ramsay said quietly. "We're together in this thing now. Wherever it leads."

"You know what we're going up against?"

"I know," he said. "I saw it in there. But I'm not going to try to convince anybody else. I would suggest that you don't either, unless you want to be locked in a rubber room."

"No," she said, "I don't imagine we could get anybody to believe us. Not anybody who could help."

"I'm afraid that's it," he said gently. "It will have to be you and me, Holly, and that's it."

She laid her head against his shoulder for a moment, then looked up at him. "I think I'd like to be kissed now," she said.

He complied.

Chapter 17

He was alone again.

Alone and running.

Malcolm stumbled blindly through the forest, tears blurring his vision. Only an ancient instinct saved him from repeated collisions with the trees. He ran on tirelessly with no thought of direction or destination. He knew only that he had to get away, far away from the terrible house where the men had done hurtful things to him. He blanked all thoughts from his mind except escape.

And he ran.

Alone and crying through the forest.

The daylight waned and night crept in and Malcolm ran on. The sky was tinted gray with the coming dawn when he finally dropped to the ground, sobbing. He had used up his youthful body, and in seconds he fell exhausted into a dreamless sleep.

When he awoke, it was night again. He was hungry. And he was cold. He still wore only the oversized pajamas provided for him by Dr. Pastory. Both top and bottom had been ripped by thorns. The legs were soaked through by the dew.

His feet were bare, though remarkably uninjured after his

wild run through the forest. Malcolm sat hugging his knees and shivering. He pushed away the panic that nipped at him and willed himself to relax.

The smell of woodsmoke was in the air. Not the greasy smoke of the raging fire he remembered from the night of terror in Drago. This was small. Almost friendly. A campfire. There was the aroma of boiling coffee. Malcolm rose and tested the air. Where there was a campfire there were people. People meant food and clothing.

Malcolm followed the smell of the campfire, moving without sound through the trees. He heard the lapping of small waves as he approached a mountain lake. At a safe distance he stopped and hid himself among a cluster of fallen fir boughs. From there he silently watched the camp at the lake's edge.

There was a tent and two men. The men sat across the fire from each other and talked with the familiarity of old friends. Their backpacks leaned neatly against the trunk of a fir. The play of the flickering flames across their faces stirred in Malcolm memories of the drunken hunters who had killed his friend Jones. As the remembered rage returned, a growl built in his throat.

But watching these men, Malcolm sensed that they were not like those others. These were fishermen, not killers. They laughed easily together and talked with rough affection of the wives they had left behind for this weekend excursion. Malcolm's anger subsided. The growl never left his throat.

It grew late and the fire crumbled into glowing coals. The men banked the dying fire carefully and laid out their sleeping bags.

"Funny, isn't it?" said one. "Here we can stay up as late as we want, and I'm dead tired at nine o'clock."

"It's the mountain air," said the other. "Anyway, we can get an early start in the morning. Get at the fish before they've had their coffee."

"You going to sleep in the tent?"

"Nah, it's too pretty out here. Nothing in these woods to worry about."

"Except the Drago werewolves."

Both men laughed. They crawled into their sleeping bags and soon fell silent.

Malcolm waited patiently until the snoring of the men assured him they were asleep. Then he stole down to their camp, placing his feet with care so there would not be the smallest sound.

His vision at night had always been nearly as sharp as in full daylight, and he quickly found the men's supplies. Their backpacks still leaned against the fir. Malcolm opened the packs carefully and took only the clothing he needed—underwear, a woolen shirt, tough denim pants and warm jacket, heavy socks, a pair of boots. Then, selecting food he could carry easily, he slipped away.

He moved softly until he was far enough from the camp so the men would not be awakened, then broke into a loping run. After a mile he stopped and rested and examined the things he had taken.

He ate a portion of the food and dressed himself in the men's clothes, carefully burying the torn pajamas. The clothes were too large for him, but he cinched up the pants and rolled up the cuffs of the shirt and jacket and the pantlegs. He put on both pairs of thick socks under the boots. Then he moved on again. More slowly this time; he had to think, to plan.

The days passed. Malcolm knew he would have to leave the area. The town of Pinyon, the county of La Reina, would never be safe for him again. Yet he had to return one more time. There was something he had to know.

He waited for a cloudy night when the moon and stars were hidden, then crept down from the hill behind the hospital. There were still searchers in the hills, but they were amateur woodsmen and easy to elude. There were no helicopters or organized parties as there had been when the doctor was killed. Several times Malcolm passed within yards of the searchers without being seen.

He found a vantage point from which he could see everyone who entered and left the building. There he waited. In the afternoon of the following day he saw the one he waited for. His friend. Holly Lang.

She walked up to the entrance of the building with the tall sheriff. They stopped to speak, then kissed briefly, and Holly went inside. Malcolm watched with a mixture of unfamiliar emotions as the door closed behind Holly and the tall sheriff walked away. There was the joy of seeing Holly and knowing she was safe. But there was also the pain of knowing he could never go to her again. Because of what he was. Holly's place was with people who were normal. People like the tall sheriff. Malcolm's place was . . . Where?

When night came again Malcolm left La Reina County for the last time and made his way to the coast above Ventura. There he left the forest and took to the highway. Hitching rides, he headed north.

In San Francisco he stopped for a time. In that city he found acceptance among the street people. Many of them were outcasts like him. They asked no questions of him, and he offered no explanations.

There were times when powerful emotions and strange hungers took over his body, and he felt the changes coming upon him. At those times Malcolm would find a hidden spot in some alley or a field and there struggle against the strange transformation that he was just beginning to understand.

In that terrible sunken room of Dr. Pastory's clinic, when the beast had crashed through the window, Malcolm knew, really knew for the first time, what he was. The beast was Derak, and Derak was Malcolm. Or what Malcolm would become.

The knowledge filled him with horror. Malcolm wanted to live among people and not be a thing of loathing to them. He despised the thought that he might lose control and attack someone who meant him no harm. During the times of changing, he fought against what he was, and while his body cried out for release, he was able to slow and finally halt the transformation, and eventually he would come back. But the effort cost him dearly.

In the city he could not live off the land, so he learned stealing and all the tricks and skills of the street boys.

It was an ugly existence, but he survived. Moving on, always moving so he would not become well known in any one place. He moved from the cities to the smaller towns and through the countryside, taking a bus when he had money, hitching rides when he didn't. Surviving. Searching. He knew somewhere his destiny waited. He would find it, or it would find him. There was no escape.

In La Reina County the sensation faded slowly into yesterday's news. For a few weeks there were reports of "werewolf" sightings, but they turned out to be somebody's dog or a tree or an unfortunate bearded hiker. The hunt continued for the sadistic killer, but official opinion was that he had left the area. The search spread beyond county and state boundaries. The hunt for the killer was based on the description of the mild-looking man who had been seen entering Dr. Qualen's office. It was the best lead they had. As for Malcolm, a runaway boy held a low priority.

For a time writer Louis Zeno was held as a possible suspect in the Pinyon killings, but he was never considered seriously. When he was released, Zeno hurried back to Los Angeles and went to bed for a week. When he emerged, Zeno avoided all discussion of Pinyon, Abe Craddock, and what he had found in the isolated cabin. He still planned one day to write that book, but for the present he was content to crank out articles about two-headed calves and movie stars' romantic problems.

Dr. Wayne Pastory was questioned at length when he returned to his isolated clinic to find a dead assistant, a missing patient, and a sheriff and lady doctor waiting for him outside. However, his transfer of Malcolm from the hospital in Pinyon to his clinic had been handled according to the rules, and there was no crime he could be charged with. Nevertheless, the new administrative chief at the hospital, replacing the late Dr. Qualen, made it clear that Pastory was no longer welcome there in any capacity.

There were changes, too, in the office of the La Reina County Sheriff. Milo Fernandez finished up his training tour and returned to school to study police science. His next assignment would be at some larger jurisdiction than La Reina County, but it could hardly be as exciting. Milo left with regret, and with good wishes from all.

Roy Nevins, having had a taste of real excitement for the first time since his early days in Oakland, had second thoughts about retiring. The law would allow him to stay an additional five years. He sold the idea to his wife by pointing out that the pension would be bigger. The real reason was that Roy Nevins, past fifty, had found a pride in his profession. He had started watching his diet and running and had lost so much weight that he had to buy a whole new set of uniforms. It was money he was glad to spend.

Gavin Ramsay watched the departure of one deputy and the transformation of the other with, respectively, regret and pride. The investigation of the local killings had largely been taken over by other agencies as the search for the killer widened, and it was the old routine again in the sheriff's office. Given Roy's new dedication to the job, one deputy was enough to handle the work load.

The sheriff found himself for the first time in months with spare time. Fortunately, he had a place to spend it—with Dr.

Holly Lang. It was natural that they should be together because of the terrible secret they shared. As they had promised each other, neither had spoken of the nature of the beast that destroyed the brutish Kruger in Pastory's clinic.

There were people around who would be only too ready to embrace the idea of werewolves in their midst. But they were the same people who believed in little men from outer space and went to flying saucer conventions. Their support could only hinder the very personal search of the sheriff and the doctor.

They did make one attempt. On a morning about a month after their return, Gavin had said, "I know one man who would believe us."

"I thought we agreed that kooks were out," Holly said.

"This guy is no kook. He knows about these things, and he might be able to help us."

"Then by all means, let's give him a try."

They went together to Ken Dowd's shop, The Spirit World, in Darnay. Ramsay was disappointed to see the shades drawn and a CLOSED sign taped to the glass on the inside of the door. He and Holly went into the neighboring leather goods store to inquire about the owner.

"Ken Dowd?" the young clerk repeated. "He closed up about three weeks ago. He made a bundle during the werewolf boom, then locked the store and split. Wish I could have had a piece of his business at the time."

"Do you know where he went?" Ramsay asked.

"Back east somewhere is all I know. Cape Cod or something like that. Him and his wife. Told me he was going into the antique business. Something that couldn't possibly scare anybody, he said. Maybe he hasn't checked the price of antiques."

"You have no address for him?"

"No. You might try the real estate company that's selling the store for him."

Ramsay thanked the young man and he and Holly left the shop.

Back out on the street, he turned to her with a shrug. "I don't think it's worth chasing him to Cape Cod. You got any suggestions?"

"Afraid not. But we've got to keep looking, Gavin. I'd feel we were abandoning Malcolm if we gave up."

"Hey, nobody said anything about giving up. I thought Ken Dowd might help us from the, well, occult end. We missed him, but we can sure as hell keep looking. I told you we were in this together, didn't I?"

"Yes, you did. All the way, you said."

"And all the way I meant. Let's go."

Ramsay received hundreds of pictures from police agencies all over the country. Pictures of boys—delinquents, runaways, pickups, strays. He and Holly spent hours going over them. Many resembled Malcolm in one small way or another, but Malcolm himself was not among them.

One evening at Holly's little house, after a session with a new batch of photos from the police chief of Seattle, Ramsay shoved the pile of glossy prints aside irritably.

"What's the matter?" she asked.

"I'm sick and tired of looking at pictures of young boys," he said.

Holly laid a hand on his knee. "I know it's boring, but it's one thing we can do."

"Well, I'm beginning to feel like a damned pedophile."

"Are you going to sulk now?"

"Sulk, hell. It's been half a year."

"You said—"

"I know, I know, and I'm not backing out on you. I understand how important Malcolm is to you, and I'm willing to make every reasonable effort to find him. But do you realize how much time we're spending looking for a boy who

166

could be anywhere in the Western Hemisphere by now? Or dead?''

"Malcolm is alive," Holly said stubbornly. "I know he is. I can feel it."

"Okay, so he's alive. He's becoming an obsession with you. We can't even go to the movies without Malcolm sitting there between us."

Holly's cheeks showed pink spots of anger. She took her hand away from Gavin's knee. "Oh, is that so? I don't remember a lot of complaining from you last night about the bed being too crowded."

"Last night was fine," Gavin admitted. "But those times are getting to be mighty rare. We started out with what I thought was a pretty good sex life. Lately it's Malcolm this and Malcolm that, and we're lucky to have an uninterrupted twenty minutes for fooling around."

Holly stood up abruptly from the couch. Gavin scrambled to his feet to face her.

She said, "If you want out, Sheriff, you've got it. Thank you very much for sticking it out this long. I'll handle it myself from here on. Good night."

"If that's the way you want it, good *night*!" he said, and stomped out the door.

Ramsay had stomped all the way down the walk to his car and had his hand on the door handle when he stopped. *Asshole*, he told himself. He squared his shoulders, turned, and walked back up the path to Holly's little house. As he reached for the bell the door opened in his face.

"They always come back," she said.

"You're too smart for your own good, lady. Want to look at the pictures some more?"

"Not tonight," she said.

"Want to go to bed?"

"Try me."

He gently closed the door behind them.

Chapter 18

The weeks passed.

And the months.

Malcolm wandered up and down the long, diverse state of California. He had been in and out of cities, towns, villages; crossed mountains and desert. Several times he had ventured near the state line. He had looked across into Oregon, Nevada, and Arizona, but he had not crossed the line. Although he was a young man without roots, he still felt that it was in California that he would find what was waiting for him. It had all begun for him in this state, and he sensed that this was where it would end.

Once, during the winter when he was seeking warmth wherever he could find it, Malcolm did travel a short distance into Mexico. He had looked hard at the verdant hills below Tijuana and felt the presence there of others like himself. Yet they were not his own people, the survivors of Drago. He had no doubt now that there were survivors. Many times he had heard the howling in the night—calling him. Though his body yearned to answer their call, he fought against it. He was not ready.

Despite the vagabond life, Malcolm's body filled out over

the year. He grew stronger. His shoulders broadened out and his chest expanded. Such work as he was able to find helped harden him. His muscles were supple, his hands rough and callused. Although he took a boyish pride in his more manly appearance, there were new problems.

In the dim outlaw world he was forced to live in, physical conflict was common. Malcolm had seen men fight to the death over half a bottle of wine. In the early days he had often been challenged by the boys and men he met in his travels. Every time, although his body ached to respond, he had backed away from a fight. He would suffer any humiliation to avoid combat.

They laughed at him and called him coward. The taunts did not bother him, nor the name. He sensed how swiftly and terribly he might destroy these people if he yielded to violent emotions. Their name for him then would be far worse than coward.

More frequently as the weeks passed Malcolm felt his body strain to change its shape when some passion gripped him. The urge to let go was powerful, but Malcolm continued to fight it. By intense effort of will he had so far resisted the full change, but he knew the day would come when he could resist no longer. He could only hope that by then he would know what to do.

While his body grew strong, the unsettled life took its toll on the young man's emotions. On a cloudless afternoon in late spring he felt he had hit bottom. He rested that day in the Inyo hills and thought about bringing his painful life to an end. But he did not even know how to do that. With his education cut off by the fire at Drago, he understood very little of his kind. There were three ways, it was said, that they could be destroyed—silver, fire, and a third, which was never mentioned. Had one of his people ever killed himself? Was such an act possible? Malcolm had no way of knowing.

Suddenly he tensed, cocked his head, and listened. Faint but unmistakable, there came a cry of mingled pain and fear.

Malcolm tested the air, determined the direction from which the cry came, and climbed swiftly up the grassy slope.

The cries ceased as he drew near. Malcolm knew that the creature in pain sensed his approach and feared him. He moved on cautiously, guided by his sense of smell.

Behind a patch of scrub oak he found it—a young coyote, hardly more than a pup. Its forepaw was caught in a trap.

Memories flooded back to Malcolm of his own anguish on that night more than a year ago when his ankle had been crushed by the trap. He knelt beside the coyote pup, his eyes filling with tears. He reached his hand out tentatively, palm up, to show the creature he meant no harm.

The trapped coyote sniffed at his fingers. Its lip drew back in an instinctive snarl, but it made no attempt to bite him. Very gently Malcolm touched its muzzle. His fingers stroked the gray-brown fur of the head between the velvety, pointed ears. The young coyote shivered under his touch.

"Easy, little guy," the boy said. "I'm not going to hurt you."

The pup whined softly.

"I know how you feel. Believe me, I do."

The coyote looked up at him with cautious eyes. Its shivering quieted.

"That's the boy," Malcolm said, speaking in a slow, soothing tone. "Now let's see how bad you're hurt."

He moved the pup gently to get a better look at the damage done by the trap. With relief he saw it was not the bone-crushing kind that had caught him in the woods outside Pinyon. This was the legal, nonmaiming trap designed to catch and hold, but not to do serious injury.

"You're a lucky fella," Malcolm said. "I know you probably don't think so, and it's no fun to be caught in any kind of a trap, but believe me, you could have it a lot worse."

He slipped his fingers between the smooth jaws of the trap and pulled against the spring. Was there no place, he wondered, where a wild creature could be left alone? Down in the valley he had seen a flock of sheep. He supposed the rancher had set out the traps to protect his flock. Malcolm could not fault the man for that. At least the man had used this less destructive trap, and he had not resorted to poison. Still, a lamb was natural prey for the coyote. Where was the right or wrong of it all?

Slowly Malcolm forced the jaws open. The young coyote drew back the injured paw but did not try to get away. Malcolm ran gentle fingers along the leg that had been caught.

"Nothing's broken. Your foot will be sore for a while, but like I told you, it could be a lot worse."

The coyote tested its weight on the paw, raised it quickly, then tried again.

"See, it works all right," Malcolm said. "You can get along back to your family now."

The pup looked up at the boy, then lowered its head and butted gently against his leg. Malcolm scratched the coyote behind one ear.

"I wish I could keep you with me, little fella," he said. "It would be nice to have somebody to talk to. And we've got something in common, haven't we?"

The little coyote licked his hand. Malcolm drew it away.

"But it can't work that way, so don't get all friendly with me. First thing you know I'll be giving you a name."

From behind him, Malcolm heard a soft growl. He turned and saw a female coyote standing with her legs braced, the fur bristling on the back of her neck.

He looked back at the pup. "I think your mama's here." The young coyote's eyes flicked from Malcolm to the female, then back to Malcolm.

"Go on," Malcolm said. "You know where you belong."

The pup hesitated a moment longer, then trotted, limping slightly, to join the female. The two of them were quickly lost from view in the scrub oak.

"I wish," said Malcolm to the empty hillside, "that I knew where *I* belonged."

He sank down on a mossy spot sheltered by a boulder and began to weep. Malcolm was not much given to crying, but there, alone and isolated, he gave himself up to the feeling of despair.

And as he wept his body began the spasms of the shape change. He could feel his downy beard growing thicker and coarser. He tasted blood as the long teeth pushed out through his gums. Because no one was around to see, this time Malcolm did not try to fight it. He was weary, and it had been a long, very long day.

It had been a long day, too, for Bateman Styles. It had, for that matter, been a long several years for Bateman Styles. A carnival showman, he was an outdated man scraping out a living in an outdated profession.

Until this year, however, he had managed somehow to find a spot every summer, even though it was with progressively smaller carnivals. In recent years he had fronted for a kootch show, an all-takers wrestler, a shooting gallery, fun house, ringtoss, wheel of fortune, and finally a freak tent. This year he had barely made it with the broken-down Samson Supershow. Or so he thought until early that afternoon when he was summoned to the Airstream Trailer of Samson himself, otherwise known as Jackie Moskowitz, former midget.

Styles had a premonition when the kid who ran the Ferris wheel told him the boss wanted to see him. It was the day before they were to open in Silverdale, and Bateman knew his freaks were at best a borderline attraction. But what the hell, he reminded himself, the Samson Supershow was not Barnum & Bailey, and Silverdale, California, was not San Francisco. Or even Eureka.

Even in its boom days Silverdale had never been much

more than a last watering hole for travelers coming down through the Inyo pass and heading for some insane reason into Death Valley. Today it did not even show on many maps. When pressed for a location, residents would say it was five miles from Wheeler. If that reference drew a blank look they would admit the town was fifteen miles out of Lone Pine. Anybody who did not know Lone Pine deserved no further explanation.

A far cry from the old days, Bateman Styles reflected as he tramped across the dusty field to Moskowitz's trailer. When he was a boy—Lord, that was fifty years ago—carnivals had played towns throughout the South, the West, and the Midwest without slowing down for nine months of the year. In those days the carnival was a big attraction in the towns, and even in cities of fifty thousand or so population. Even with the Depression, people found dimes to spend riding the Octopus or trying to win a Kewpie doll.

It was a lot different now. But hell, what wasn't? Bateman himself had been slowing down steadily for several years. He didn't have a lot of time left, but he always said he wanted to go out running a pitch somewhere. Only suckers die broke in bed.

He reached Jackie's trailer and banged on the aluminum door.

"It's open," piped a squeaky voice from inside.

Bateman entered. Jackie Moskowitz sat on a bench at a fold-down table playing solitaire. He brought himself up to table-level by sitting on two copies of the Los Angeles Yellow Pages. He did not look up immediately.

Bateman remembered Jackie from the days when he was Major Tiny, an ill-tempered midget with Gallagher's Greater Shows. That was in the fifties. It was a phaseout time for carnivals, and just as well for Major Tiny, whose faulty pituitary gland unexpectedly betrayed him. In a period of less than a year he grew to four feet eleven. Not a big man in the outside world, but laughably tall for a midget.

173

Luckily for him, Jackie had saved his money and was able to buy a piece of the Gallagher's show when he got too big to work. It had since declined steadily until the ragtag collection of grifters, kids, and burnouts that made up Samson was all he had left.

"What's up, Jackie?" Bateman said, squeezing his paunch into the narrow space behind the table across from Jackie.

"I gotta cut back," said the little man.

"Oh?" Styles braced himself for the bad news.

"Your show's gotta go."

"Why mine?"

"Because it's the weakest in the whole shebang. I carried you last year for old times' sake. I was ready to do it again, but I got to lookin' at the bills, and I can't hack it."

"My tent's better than the kootch show," Bateman protested. "Those bimbos couldn't give a hard-on to a Mexican sailor. Or what about the Wheel of Fortune? Umbach's got his foot on the pedal so heavy it raises smoke when he stops the thing. Even the yokels aren't going for that."

"Forget it, Bateman," squeaked the little owner. "You're gone."

"Why me? Just give me a reason."

"Okay. That bunch of so-called freaks you carry around wouldn't get a second look at a Kiwanis convention. Your giant, what is he, six-seven?"

"Six-eight-and-a-half," Styles protested.

"Some giant. The yokels can see kids bigger than that at any high school basketball game. And your bearded lady— you call that a beard?"

"You would if you kissed her."

"God forbid. That five-o'clock shadow don't impress anybody, not even when she darkens it up with pencil shavings."

"She's got three kids."

"That don't make her no freak."

174

"I mean, how's she going to take care of them?"

"That ain't my problem. Let her do shave cream commercials. And your sorry fire-eater—what's he call himself, Torcho?"

"Flamo."

"It's always one or the other. Do you know how old his shtick is? I mean, blowing lighter fluid out of your mouth went out with handlebar mustaches."

"Handlebars are back."

"Don't confuse the issue."

"So my people aren't exactly New Wave. What of it? Most of the carnival is things that's been around for years. Nostalgia, that's what brings the folks in."

"Well, in your case it ain't bringing enough of 'em in. You and your freaks are out, Bateman. Sorry, but that's the way it is. In another year I'll most likely be out, too. You and me, we're the tail end of this business."

Styles seemed to crumble where he was wedged into the small seating space. He stared blankly down at the worn cards laid out before Moskowitz.

"Can't you give me a week?"

"No way. Everything's too tight. Hell, Bateman, you can probably collect more on Social Security than you make traveling with a tin-can outfit like this. You're sure as hell old enough for it."

"They tell me that to collect any of that you have to show you put some in over the years."

"No bull? How chickenshit."

"What if I come up with another gimmick?"

"I don't want your freaks, period."

"Okay, if they got to go, that's it. Maybe I can come up with something else."

"Come up with what? We open tomorrow."

"Lemme think about it, okay?"

"Sure, you think about it, Bateman, but I don't want to see those freaks in the morning."

175

"I'll give them the word."

"Good."

Moskowitz returned his full attention to the solitaire game. Styles levered himself out from the confining seat and left the trailer.

Breaking the news to his people—like most old-time carnies, Styles would never call them freaks—did not go too badly, all things considered. Colossus shook his hand, thanked him for a year of work, and said he'd have no problem getting a dishwasher job in some joint. They liked to have a big guy who could come out from the back if the bouncer got into it with somebody tougher than he could handle. Colossus was no fighter, but he was big and looked mean, and that was enough to discourage a lot of mouthy punks.

Flamo said little when Bateman gave him the bad news. He merely belched and chewed his Maalox tablets. He guessed maybe he could go back to his wife in Bakersfield if she had kicked out the twelve-string guitar player she'd been shacking with.

With Rosa it had been tougher. Tears had welled in her great brown eyes and rolled down into her inadequate mustache. Bateman took her aside and slipped her enough for bus fare back to Flagstaff, where she had parked the kids with a sister. It was the best he could do.

Now, walking in the late afternoon on the hill above Silverdale, Styles missed all of them. In his years as a showman he had seen a couple thousand people come and go. He could never get used to it. They were his family. And in his heart he knew, once somebody left the carnival, you never saw them again. It was like they died.

Speaking of which, unless he could come up with some fast spiel for Moskowitz by tomorrow morning, Bateman Styles would himself be leaving the carnival. When he'd made the pitch in Moskowitz's trailer he had some half-ass idea about selling the midget on a flashy new idea. The trouble was, he didn't have one. All the ideas were used up.

Bateman stopped frequently to rest as he walked. The hills were steeper than they used to be. And it was hard for a man to catch his breath at this altitude.

He sat on a rock and looked at the view. Silverdale might not be much shakes as a town, but you couldn't buy the view for a million dollars. To the east, flat and parched, stretched Death Valley. It shaded delicately from gold to chocolate brown. To the west, just beyond the Inyo foothills, stood big-shouldered Mount Whitney.

His contemplation of the scenery was interrupted by a sound very close to him. Not quite a sob and not quite a growl, but a little of each. Bateman stood up and looked behind the rock he had been sitting on.

There on the ground lay a boy, or young man, his body twisted into an unnatural position. He was huddled there, his face away from Styles, his limbs twisting and jerking as though yanked by invisible wires. It was the boy who was making the sob-growl sounds.

Styles's first thought was that the kid was having an epileptic seizure. He had once worked with a high-diver who was an epileptic. They all figured someday Carlo would throw a fit while he was up on the tower, looking down at the tub. Sure enough, one day he did. Carlo's last dive was by far his most spectacular.

Bateman knew you were supposed to keep an epileptic from swallowing his tongue. He leaned down and tried to roll the young man over onto his back. Then he saw the face, and forgot all about epileptic seizures.

Ten minutes later the young man was looking reasonably normal. All muddy and soaked with sweat, but not a bad-looking kid. Styles leaned against the rock, smoking an unfiltered Camel.

"Hi," said the showman.

The boy said nothing.

"You got a name?"

"M-Malcolm."

"Mind telling me how you do that, Malcolm?"

"Do what?"

"Make yourself go all hairy and fierce-looking like you just did."

Malcolm stared at Bateman Styles. He was silent for a minute as he seemed to make up his mind about something. Finally he said, "I don't do it on purpose. It just . . . happens. Sometimes I can control it."

"Anything special that makes it happen?"

"When something makes me feel really sad. Or really mad. Then . . . things happen to me."

"No kidding. What makes you mad, Malcolm?"

"I don't know. Lots of things."

"How about being in a cage with people standing around looking at you, pointing, saying things about you?"

The moment he said "cage" Styles knew he'd hit it. The boy's eyes deepened to a dangerous shade of green, and his lips pulled away from his teeth like an animal. Then he got hold of himself.

"Yeah," Malcolm said. "That would make me mad."

Bateman Styles drew in deeply on his cigarette, coughed, and said, "You want a job?"

Chapter 19

Bateman Styles leaned back from the fold-down table and lit up a Camel. He coughed. He watched as the boy Malcolm shoveled in the beans and sausage he had heated on the small butane stove. It looked like his grocery bill was going to go up fast, but if the kid could manage that trick he saw today, he'd soon pay for it.

"That was good, Mr. Styles," Malcolm said when at last his plate was empty. "Thanks."

"Sure it was enough?"

"Well . . ."

"It'll have to be," Styles said quickly, "until I can get to the store."

"I wish I could help pay," Malcolm said.

"You will, my boy, you will," Styles said. "However, before we start making permanent arrangements, we'd better go see the boss about taking you on."

"You're not going to ask me to, you know, do it for him, are you?"

"Not if you don't want to, my boy. That act's our bread and butter, and there's no use giving it away, not even to the boss."

"It isn't that I don't want to, Mr. Styles; it's just that I can't, like, make it happen just any time."

"I get the picture, lad. You need the stimulus. Anger, despair, some powerful emotion. We'll work that out. By the way, 'Mr. Styles' makes me nervous. Call me Bate."

Malcolm grinned shyly and nodded.

"What we need now is a name for you."

"I have a name."

"No, no, no. Malcolm definitely does not fill the bill. We need something to draw in the marks. Something to whet the people's appetites for what they are about to see. Like Flamo the Fire-Eater."

"I don't eat fire."

"I know that, boy. I was merely using it as an example. As a matter of fact, it didn't do much for Flamo either." Styles was silent for a long minute. He closed his eyes, laid his head back, pursed his lips, and passed a hand over the wisps of gray hair that remained on his scalp. Suddenly his eyes popped open. He smiled broadly, showing brown-stained teeth.

"I've got it. Wolf Boy. Grolo the Wolf Boy." He waited for a reaction.

Malcolm frowned.

"Something wrong?"

After a moment's hesitation Malcolm shook his head. "I don't want to be called that."

"What's the matter with Grolo?"

"That's okay. It's the other part."

"Wolf Boy?"

Malcolm nodded.

"Judas Priest, why not? It's short, descriptive, and has a nice scary ring to it."

"I don't like it." There was a new, cold note in the boy's voice.

"Then we shall discard it," Styles said decisively. He again went into his thinking posture—eyes closed, head

180

back, lips pursed. This time he was out of it in thirty seconds.

"Animal Boy." He studied Malcolm through narrowed eyes. "Can you live with that?"

"I guess so."

"Then it's Grolo the Animal Boy. I don't think it has the same appeal as Wolf Boy—"

Malcolm's eyes darkened.

"But, after all, you are the attraction here, and we'll call you anything you like."

They left Styles's antiquated trailer together and tramped across the dark field toward Jackie Moskowitz's Airstream. The concession stands were up, the tents in place, the small Ferris wheel erected, all ready to go at ten the next morning. Some of the attractions, like the kootch show and Bateman's tent, would not open until evening.

In the back of the food tent the perpetual poker game was in progress. The laughter and good-natured cursing of the carnival hands floated through the clear night. Elsewhere it was quiet. The town of Silverdale, immediately to the north, showed only a sprinkling of lights.

The showman and the boy came to a stop at the owner's blimp-shaped trailer. Styles gave Malcolm a reassuring wink and banged on the aluminum door.

The little owner was wearing yellow pajamas and a cutoff robe when he opened the door. He looked at Styles and the boy with distaste.

"Jesus, Bateman, is this important? I just took a sleeping pill."

"I told you I'd get a new show."

"Well?"

Styles swept his hand in a grand gresture toward Malcolm. "I give you Grolo the Animal Boy."

Moskowitz squinted up at them. "Come in here in the light."

Styles urged Malcolm into the trailer, then followed. The

showman stood back while Malcolm shifted nervously from foot to foot. Moskowitz walked slowly around the boy, examining him from all angles.

"Animal Boy? What the hell does that mean? He's not a geek, is he?"

Styles was offended. "Jackie, you've known me long enough to know I wouldn't bring you a geek. Grolo here will turn into a raging, roaring, frothing animal before the eager eyes of the paying customers. He will be a sensation."

"Yeah? What's the trick?"

"Jackie, please. Would you ask Houdini how he did his Water Torture escape?"

"I would if he was looking for work."

"This is by way of a trade secret. Even I do not know how he does it."

"Okay, okay, so don't tell me." Jackie picked up one of Malcolm's hands and examined it. "He don't look much like an animal."

"Not now, he doesn't. Just wait until tomorrow night when there's a tent full of marks waiting to see him."

"I don't know, Bateman. I was thinking of using your space for a baseball pitch. I haven't had one for two years."

"A baseball pitch? Can you imagine people paying more to knock over weighted metal milk bottles than to see a genuine, bona fide Animal Boy?"

"People like to throw baseballs."

"They like to be scared, too. Why do you think horror movies clean up?"

"Well . . ."

"Jackie, let me try it for this one week in Silverdale. I'll guarantee you a minimum."

"Guarantee?"

"More than that. If we don't outdraw the kootch show *and* the ringtoss, I'll make up the difference out of my own pocket. And if we bomb, you can leave us here and you're out nothing."

"Are you sober, Bateman?"

Styles held up a right hand. "Not a drop since early this afternoon."

The little man cracked off a huge yawn. "Okay, you got a deal. I want to see this act myself. But remember, if your animal boy is a dog, it's adiós."

"Fair enough, Jackie, fair enough."

"Now get out of here and let me get some sleep." He looked up doubtfully at Malcolm. "Uh, so long, Grolo."

"Good night, Mr. Samson," Malcolm said.

As they walked back across the field together Styles clapped Malcolm on the back. "Congratulations, my boy, you're in show business. This calls for a toast to our future success. Or do you indulge?"

"I don't drink, but you go ahead, Bate."

"Thank you, my boy, thank you. I believe I will. Then perhaps I'll take a stroll over to the kootch girls' trailer. Care to join me in that?"

Malcolm flushed. "Well, I, uh, don't know if I, uh . . ."

"That's all right. Plenty of time for sport. Probably better for you to get a good night's sleep. I'll fix you up with a blanket roll in the trailer and try not to wake you when I come in."

Malcolm jolted out of a light sleep when Bateman Styles returned to the trailer sometime after midnight. It took him a moment to realize where he was, then he closed his eyes and feigned sleep as the showman bumbled about the trailer, trying clumsily to be quiet. Soon Styles was in his bed, snoring. Malcolm dozed off again with a tiny, contented smile on his lips.

Bateman was up at dawn, apparently none the worse for his night's carouse. He scrambled some eggs and made hash browns for the two of them, then left Malcolm alone.

The sounds and smells of the carnival as the people

started coming in were enticing, but Malcolm stayed in the trailer. He was not yet ready to move among people again.

In midafternoon Styles returned, looking pleased with himself.

"Good news, boy. At virtually no expense, I have procured a cage," he said. "We can't convince the good people you're dangerous without a cage, now can we?"

He saw Malcolm's expression darken and went on quickly. "It isn't much of a cage, really. It would barely hold a determined pussycat. However, it will do until we can find something more impressive. It was lucky that Clete Matthews still had it from the time he was carrying a chimp act. The thing still smells faintly of chimpanzee, but I daresay we can get used to that, right?"

"Sure, I guess so."

Bateman studied the boy for a moment, then sat down on the rumpled bed. "Kid," he said, "I want you to understand what's going to happen tonight. You'll be in the cage inside the tent with a curtain pulled to hide you till we're ready. I'm out front talking, turning the tip, as we say, to get the marks to part with their coin and come inside. Then I come in and say a lot of things to you and about you that won't sound nice. Don't you pay any attention. It's show business. I want to get the marks riled at you so you can work up enough passion to . . . do the thing you do. You just . . . let yourself go, or whatever it takes, okay?"

"Okay, Bate."

"Fine. We're going to make us a few bucks, my boy. And maybe have some chuckles along the way." He pulled out an old-fashioned turnip watch. "Are you ready to go at it?"

"I'm ready if you are."

"Then let us proceed."

Styles put up the same garish canvas paintings that he had used for his dismantled freak show. There had been no time

184

to prepare a new one, and Bateman reasoned that any pictures were better than no pictures. He climbed up on the platform and observed for several minutes the trickle of locals who passed on the sawdust walkway below him. Then he blew into his hand mike, heard the resultant blast from the speaker, and began to improvise a spiel.

"Inside, ladies and gentlemen, inside, inside, inside. Inside this tent you will positively *not* see"—he pointed to the garish pictures in turn—"Colossus the Giant. You will *not* see Rosa the Bearded Lady. You will *not* see Flamo the Fire-Eater. All this I promise you. What, then, you ask, *will* I see on the inside for the price of one lonely dollar? A fair question. I would tell you, my friends. I would describe in detail the wonder inside, but frankly, you would not believe me. You would not believe me, and I would not blame you. For inside, inside, inside, for the price of one dollar, I have for you the most inconceivable, incredible, impossible, astounding, amazing, astonishing sight on the face of the earth."

A few strollers stopped to listen to the spiel, grinning at the cascade of superlatives. Styles noted that nobody was reaching for his wallet yet.

"At monumental expense and superhuman effort the Samson Supershow has brought from faraway shores the most bizarre attraction ever presented in the Western world. Yes, in this very tent, my friends, blessedly caged to keep us from being attacked, is Grolo . . . the Animal Boy!"

The tip was building, but not fast. The Wheel of Fortune across the way had twice as many waiting to dump their coins on Umbach's crooked wheel. Styles forged on.

"Before your very eyes—no mirrors, no tricks with the lights—before your very eyes Grolo will become the fearsome, the terrible, the fantastic . . . Animal Boy!"

The showman continued to improvise in this vein while a few people payed their dollars and straggled into the tent. For the first time since he had watched Malcolm's remarkable transformation this afternoon, Bateman began to have doubts. What if the kid couldn't do it? What if he hadn't really done it in the first place? Styles *had* put down a few belts of Old Overholt earlier to brace himself for delivering the bad news to his people, and it would not be the first time he had seen things that did not happen.

He pulled aside a flap and peeked into the tent. One good thing—if the kid did funk out on him, he wouldn't have a lot of money to refund. Not more than a dozen people stood on the dirt floor waiting for the show. Might as well get on with it, he decided.

Styles broke off the spiel and entered the tent. He stepped up onto the low platform at the far end and paused dramatically with a hand on the worn velvet curtain.

"My friends, in the next few moments you are going to see something no other human eyes have—"

"Get on with it, old man," said a teenager who had come in with two friends. "We already heard the bullshit."

"Yeah," said a man with the weather-beaten face of a farmer. "Let's see what you got back there."

"Very well, my friends," said Styles without breaking stride. "Your impatience is understandable. Without further ado I give you . . . Grolo the Animal Boy!"

He snatched aside the curtain to reveal the chimp cage. Seated inside, for the top of the cage was too low to allow him to stand, was Malcolm. He looked around at the small crowd, his eyes large and apprehensive.

After the first intake of breath, a muttering rose in the crowd.

"That's an animal boy?" somebody said.

"What else does he do?"

"It's just another phony!"

"Fake!"

"I want my money back!"

The last comment triggered Bateman Styles to action. He

186

glared into the cage, giving Malcolm a wink that the marks could not see.

"I don't blame you one bit, my friends, and believe me, every penny will be refunded to you. You see, it is not only you but myself as well that has been flimflammed here. I was given the most solemn assurances that this was, indeed, the authentic Animal Boy you may have read about or seen on television. I am embarrassed to admit to you that this young imposter hoodwinked me."

Speaking directly to Malcolm, he said, "Young man, you are a liar. A cheat. You misrepresented yourself to me and you have tried to steal the money from these good folks out in front. You are nothing more than a contemptible juvenile hoodlum. You should be caged in prison."

To the people out front, who were enjoying his tirade, Styles added, "Go on, friends, tell this young imposter what you think of him and his type." Searching for a reference they could relate to, he added, "This is the same kind of punk who tears in here on a motorcycle, freaked out on drugs and who knows what all, and rips up the landscape, then goes roaring back to the city, leaving you to clean up his mess. Go ahead, tell him what you think of him and his kind."

The people watching understood that this was somehow part of the show, yet they were carried along by Styles's florid speech.

"Boo!" came the first tentative yell.

"Get out of here!"

"Dirty biker!"

"Go home, faggot!"

Someone picked up a small stone from the ground and threw it. The stone clanked off the bars of the chimp cage.

Malcolm listened to the shouts and jeers and tried to concentrate on what Bateman Styles had told him to do. Styles had been kind to him and asked no questions, and he did not want to let the showman down. He concentrated. Nothing happened.

The boos got louder. Styles began to sweat as he anxiously watched Malcolm through the bars. The marks were getting carried away by their own voices. One of them heated a penny with a cigarette lighter and tossed it into the cage.

Malcolm blanked Bateman Styles out of his mind. He got off the stool and walked forward in a half crouch to seize the bars. He looked down into the taunting faces and summoned back a series of images. The fire. The trap. The hunters. Dr. Pastory and the table. Kruger and the cattle prod. Kruger hurting Holly.

He felt it begin.

The jeers of the crowd died in their throats. For a moment there was silence in the tent. Bateman Styles, along with the paying customers, stared in awe at the boy in the cage.

"What's happening to his eyes?" a plump girl asked her boyfriend.

"Look at his face," somebody else said in a strangled tone.

"And his hands! My God, they're *growing*!"

"The teeth! Holy shit, the teeth!"

Styles watched the contortions of the boy in the cage. Even though he had seen the process before in reverse, he was stunned by what was happening in there. The growls that came from the boy could surely not be human.

He let the transformation continue until blackened hairy hands started to bend the inadequate cage bars. Then he caught the message flashed from the dangerous green eyes. This must go no further. Without ceremony the showman snatched the curtain back in front of the cage.

"That's it, my friends. I think each and every one of us can agree that we got our dollar's worth here today. Grolo the Animal Boy. There will be another show in one hour by the clock. Tell your friends. I thank you."

The dozen people who had witnessed the performance filed out silently. Once outside, they all began to talk at once, the general topic being speculation on how it was done. They scattered excitedly over the small carnival grounds to spread the word.

When he had seen the last of the customers leave, Bateman Styles hurried back through the curtain and helped Malcolm out of the cage. He was relieved to see that the boy looked normal again, if somewhat sweaty. Malcolm gave him a tired smile.

"How did I do, Bate?"

"Lad, you were sensational. We will never again have a crowd that small, or I do not know this business. How do you feel?"

"Okay. A little tired."

"Think you can do it again in an hour?"

"Yeah. I found out there's a kind of a trick I can use to make it easier."

"Whatever the trick is," said the showman, "don't tell me. There are some things a man should not know. Go catch a nap in the trailer if you want. I'll call you in time for the next show."

"I think I'll just walk around, if that's all right."

"Sure. If you want to see any of the shows, take a ride, tell 'em you're working with me. You're one of us now."

One of us. Beautiful words. He really wasn't, of course, but it was as close as Malcolm had come to belonging anywhere in a long time. He strolled around the small carnival, savoring the tinny music from the merry-go-round, the thumping drum from the kootch show. He inhaled with pleasure the raw smell of sawdust mingled with cooking grease and cotton candy. He gazed happily at the colored lights strung above the walkways. When he told the other carnival people he was working with Bateman, they accepted him without question. Nobody asked what he did or where he came from. He was *almost* one of them.

189

As Styles had predicted, the crowd was much larger for the second show. Many who had been at the opener came back to see it again. Jackie Moskowitz himself came in, positioning himself in the front row, where he would not have to look through people's armpits. Styles shortened his spiel this time and let the act speak for itself. Again the Animal Boy was a sensation.

When they closed out the week in Silverdale, there was no more talk of leaving Bateman Styles behind. The Animal Boy *did* bring in more than the kootch show and the ringtoss combined.

The sponsoring civic organization was so pleased with their share of the carnival's take that they invited the Samson Supershow back to Silverdale for another stand late in the summer. Jackie Moskowitz, with holes to fill on his schedule, was only too happy to oblige.

As they traveled north with stops at Manzanar, Crestview, Mono Lake, Markleeville, Sattley, Ravendale, and a dozen other California towns nobody ever heard of, the fame of Grolo the Animal Boy spread. People were driving fifty or a hundred miles to see the amazing change of boy into beast. Bateman Styles was supremely happy. He had a real attraction again. Jackie Moskowitz was talking long-term contract.

As for Malcolm, he was as close to being content as he could remember since childhood. Sometimes he would awaken in the night from a terrifying dream, then relax as he recognized the tacky trailer of Bateman Styles. There was still the nagging worry that someone would find him and take him back to answer for the business at Pastory's clinic, but over the weeks that faded, too.

It happened in mid-July. The Samson Supershow was playing a small town outside Red Bluff. Two men from Los Angeles paid their dollars and walked into the show, and Malcolm's life was about to be changed forever. By mid-

July, with the Samson show playing a town called Castle Rock, Malcolm had relaxed enough to laugh out loud, something he had not done since his days with Jones. He felt sometimes that his life here was too good to last.

He was right.

Chapter 20

"What am I doing here?" Louis Zeno complained. "What's the name of this town again?"

"Castle Rock," said Ted Vector. He was a bony, loose-jointed man with quick eyes. He wore a bag of camera equipment slung over a shoulder.

"Castle Rock," Zeno repeated. "That's not a town; that's a dance craze from the thirties."

"Don't be so negative. Once you see what I've got for us here, you will forever remember Castle Rock as our El Dorado."

Zeno came to a stop on the sawdust midway and stared at his companion. "Tell me something. What made you think of me, anyway?"

"Actually, it was Ed Endicott who suggested you."

"The editor of *National Expo*?"

"Do you know another Ed Endicott? He said he liked the way you were handling that werewolf business down in Pinyon until you got yourself in trouble."

"Yeah, trouble. I could have got myself eaten," Louis Zeno muttered.

"So when I told him what I had here, he said you'd be the perfect one to write it."

"Wonderful. Now I'm the *National Expo*'s werewolf man."

"You would rather be the two-headed-calf man?"

"Okay, okay." They walked on a short distance in silence. Then Zeno said, "You really think this Animal Boy is legitimate?"

"What the hell, he's close enough. They're talking about him all over the state. Ed Endicott was convinced enough to give me an advance, and you know the *Expo* don't throw money around."

Zeno sighed. "Let's get on with it, then. This'd better not turn out to be some turkey in a rubber mask."

Grolo the Animal Boy had his own sign outside the tent now. Two garish paintings flanked the platform where Bateman Styles was delivering the pitch. One showed a figure with the body of a boy and the head of some nightmare animal with huge tusks leering out from between two trees. The other had the Animal Boy carrying off a terrified, near-naked woman in the tradition of 1940s horror movies.

Zeno stared up at the pictures. "For *this* you had me drive up from L.A.?"

"Lighten up, pal. You can't spend your life writing about Burt Reynolds and Bianca Jagger," Vector told him. "Anyway, it's what's inside that counts."

The photographer stopped to click off several pictures of the front of the tent, then they joined the large crowd listening to Bateman Styles.

". . . It is my duty to warn you, friends," Styles was saying, "to stay well away from the front of the stage. Grolo is inside a sturdy cage of tempered steel, but his full strength when the rage is upon him has yet to be tested. Therefore, for your own safety, please stand clear. Everyone will be able to see everything that happens."

He paused and made a mental count of the spectators. "Now let us go in for the first show of the evening. For those of you who cannot fit inside the tent this time, your tickets will entitle you to first admittance at the next show one hour from now by the clock."

The showman stood next to the girl selling tickets and smiled contentedly. When he spotted Ted Vector's camera bag he leaned down from the platform.

"Sorry, sir, no pictures."

Vector looked up in innocent surprise. "What?" Then he smiled and tapped the camera bag as though he had just remembered he was wearing it. "Oh, this? I don't plan to take any pictures inside. I'm a tourist, you know. Never go anywhere without my camera."

"Well, as long as you leave it in the bag . . ." Styles said doubtfully.

"Absolutely," said the photographer. He and Louis Zeno paid their money and filed into the tent with the rest of the crowd.

The people were packed shoulder to shoulder in the tent. There was no air circulating except that flowing in through the entrance. The combined body heat was oppressive.

Zeno tucked himself in behind Vector and followed the photographer as he pushed his way to a position near the front. He mopped perspiration from his neck with a handkerchief and stared gloomily at the moth-eaten velvet curtain.

"This'd better be good, Ted. Remember, I could be home among the Beautiful People covering some swinging Hollywood party."

"Sure, sure, I know how you cover those parties—you open a can of beer, sit in your bathtub, and fantasize. Watch now, here comes the man."

Bateman Styles made his appearance at one end of the

curtain. It was a refinement he had added since the crowds became too big for him to walk easily through from the entrance to the stage.

"Ladies and gentlemen, welcome to the most astounding, the most amazing, the most incredible phenomenon on view in America today. In a very few minutes I am going to pull this curtain aside and reveal to you the Ninth Wonder of the World!"

"What happened to the eighth?" Zeno whispered to the photographer.

"Wasn't that King Kong?"

"Of course. How could I forget?"

Styles gave the two men a stern glance and they fell silent. Then the showman went on with his pitch, the grandiloquent speech rolling smoothly off his tongue in effortless flowery sentences. After many years in the business, Bateman Styles no longer had to think about what he was saying. The sentences, each with a verbal exclamation point, formed themselves and marched out of his mouth while he thought of other things.

He wound it up. "And now, ladies and gentlemen, the moment for which we have waited in an agony of growing suspense! I give you . . . Grolo the Animal Boy!"

He swept aside the curtain to reveal Malcolm seated on the stool in the confining chimpanzee cage. The boy gazed shyly out at the crowd.

By this time people knew the routine of the act from the reports of others who had seen it. They launched into the derisive hoots at Malcolm without prompting from Styles.

"That's no animal."

"Get off the stage, you fake."

"He doesn't even shave yet."

"Course not, it's a girl!"

"Refund . . . refund!"

"Booo!"

Louis Zeno took no part in the harassment of the boy in

the cage. Nor did he pay any attention to Ted Vector, who was fumbling in his camera bag. Something about the boy's luminous green eyes as they locked on his for a brief moment made the writer acutely uncomfortable.

"Let's get out of here," he whispered to the photographer.

"Are you crazy? The show hasn't even started. Take notes or something."

As always, when the boy began to change, the jeers of the crowd died abruptly. No matter how prepared they were for what was about to happen, the actual transformation on the small stage never failed to shock.

"Jesus," Zeno muttered through clenched teeth.

"See? See? What did I tell you?" Ted Vector had his camera out of the bag now and was holding it down low where it would be concealed from Bateman Styles.

The writer was not listening. He was back in the cabin at the moment he entered and saw torn bits of Abe Craddock everywhere. His stomach lurched, and for a moment he thought he was going to vomit.

"I've seen enough," he said. "Let's go."

"What do you mean? Aren't you going to interview the pitch man or anybody?"

"Who needs interviews? I can make up the quotes, like I always do. Let's go."

"At least let me get some shots of Grolo. Your story is worth shit without pics."

"Well, hurry it up."

Zeno tried not to watch what was happening in the small cage, but a terrible fascination kept pulling his eyes back. The boy's face had sprouted a coarse black hair. His body had broadened and stretched and changed its shape with a crackling of bones. He had to bend far over as he clutched the bars to keep from banging his head on the low ceiling. The eyes glowed with deep green fire. The teeth . . . visions of Craddock's savaged remains swam back up in Zeno's mind.

Vector brought the camera up with no further attempt at concealment and began clicking pictures. The creature in the cage caught the tiny sound. The ears pricked and the great head swiveled toward the source. It gave an inhuman growl; the taloned hands gripped the bars and began to bend them apart.

"You!" Bateman Styles jumped to the center of the stage and stabbed an accusing finger at Ted Vector. "Out! I told you no pictures!"

"Come on," Zeno said, tugging at his friend's arm.

"Just one more."

Click.

The bars separated. A powerful black-haired arm reached through.

"Shit, he's coming out!" someone yelled.

Styles's voice rose above the others. "Get that camera out of here before you get somebody killed!"

Zeno took a firm grip on the photographer's arm and tugged him back through the tense crowd and out of the tent.

"I got some great stuff," he said when they were back out on the midway.

"Yeah, you almost got us ripped apart, too."

"You convinced now?"

Zeno modulated his voice. "It's a good trick. Looked real in the dim lights in there."

"Bet your ass it looked real. How soon can you have the story written?"

"Tomorrow morning."

"Good. I'll develop this stuff tonight and we can hand the whole package to Endicott and collect the rest of the bread." The photographer gazed around the carnival. "You feel like seeing anything else? A couple of the girls in the kootch show aren't too bad, and they go all the way."

"What I feel like," Zeno told him, "is getting the hell out of here. Now."

CAGED ANIMAL BOY TERRORIZES CARNIVAL

The headline sprang out of the copy of *National Expo* being browsed by the shopper ahead of Holly Lang in the Safeway checkout line. And the picture—a horribly distorted mingling of human and animal features. But the eyes . . . she knew the eyes. Beyond any doubt, it was Malcolm.

Holly snatched her own copy of *Expo* from the rack and paid for it along with her groceries. She got into her car and drove directly to the sheriff's office.

Gavin Ramsay frowned at the half-tone photo in the tabloid. He said, "Are you sure this is Malcolm?"

"Of course it is. Don't you see it?"

"Frankly, no. They do some wild things with makeup these days."

"Damn it, Gavin, you're just being obstinate. You *know* it's Malcolm."

"Well, there's a chance."

"So let's go. We'll find that carnival and get him out of there."

"Right now? Just like that?"

"Why not?"

"For one thing, we don't know how old this photo is or where this"—he scanned Louis Zeno's story—"Samson Supershow is playing. It doesn't sound like a very big outfit."

"You can find out, can't you? You're a cop."

"I suppose I can," Ramsay admitted, "which brings me to my second point. I have a job here, and the taxpayers would probably not approve of me rushing off to do some private business on their time."

198

"I can go," Holly said. "You don't have to come along."

"Uh-huh. I remember the last time you rushed off to handle things on your own. As I remember, you were in kind of a fix when I got there."

"This is different," she said. "I won't have a Wayne Pastory to contend with. Chances are these carnival people don't know what they've got. All I'll do is go to the carnival, find Malcolm, and bring him back."

"Assuming that this *is* Malcolm," Ramsay said, "what if he doesn't want to come back?"

Holly was flustered for a moment. It was a possibility she had not considered.

"In that case I'll . . . I'll let him decide for himself. The least I can do is tell him he's not in any trouble over what happened at Pastory's."

"I don't want you to get in any trouble either."

She softened her tone. "I promise, Sheriff, if there is the least hint of any rough stuff I'll come running back for reinforcements. Okay?"

He could not hold the stern expression, and relaxed into a smile. "Okay, Doctor. Let me see if I can locate this Samson Supershow for you."

He made a call to the sheriff's office in Los Angeles County. A deputy he knew there said he would check with the theatrical booking agencies. Half an hour later the L.A. deputy called back with the information.

"He says Samson is booked this week in some place called Silverdale over in Inyo County," Gavin told Holly. "If you want to wait a couple of days, maybe I can arrange to go with you."

"Thanks, Gavin, but I don't want to let any more time go by. It's been over a year since we last saw Malcolm at the clinic."

"Then what difference would a couple more days make?"

"I just don't want to wait, that's all."

199

"You *will* call to let me know what's happening."

"That's a promise. I'll call as soon as I know anything." She came around the desk and gave him a warm, affectionate kiss. "Thanks, Gavin."

"Don't mention it."

She skipped out of the office to her waiting Volkswagen. Ramsay sat watching her, a worried frown on his face.

It had not been a good year for Dr. Wayne Pastory. After the unpleasantness at the clinic and his dismissal from La Reina County Hospital, he had been unable to get a practice started anywhere else. His reputation in the medical community, never the best, had fallen to a new low.

He was living in Stockton, eking out a living providing uppers and downers to minor league ballplayers. As he pondered his reduced circumstances, Pastory nourished an ever-building rage. His chance for a real breakthrough—a study on an advanced case of genuine lycanthropy—had literally been stolen from him. Those people had had no right to break into his clinic and make it possible for Malcolm to escape. Yet it was he, not they, who suffered the ostracism. The injustice of it ate away at his mind like a steady drip of acid. Someday . . . someday he would make them all pay.

When he saw the picture and story of the "Animal Boy" in the supermarket tabloid, Pastory could have cried out for joy. It was Malcolm. Malcolm as Pastory had seen him when he applied the electrical charges, only further along in the transformation. What must be happening to him now in the hands of some unschooled carnival showman?

It was an easy matter to learn where the carnival was playing. Wayne Pastory locked up the small apartment that was serving also as his office and headed for the town of Silverdale.

Chapter 21

An authentic carnival, even a rinky-dink outfit like the Samson Supershow, was a new experience for Holly Lang. She had grown up a city girl, and the closest she had come to the carnivals of small towns were theme parks like Disneyland and Magic Mountain. Those had been exciting at the time, but there was always a sense of antiseptic unreality. People dressed in oversized animal costumes. Here in the carnival the sights and smells were real. The people were real. And always just beneath the surface of cotton candy and jangly music there was a sense of danger. Things could happen in a carnival that would never be allowed at Disneyland.

These thoughts danced in and out of Holly's mind as she made her way along the sawdust midway. The carnival was an experience she would like to take the time to savor one day, but tonight her entire attention was given to finding Malcolm.

She had no trouble locating the tent. It was the largest on the grounds, and the crowd outside it was bigger than any of the others. Jungle sounds blared from a loudspeaker that Bateman Styles had recently added.

As Holly approached, the entrance flap was pulled back and a crowd of people spilled out. Apparently the show had just ended. From their expressions, it appeared the audience had enjoyed themselves.

Holly frowned up at the huge paintings flanking the entrance. She listened to the comments of a couple who were just coming out.

"I wonder how they do it," the woman said.

"Search me," the man answered. "I was watching him like a hawk the whole time and I didn't see anything funny."

"You don't think it could be real?"

"Are you kidding? People don't turn into animals except in the movies."

"Yes, but in the movies they can use camera tricks. This wasn't any picture."

"Well, it *looked* real. I'll say that."

"I know. I thought for a minute he was coming right through the bars."

"It's all part of the act."

"Well, I hope so."

The couple drifted off toward the food tent. Holly waited until the last of the crowd had come out, then she started toward the entrance.

She pulled aside the tent flap and was met by a fat man with a red nose. He wore a bright checkered vest and straw hat.

"Sorry, Miss, the show has just ended. There will be another in one hour. You may buy your ticket now, if you wish, and be guaranteed of getting in."

"Are you Mr. Styles?" Holly asked.

The man's expression turned guarded. "Do I know you from somewhere?"

"We've never met. I read the story about you in the *National Expo*."

"Ah, yes, that piece of drivel. Since that was published I

202

don't even allow a camera into the tent. I would ban writers, too, if there was a way to tell them from other layabouts. How may I be of service to you?"

"I, er, think I know your . . . Animal Boy."

"Grolo? I hardly think that's likely, Miss . . ."

"Dr. Lang."

"Doctor," Styles amended. "What makes you think you are acquainted with my protégé?"

"In the first place, his name is Malcolm."

"I'm afraid you've made a mistake, Doctor. I don't know any Malcolm."

"Holly!" The joyful cry came from the rear of the tent. "I thought I recognized your voice."

Holly and Bateman Styles turned. Malcolm jumped down from the stage and ran toward them, smiling broadly.

"You know this lady?" said Styles.

"It's all right, Bate," the boy said. "She's a friend of mine."

As he reached them Malcolm stopped, suddenly shy. Holly opened her arms and he responded with an enthusiastic hug.

"Malcolm, Malcolm, where have you *been*? I've been looking for you for more than a year."

"I've been a lot of places. Since May I've been traveling with Mr. Styles. How did you find me?"

"A story in the paper."

Malcolm frowned. "That one with the awful picture?"

"Yes."

"It was just a lot of made-up stuff."

"I was sure of that," Holly said, "but I thought it might be you."

Styles cleared his throat. "If you will be good enough to excuse me, I have a number of errands to run, and I'm sure you have things to talk about. Malcolm, why don't we skip the next show and close out with the ten o'clock."

"Can we afford it?"

"Don't worry about that, my boy; we're well ahead of the game. A reunion with your friend certainly takes precedence."

"Well, thanks, Bate," Malcolm said.

"Think nothing of it. I will see you at ten." He touched the brim of his straw hat. "Good evening, Doctor."

Holly nodded to him, and she and Malcolm walked off up the midway arm-in-arm.

"I can't tell you how happy I am to have found you at last," Holly said.

"So am I," said the boy.

"You've grown."

"I guess so."

Holly squeezed his arm. "If you can get your things together, we can leave right away and be back in Pinyon in the morning."

Malcolm's happy expression faded. "Are they looking for me back there because of, you know, what happened at that clinic?"

"Nobody is looking for you, except to help you, Malcolm. What happened up there at Bear Paw was not your fault. Everybody knows that."

"They do?"

"You have my word for that. You trust me, don't you, Malcolm?"

"Yes."

"Good, then shall we get started?"

The boy looked doubtful. "I don't like to leave Bate just like that."

"Why on earth not? The man has been exhibiting you like some kind of a freak."

"It's not that way, Holly. Mr. Styles has been good to me. I was feeling really bad when I met him, and he gave me something to do with my life. Besides . . ." He hesitated.

"What is it?" Holly prompted.

"I *am* some kind of a freak."

204

Holly came to a stop and turned to face him. She spoke sharply. "Don't you ever talk that way again, Malcolm. You are . . . different, through no fault of your own. Some people are born with terrible deformities. They can't help it either. But you are *not* a freak. Not something to be put in a cage and shown to a lot of curiosity seekers."

"It really isn't that bad," Malcolm said. "I don't even think about the people who come to see me. When I'm up there on the stage I think about . . . other things."

"You don't want to go on doing it, though, do you?"

"No, I . . . I guess not. I'm always afraid that someday I'll lose control for real."

"Then come back with me, Malcolm. Let me try to help you."

"Do you think I could ever be . . . cured, Holly?" His eyes searched her face.

Holly hesitated before she answered. "I don't know, Malcolm. I want to be honest with you, and not give you any false hopes. Your case is so different from anything doctors have dealt with that no one can say if there is a cure. One thing I will promise you: I will do everything I can, and so will a lot of other concerned people, to help you in any possible way. Okay?"

"Okay," he said. They smiled at each other.

"One thing, though," the boy added. "We're still booked here for tonight and tomorrow. I'd like to stay and do those shows for Mr. Styles."

"He is important to you, isn't he?" she said.

"I never knew my real father. I would have liked him to be like Bate."

"All right," Holly said. "I'll take a motel room in town. Maybe I'll come down and watch your act."

"No," he said quickly. "Don't do that."

"Not if you don't want me to," she said.

"I'd rather you wouldn't. This is a different part of my

life. It doesn't have anything to do with you, and I want to keep it that way.''

"Then I'll just stay in my motel room until you're ready to go.''

"Thanks, Holly,'' he said, relieved.

"Well,'' she said brightly, "we have a couple of hours to kill. What would you like to do?''

"Let me show you around the carnival. We can go on the rides free, since I work here.''

"That sounds like fun,'' she said. "Shall we try the Octopus?''

When Malcolm came back to the tent for the ten o'clock show he found Bateman Styles sitting on the front of the stage with his legs dangling. Beside him was a bottle of Old Overholt and a plastic cup from the food tent. The showman seemed to be studying the shine on his shoes.

"Hi, Bate,'' Malcolm said cheerily.

"Hello.'' He did not look up.

"Something wrong?''

"Wrong? What could possibly be wrong?''

"You're mad, aren't you?''

Styles poured rye whiskey into the cup and swallowed it. "No, Malcolm, I'm not mad. I always knew you had a life of some kind before I found you, and I'm not surprised that it would catch up with you someday and pull you back. You *are* leaving, aren't you?''

"Yes.''

Styles hopped down from the stage and came over to stand beside him. He clapped a hand on the boy's shoulder. During the summer Malcolm had grown an inch taller than the showman.

"I want to wish you the best of luck, my boy. If you have something to go back to out there, I don't blame you. The

206

carnival is no place for anybody who has roots. We did have a good season together, didn't we?''

"A good season," Malcolm agreed. "Bate, I want to finish out the date here. I'll do tonight's show and tomorrow's."

"You don't have to do that. I imagine you're anxious to get going with your friend, the doctor."

"I want to do it," Malcolm said. "You can pitch it as a farewell appearance and jack up the admission price."

A smile spread slowly over Styles's ruddy face. He began to laugh, then subsided in a coughing fit. When he recovered his breath he said, "Malcolm, my lad, you are beginning to sound like a real carny. Go and get yourself ready while I step out front and turn the tip." He laughed again. "Farewell appearance. I'm proud of you."

Malcolm stepped behind the curtain and changed into one of the sets of cheap shirts and pants Bateman had bought for the act. There was no sense wearing anything good, since when his body changed it pushed right out through the clothes.

Lately the change had seemed to go further each time before he could reverse it. It had begun to worry Malcolm, and he was glad to be going with Holly. If there really was help for him, he knew Holly would find it.

As he buttoned up the shirt and tucked it down into the pants, he heard Styles warming up to his spiel out in front.

"Yes, ladies and gentlemen, tonight and tomorrow are absolutely the last and final opportunity you will have to see the Ninth Wonder of the World! The sensational what-is-it that people all over the country are talking about! The inimitable, the incomprehensible, the indescribable . . . Grolo the Animal Boy!"

Malcolm smiled. Over the weeks he had built a real affection for the showman, and he sensed that Styles liked him, too. In other circumstances he would be glad to stay with the carnival as long as Bate wanted him, but his future was too uncertain. What they were doing might be just a fun-scary show to the marks, but Malcolm knew they were playing a deadly, dangerous game.

"Yes, my friends," Styles continued out in front, "tonight and tomorrow are absolutely and irrevocably the farewell appearances of the Animal Boy! Never again on this continent or any other will you have the opportunity to see this amazing metamorphosis! Therefore, my friends, since you will be witnessing something no one will ever see again, the admission for tonight and tomorrow's shows will of necessity be slightly higher, a still very reasonable five dollars! And if any of you think you can get a better buy today for five dollars, please tell me and I'll go with you!"

Malcolm heard the crowd laugh with Styles and he knew the showman had them in his pocket. He was glad that Bateman would make a few extra dollars these last two days. It would be partial repayment for the happy time this summer that Styles had given him.

He finished dressing and entered the old chimpanzee cage. Styles had talked about getting a more elaborate cage but had not got around to it. Malcolm had developed a feeling almost of affection for the cage. The door in the back was never locked, of course, and when the power of the beast flowed through his body he could have easily ripped it apart. The marks did not know this, of course.

He sat on the stool and listened to the babble of voices beyond the curtain as the crowd streamed in.

When the tent was full, Bateman slipped in through the rear and winked at Malcolm. "Everything all right, lad?"

"Everything's fine, Bate."

"Good. Let's give 'em their five dollars' worth."

Styles stepped through the curtain for his introduction speech. He was in masterful form, and he had the marks howling for action even before the curtain was pulled aside. Malcolm smiled happily.

"And now the moment for which we have all waited . . ." Styles intoned.

"And paid our five dollars for," somebody in the crowd added.

"I give you, for the very last time, in his farewell appearance . . . Grolo the Animal Boy!"

He pulled back the curtain and Malcolm assumed the puzzled and rather embarrassed look they had perfected over the summer. He sat on the stool, hands folded in his lap, and tried not to smile as he thought about rejoining Holly Lang.

"Well, what's the matter, Grolo, off your feed tonight?" Bateman said in his tone of mock anger. "Surely this is not what the good people paid to see."

The crowd joined in enthusiastically.

"Yeah, what a phony!"

"Do something, stupid!"

"What is it, a wax dummy?"

"Give us our money back!"

"Look, he's even smiling!"

Malcolm left the stool and walked in a crouch to the front of the cage. There he clutched the bars as he always did and stared out at the people hurling insults at him. He tried, as he had taught himself, to summon up the hateful, painful things that had been done to him in the past. But tonight, try as he might, all he could think about was going back with Holly and maybe . . . just maybe finding a cure that would make him normal, like other boys.

After several minutes of no action the tone of the crowd changed. Where the insults and jeers had been good-natured, a part of the act, they began to turn ugly as Malcolm stood gazing out over their heads with a half smile on his face.

"Come on, we haven't got all night!"

"What's the matter with him? I thought he was supposed to change into an animal."

"Hell, he's not doing anything!"

"We've been robbed!"

"Come on," a burly tattooed man yelled, "let's pull him out of there and *make* him do something!"

Bateman Styles, who had been watching Malcolm anxiously, turned quickly to the crowd when he heard the last comment.

"Ladies and gentlemen, I'm very sorry, but the Animal Boy is not feeling well tonight. He will be unable to perform."

"Bull! It's part of the act."

"I assure you, young man, this is an unscheduled interruption. If you will kindly file out, I will personally hand each and every one of you a pass to tomorrow's show."

"Pass, hell, what if there ain't no show tomorrow?"

The crowd shifted, looking as though it might advance on the stage.

Styles said quickly, "You're absolutely right. Your money will be refunded out in front; each and every dollar will be returned with my sincerest regrets."

"You can stuff your regrets," somebody said. "Just give us our money."

The crowd laughed, and the ugly moment had passed. They trooped out of the tent and Styles followed with the cash box. As he passed through the entrance flap he turned for a long, sad look at Malcolm, then continued outside to return the money.

When the showman returned Malcolm had left the cage and was sitting slumped in a wooden chair behind the curtain.

"I let you down, Bate," he said. "I'm sorry."

"Nonsense, my boy, nonsense," boomed Styles. "You could no more help yourself than I could jump over the Ferris wheel."

"I tried. Really I did."

Bateman pulled the stool out of the cage and sat next to

him. "I know that, Malcolm, and I think I know why it didn't work. You're happy, aren't you?"

"Well, yeah, I guess so."

"Of course you are. I could see it in your eyes when you came out and saw that Dr. Lang tonight. You like her a lot, don't you?"

Malcolm nodded. "Holly was a friend when I needed one. Like you, Bate."

"Thank you, my boy. I appreciate being included in that company. However, as they say, sometimes friends must part, and I guess this is the time for you and me, right?"

Malcolm swallowed hard. "I guess it is. Holly's a doctor, and she's going to try to cure me. Make me normal."

"Unquestionably a worthwhile endeavor."

"If it works out, and I'm just like everybody else, I'd be no good to you, would I?"

"Utter nonsense, my boy. You are a natural for the carnival life. Anytime you want to come back, just look up Bateman Styles and we'll work something out."

"Sure, Bate. Thanks."

Styles lit a Camel and coughed into a handkerchief. "I'd better go clean up out front. Will you be staying in the trailer tonight?"

"If it's all right. Then I'll leave tomorrow with Holly."

"Of course it's all right. I may be in a bit late myself. I'll try not to wake you."

Styles pushed through the curtain and eased himself down off the stage. He started for the front of the tent, slowing down when he saw a man standing in the entrance flap.

"Sorry, bud, the show's over. No more shows tonight."

"I know," the man said. "I saw the last one."

"What's the problem? Didn't you get your money back?"

"I don't want my money back. I have a proposition for you."

Styles looked more closely at the man. He was not big,

211

but he was wiry and seemed charged with nervous energy. His hair was slicked back, his eyes bright and a little too close together.

"What kind of a proposition?"

"First let me introduce myself. I am Dr. Wayne Pastory."

Chapter 22

It seemed to be his day for meeting doctors, Bateman Styles decided. The first had taken away his livelihood; now this one was offering him a proposition. Holly Lang appeared to be authentic, but Bateman was inclined to be skeptical about Wayne Pastory. He had known too many self-proclaimed ''doctors'' who used the title as part of a scam. And this wiry man had the overintense look of somebody not playing with a full deck.

''You say you have a proposition, Dr. Pastory,'' Styles said carefully.

''Yes, I think it might be of some interest to you. Is there somewhere we can talk?''

''Right here is as good a place as any.''

Pastory looked back doubtfully at the entrance. ''We won't be disturbed?''

''There won't be anybody coming in,'' Styles told him. ''The rest of the shows have been canceled.''

''Ah, yes, so I understand. That rather undercuts your income, I would guess.''

''You could say that.''

''Perhaps I can make that a little easier for you.'' He

looked quickly at Styles. "I don't know what your relationship has been with this, er, Animal Boy, but I assume he is of no further use to you."

"The relationship has been a professional one," Styles said slowly. "And no, it doesn't look like we'll be performing again."

"All right, here's my proposition—I'll take him off your hands."

"Off my hands," Styles repeated.

"Exactly. We both understand he has no future with you. Oh, I expect to compensate you, of course, but inasmuch as he is worth nothing to you now, I wouldn't think we'll have to do a lot of haggling over the price."

"No, I wouldn't think so," Styles agreed. He tilted his head to one side and stared down into Pastory's bright little eyes. "May I ask, Doctor, precisely what your interest is in the Animal Boy?"

"I don't see as that is of any importance to our transaction."

"Call it curiosity."

Pastory sighed and spoke rapidly, like a man who knows he is talking over his listener's head. "I am a researcher in psychobiology. The, er, phenomenon of the boy's physical change is of great interest in my field. I want to complete a series of experiments that will shed greater light on his condition."

"And maybe make you a few dollars?"

"I am a researcher, Mr. Styles. Monetary gain is not important to me."

"Ah, yes, of course. Forgive me."

Pastory nodded brusquely. His eyes flicked hungrily up to the curtained stage.

"But as you saw tonight," Styles continued, "this phenomenon, as you call it, is not so reliable."

"There are laboratory methods of triggering the process," Pastory said. "Shall we get down to business?"

"I'd like to hear more about these laboratory methods," said Styles.

"I don't think they would be of much interest to you. Highly technical, you understand."

"That so? What makes you think these methods of yours will work?"

"Because they have before." Pastory was losing patience. "I assure you it is nothing you could duplicate here. The boy was in my care for a short period about a year ago and I was making significant progress until an interruption by outsiders brought my experiment to an end."

"What a shame," Styles commented.

"Yes, yes, but that's not important now. I can pick up where I left off. How does a hundred dollars sound for transferring the boy to me?"

"A hundred dollars. My, my." Styles rubbed his nose thoughtfully.

"I'll make it two hundred just because I am eager to resume my work with the boy."

"You must be."

"That's cash, of course."

Pastory reached for his wallet. He opened it and slipped out four fifty-dollar bills. He was careful not to let Styles see how much more he was carrying.

Bateman took the money. "Ah, yes, two hundred United States dollars." He held the bills up one at a time to the light bulb that was suspended from the top of the tent. He grasped them by the edges and snapped them out. "Crisp new currency; yes, indeed."

"The money is quite genuine," Pastory said. "Can I see the boy now?"

Even from behind the curtain Malcolm recognized the voice of Wayne Pastory immediately. He felt that his past was catching up with him from all directions.

He parted the curtain just a crack and peered out into the

tent. The sight of the doctor made him shiver with remembered terrors.

As the conversation continued between Pastory and Bateman Styles, Malcolm's high spirits of a short time ago plummeted. The showman, his friend, was actually dickering to sell him out. Malcolm felt a sob rise in his chest. He forced it back. His vision blurred as tears squeezed into his eyes.

He let the curtain close and sank slowly to his knees. His face was feverish, yet his body shook with a chill. He felt the muscular spasms that preceded the change. He ground his teeth and fought for control.

Be reasonable, he told himself. He couldn't blame Bateman for taking a few dollars from Pastory. Malcolm knew he would never go back to that hateful clinic anyway. Holly was waiting for him. Why did it matter to him what kind of a deal Bateman made with Pastory? His body jerked convulsively.

"Do we have a deal?" Pastory said.

Styles continued to hold the bills in both hands. "Let me be sure I understand," said Styles. "You are offering me two hundred dollars for the boy. I take the money and you take Malcolm."

"Yes, yes, can we get on with it?" The doctor looked at his watch. "My time is limited."

"Yes, well, so is mine. So let me tell you without further palaver what you can do with your two hundred dollars. You can take these bills, roll them up, and stuff them one at a time up your ass."

Pastory blinked. He stared at the showman. "I don't think I understand what you're saying."

"I don't know how I can make it any plainer."

"Is it a matter of more money?"

"It is a matter of you getting the hell out of my sight. So you're a doctor. Good for you. I'm a carny. Been one all my life. I'll tell you something about carnival people, Doctor: we have a code of our own, and we try to live by it. Sure, we

216

may work a scam here and there, put pictures out front of attractions we don't have inside, weight the milk bottles so they won't tip over. But there are some things we do not do. We don't sell human beings. Not for two hundred lousy dollars. Not for any price. Now get the hell out of my tent.''

Styles let the four fifty-dollar bills flutter to the dirt floor. Pastory stared at him for a moment, then bent to pick them up. When he straightened again his face was mottled with anger.

''You don't know what you're doing. Malcolm is not just another boy. He is a unique specimen of active lycanthropy. I want him.''

''Get out of here,'' Styles said. ''I can't stand to look at you.''

Pastory reached out and seized the lapels of Styles's brightly checked coat. ''Damn you, old man, you can't do this to me. I want that boy. I will have him!''

Styles opened his mouth to shout, and Pastory's fingers moved up to clamp around his throat, shutting off his air. The smaller man squeezed. The tendons stood out like cables in his forearms.

Styles's eyes bulged. His face turned an unhealthy bluish color. He scrabbled ineffectually, trying to pry loose Pastory's fingers. He staggered backward, Pastory following, until the smaller man's grip was broken.

Styles pulled in a wheezing breath. He gave a strangled cough, clutched at his chest, and staggered into one of the tent supports, making the canvas shiver. His eyes rolled up into his head and he fell heavily to the dirt floor, his chest heaving. Pastory came over and stared down at him. Styles body bucked once, twice, then lay still.

Pastory looked quickly toward the entrance to the tent. Assured that no one had heard the short scuffle, he ran to the stage at the far end, mounted it, and pulled aside the curtain.

The hate-filled face that glared up at him from the crouching figure only faintly resembled the boy Malcolm.

217

The muzzle was pushed well forward, the eyes slanted and deep green, the ears pointed and cocked. The black upper lip curled back to show the outsized killing teeth. It growled.

Pastory spread his hands as one does with a strange dog to show he carried no weapon. He advanced slowly.

"It's all right, Malcolm. No one is going to hurt you. You remember me, don't you? I'm your friend. You know that. I'm going to take you back with me to where no one will hurt you again."

Another growl. The creature drew back slightly. The shoulders and deep chest were covered with coarse hair. The clothing he had been wearing hung in tatters.

Pastory could barely contain his excitement. This was the furthest along in the change he had yet seen the boy. He ached to get Malcolm back to the laboratory. This time there would be no bungling Kruger to mess things up.

"Come along now," he said, putting just the right note of authority into his voice. "There is nothing more for you here. Your place is with me."

The answering growl this time was deeper. The teeth seemed to have grown.

For the first time, Pastory felt a small doubt about his ability to control the boy. He took a step back. "I'm here to help you, Malcolm. Now stop this foolishness and come along."

The attack was so swift that Pastory had no time to cry out. From the crouching position on the floor Malcolm sprang at him. The flashing teeth seized him by the throat; the powerful jaws clamped together. Pastory felt the hot splash of blood down the front of himself. He screamed, but all that came from his gaping mouth was a soft bubbling sound. He had a last impression of the hot, snorting breath of the beast on his face, then the life drained out of him.

The beast, with its jaws still clamped on the man's throat, worried him the way a dog does a rabbit. Blood spattered the wooden floor of the stage, the velvet curtain, the canvas of the tent, the cage. Finally he dropped Pastory's pale and broken body with a thump.

He came through the curtain and in two long bounds was at the side of the still figure of Bateman Styles. The muzzle poked down close to the showman's livid face and snuffled questioningly. There was no answer from Styles. No movement, no breath, no heartbeat.

The beast whirled from the body of the showman and ran out through the opening in the rear of the tent. Outside he lifted his bloody muzzle to the night sky and he howled.

It was a sound Malcolm had heard many times from others in the night. He howled again—a long, ululating cry of loneliness and rage and despair. From up in the distant hills, faint but unmistakable, came an answer.

Along the carnival midway people stopped and turned to stare toward the unearthly howling. Small children began to cry. Women pressed closer to their men. The men glanced at one another, each waiting for someone else to make the first move. Then several of the carnival people started toward Bateman Styles's tent.

Malcolm heard them coming. He swung his great beast's head to and fro, searching for a way out. Seeing a path that led off toward the town between the parked trailers and trucks, he ran. Ran with ground-devouring strides. If any of the carnival men saw the powerful figure loping across the field, they did not try to give chase.

Chapter 23

Gradually Malcolm's pace slackened. His breathing grew labored. He became aware of an ache in his muscles and the slap of his bare feet on the pavement. He slowed to a walk, watching behind to be sure there were no pursuers.

The shadows seemed to deepen. He listened to the tiny chirps and rustlings of the night creatures. The air was cold on his skin where the clothing was torn, and he realized that the transformation had reversed itself. Once again his appearance was that of a normal human.

He gathered the torn remains of his clothing about him and looked around to get his bearings. He saw he was on the state highway that formed the main street of Silverdale. A mile ahead he could see the scattered lights of the town. A couple of hundred yards before him was the neon sign for the motel where Holly Lang was staying. He hurried on.

There were only four cars pulled into the spaces to accommodate the twelve rooms of the motel. Curtains were pulled across the windows in the occupied rooms. In the office Malcolm could see a young Oriental woman working on a crossword puzzle.

He crept along the wall to the motel room with Holly's Volkswagen parked before it. Softly he knocked.

When Holly opened the door her shocked expression reflected the boy's disheveled appearance.

"Malcolm, what happened to you? Are you all right?"

"Can I come in?"

"Of course." She stood aside while Malcolm entered the room. She led him to a chair, then snapped off the old movie that was playing on television.

Malcolm sat stiffly in the chair for a moment, breathing hard. Then he started to cry. At first he made an effort to hold back the tears, then gave in to them. All the pent-up sorrows. frustrations, and pains of his young life burst forth in uncontrolled sobs. Holly took a chair across the room and sat quietly, letting him cry it out.

After a while he subsided. He used the tattered sleeve of his shirt to wipe his eyes, and looked shyly over at Holly.

"I've never done that before," he said.

"Then it was about time you did. Everybody has to let the hurt come out once in a while."

"It does feel better."

"Of course it does. People shouldn't hold those things inside."

The boy's faint smile faded. "Oh, Holly, it's all over now. I've ruined everything."

"Why don't you tell me about it."

The boy spoke haltingly, glancing at Holly's face from time to time for a reaction. Mostly he kept his eyes downcast.

"Dr. Pastory came to the tent tonight."

"How did he . . ." Holly interrupted, then caught herself. "No, never mind. Go on."

"He . . . he wanted to take me back. He offered to buy me from Mr. Styles. For a minute I thought Bate was going to do it, but he never would have. He told Dr. Pastory to get out. Pastory grabbed him and there was a scuffle. Mr. Styles choked and fell down. I was behind the curtain and heard the whole thing.''

The boy paused. His gaze drifted off to a corner of the ceiling, as though seeing there again the events of the night. ''I didn't want it to happen to me then, Holly. I didn't want to change. I tried to fight, but I couldn't help it. When Dr. Pastory came to get me, I couldn't help myself.''

''There's blood on your shirt,'' Holly said. ''Did he hurt you?''

Malcolm shook his head. ''It isn't my blood. It's his. Pastory's.''

''You . . . attacked him?''

''I killed him, Holly.''

''Oh, Malcolm, are you sure?''

''I killed him, all right. And do you want to know what else?''

''What?'' Holly said quietly.

''I liked it. I hated him so much, both for what he did to me and for hurting Mr. Styles, that all I wanted was for him to die. And when he did I was happy.''

Holly stretched out a hand and touched him on the shoulders. ''Oh, my poor, poor Malcolm.''

''Then I went to Mr. Styles and I saw he was dead. If I could have killed Pastory again right then, I would have. I ran out. People started coming toward the tent. I just kept running until I got here.''

''I'm glad you came to me,'' Holly said.

''I shouldn't have. They'll be looking for me soon. I'll just get you in trouble, too.''

''You mustn't think that way, Malcolm. What happened was not your fault. Wayne Pastory was an evil man. Whatever happened to him I'm sure he provoked.''

''But I killed him, Holly. I turned into an animal and I killed him. If they catch me, they'll lock me up.''

''Not if I can do something about it,'' she said. ''Come

with me, Malcolm. Now, tonight. We'll go where there is help for you.''

''Why should anyone want to help me?'' he said.

''You are not to blame for what happened. You have to remember that. What you have is like a sickness. And sickness can be cured.''

''But this is . . . I'm . . . different,'' the boy said.

''Yes, Malcolm. And it is because you're different that you can't be held responsible.''

''It could happen again,'' he said.

''We must see that it doesn't. You were put under unbearable stress tonight. The man you most hated attacked and killed a good friend. A lot of so-called normal people would have lost control, too.''

Malcolm was silent for a long minute. Then he said, ''What can we do, Holly?''

''The first thing is to get out of here. I can pack in ten minutes, then we'll start back to Pinyon. There are people there we can trust.''

Malcolm looked at his torn, blood-spattered clothes. ''I can't go like this.''

''I doesn't matter, Malcolm,'' Holly said. ''No one but me will see you.''

''I don't want to,'' he said, trying to cover himself.

Holly sighed. He was, after all, an adolescent boy with the normal adolescent's dread of being embarrassed. She said, ''I might have something you can wrap yourself in, at least until we get to Pinyon.''

''I have some things in the trailer,'' Malcolm said. ''Mr. Styles's trailer. I can go and get them.''

''Do you think that would be safe?''

''I'll be careful. If there are people around, I won't go near it.''

''I think you're taking a big risk just to pick up some clothes.''

''They're kind of special,'' the boy said. ''Mr. Styles

223

bought them for me. I don't have anything else to remember him by.''

''All right, Malcolm, if you feel you have to. Promise me you'll be very, very careful.''

''I promise,'' he said.

They walked together to the door. Holly looked out to be sure no one was around. Then she gave the boy a hug, and he slipped away into the night.

He stayed in the shadows of the brush at the side of the road as he made his way back toward the carnival grounds. Circling the perimeter, he saw that all normal activity had come to a stop. The lights still blazed, but the sounds of the carnival—the jangly music, the rumble of the rides, the talkers, the laughter of the people along the midway—were missing. A car from the Inyo County Sheriff's Department was parked near the entrance gate.

Malcolm slipped onto the grounds between the food tent and the shooting gallery. He could see a crowd milling around in front of the Animal Boy tent. A man in a sheriff's uniform stood guard out in front to keep back the curious. So far there seemed to be no one back where the trailers were parked.

As he made his way toward Bateman Styles's battered old trailer, Malcolm stopped suddenly. The breath caught in his throat. Ahead of him a man-size shadow detached itself from the others and moved into his path.

''Hello, Malcolm.''

It took a moment for him to make out the sandy-haired, mild-looking man who stood regarding him calmly. Then recognition came with a jolt.

''Derak! How did you find me?''

''We've known where you were for months,'' he said. ''One or more of us was always nearby, waiting for you to call and tell us you were ready. Tonight you did.''

''I called you?''

''We heard it from the hills. The howling.''

"I didn't mean to do that," Malcolm said. "I couldn't help myself."

"I understand," Derak said. "The fact remains that you called to us. By now you have learned that you cannot live among the others as one of them. It is time for you to join us."

"H-how many of you are there?"

"More than you might think. There is a band of us now in the hills above this town. Some of them you will recognize from Drago. We're all waiting for you, Malcolm."

The boy peered into the darkness. He thought he saw movement among the shadows. "Are there others here now with you?"

"Yes. You will meet them all when you join us. Come, let's waste no more time."

Malcolm hung back. "Derak, I-I'm not sure this is what I want to do."

The eyes of the sandy-haired man lost their mild look. They glittered, reflecting the lights of the carnival. "My son, you have no choice."

"But I do. I have a friend who says there may be a cure for me."

"*Cure!*" Derak snapped the word off like the crack of a whip. "Cures are for sick humans. You are not sick. And Malcolm, you are not human. You belong with us. It is your only hope for survival."

Malcolm pulled in a deep breath. Although Derak seemed to draw him like a powerful magnet, he was determined to assert his own will.

"Dr. Lang has promised to help me."

Derak snorted in contempt. "Dr. Lang? That woman in the motel room? What do you think she can do for you?"

"I don't know," Malcolm admitted. "But she promised to try, and I believe her."

"You're a fool. She will only exploit you like that other doctor."

225

"No," Malcolm said stubbornly. "Holly is different. I trust her."

"You have much to learn," Derak said. "Not only about humans but about yourself."

"I'm going with her," Malcolm said. "You can't stop me."

"Can't I?" Derak said darkly. "You don't know how easily I could take you right now."

"Then you'll have to do it that way." The boy braced his feet wide apart and faced the man.

Derak made a sound deep in his chest. He took a step toward Malcolm. For a moment the light gleamed off his teeth, suddenly grown longer. Then he stepped back into the shadows.

"No, Malcolm, I will not take you by force. I want you to join us of your own choosing. I ask you once more—come with me."

Malcolm shook his head. "No. If there is a chance I might be helped, that I might live as a normal human being, I have to take it. I'm going with Dr. Lang."

Derak's eyes glowed dangerously. "Very well. It is a foolish choice, one you are going to regret. However, the choice is yours to make. When you are ready to come to us, you know we will be near."

As Malcolm watched, Derak seemed to vanish into the darkness. A second shadow shape moved, too, and the boy was left alone.

He continued to Styles's trailer, relieved to see there was still no one around. He slipped inside, leaving the door ajar. For a moment he was overwhelmed by the familiar surroundings that had been his home during the happy summer months. He moved about, running his fingers lightly over the cupboard where they kept their supply of food for the butane stove, the board where the old man had been teaching him chess, the perpetually rumpled bed where Bateman slept, his own bedroll neatly tucked away under the fold-

226

down table. Even the stale smell of Bate's Camels brought back happy memories.

Malcolm shook himself out of the mood and quickly selected a few articles of clothing. He slipped them on, taking the tattered old ones with him to dispose of along the way.

He made his way back to the highway, buoyed by the thought that in an hour he would be back with Holly. Then they could be on their way to a new life for him.

At that moment, however, someone else knocked at the door of Holly's room. Expecting Malcolm, she opened it to a surprise.

Chapter 24

Malcolm quickened his steps as he approached the motel. The same cars that had been there before still stood in the parking spaces. The Oriental woman dozed in the office. Holly Lang's Volkswagen waited outside her room.

He stopped. There was a prickling of his skin as when someone draws a fingernail down a blackboard. Everything looked the same, yet something was different. He could sense it. Something unknown was waiting for him behind the drawn curtains of the motel room.

He approached slowly, looking in all directions, listening, sniffing the air. Nothing moved in the night. There was no sound. He could detect no foreign scent. And yet, he had this feeling . . .

He knocked lightly at the door, his muscles tense, nerves jumping.

The door opened.

The woman who stood in the doorway was not Holly Lang. She was two or three inches shorter than Holly. Her compact body was beautifully rounded and displayed to good advantage in a tight skirt and top of black leather. The woman's hair was black as midnight, her mouth wide and inviting. She smiled. Her eyes were wide-set and playful. They were green. Deep, deep green.

"Hello, Malcolm," she said.

The impact of the woman in the doorway kept him from speaking for a moment. He felt very young and clumsy.

"Are you going to stand out there staring all night?"

"Who are you?" he managed finally.

"I am Lupe. I've been waiting for you. Come in." She stepped aside and watched him with amusement.

Malcolm entered the room hesitantly. No one else was there. He saw Holly's suitcase lying open on the floor, her things packed neatly inside.

"Where is Holly?"

"We have her now."

"We?"

"Oh, come, Malcolm, you know me. We can always recognize each other."

"What do you mean you have Holly?" A blade of fear stabbed into him.

"Oh, not *that* way," Lupe said. "She's still all right, as far as I know."

"You're one of Derak's people?"

"Yes, of course. Derak has your friend."

"Where has he taken her?"

"To the hills. I can show you."

"Well, come *on*!" He started toward the door.

"What's your hurry?" The dark woman's voice was husky and insinuating. "He won't do anything to her. Not until you get there, anyway."

"What do you mean?"

"I think you'd better hear the rest from Derak. We'll go after them in a little while."

"Why not now?"

"There are other things we can do now." She reached up and undid the top button of the leather blouse. "How old are you, Malcolm?"

229

"Almost sixteen."

Another button.

"Have you been with a woman?"

"Yes."

The third button.

"Many?"

"No."

"I'll bet you have never been with a woman like me."

She undid the last button and dropped her arms. A shrug and the leather top was on the floor. She wore nothing underneath. Her breasts were large and firm and proud. Malcolm could not pull his eyes away.

Lupe reached for the fastening at the side of her skirt. "Have you?"

"What?" Malcolm's mouth was dry.

"Have you been with a woman like me?"

"No."

"I didn't think so."

A soft snap, a zip, and the leather skirt joined the top on the floor. Lupe stood straight before him. She touched the dark triangle of pubic hair, slid her hand up over the rounded belly, and cupped one heavy breast. Her finger played with the nipple until it stood erect.

"Do you like me?" she said.

"I-I have to find Holly."

"I told you I'll help you. But first, wouldn't you like to get to know me better?"

She came toward him, stopping inches away. He could feel the heat of her naked body. There was an ache between his legs.

"I can make you feel really good," Lupe said. "Would you like that?"

She reached down and touched him. His erection grew under her fingers.

"Well, what do we have here?" she teased. "And only

sixteen years old. You are going to be quite a man, Malcolm."

He began to perspire. He could feel his shirt going damp at the armpits. Conflicting emotions ripped him. He wanted to take the hand of the taunting woman away, and he never wanted her to move it.

She opened his pants and slipped her hand inside. The sensation was unbearable pleasure.

He tried to speak, but all that came out was a long "Aaahhh!"

"Take those things off," Lupe told him. "Come into bed with me."

She peeled back the spread, blanket, and top sheet, then lay down, spreading her midnight hair over a pillow. She cocked one knee and massaged the velvety inside of her thigh with gentle strokes of her fingertips.

"Hurry," she said in a husky whisper.

With his eyes never leaving the woman in the bed, Malcolm stripped off his shirt and pushed the pants and shorts down his legs. He pulled off shoes and socks and lay down on the bed beside her.

Instantly Lupe was on him. She kissed his mouth, her tongue probing deep. Her hungry lips nibbled at his chin, his throat, and down across his chest to his belly. The green eyes looked up at him teasingly.

"Feel good?"

"Y-yes."

"Want me to stop?"

"No."

"I told you so."

She took him into her mouth then. Her tongue and lips worked on him, her white little teeth giving him gentle love bites. Her cheeks hollowed as she sucked. Malcolm felt as though he were being pulled inside out.

Just when he thought he could not last a second longer, she drew her head back, her mouth making a little popping

231

sound as he slid out. She rubbed the length of her body up along his, the flesh lubricated by their mingled sweat. She raised her head and looked down on him. Her hair was a shiny black curtain framing her face. She smiled. Her teeth were very white and very sharp. And not so little anymore.

Slowly, tantalizingly, she lowered herself down on him and took his length inside her. He felt the heat radiate through his body.

"Good?" she said, her breath moist on his face.

He could not answer.

She began to ride slowly up and down on him, pausing at the top just before he would have slipped out, then sinking gradually to swallow him up again.

Malcolm closed his eyes, giving himself to the sensations of his body. Sitting on him, riding him, Lupe stepped up the rhythm and the vigor of their joinings until her buttocks smacked his upper thighs with a report like a pistol shot.

His climax came a second before hers. She dropped down on him, her arms wrapped about his neck, nails digging furrows in his back. They cried out together and rolled back and forth over the king-size bed until his seed was spent. Then they continued to cling to each other like drowning children as their breathing slowly returned to normal.

Lupe was the first to speak. "I told you you'd never had a woman like me."

"Mmmm" was all Malcolm could manage.

"It gets better."

"I don't believe it."

"Oh, yes. When you really know about yourself and about what we are, there are ways to make it much better."

Malcolm opened his eyes. He rolled to one side and pushed the woman away. "You said you'd take me where Derak went with Holly."

"Did I say that?" Lupe's eyes danced with mischief. "I don't know why you're so anxious to see Derak."

"We have to settle something."

232

"You're not thinking of challenging him?"

"Why not?"

"Because you are just a pup. Derak has been a leader of his people for a long time. You're lucky he has let you come this far on your own."

"Let me?"

"Of course he has. He could have taken you many times over the past year."

"Then why didn't he?"

"You don't know?"

"I'm asking."

"Because he is your father."

Malcolm sat up and stared at her. Derak, his father? The knowledge hit him like a fist. Malcolm knew him as a leader, a teacher, one to be respected. And perhaps feared. But a father? How was it possible? He felt closer to Holly, to Jones, to Bateman Styles, than to the quiet-spoken man with the deep green eyes.

"Don't start thinking that makes you too special," Lupe went on. "Derak was father to half the children in the village of Drago. Of course, many of them did not survive the fire. Maybe that is why he is so patient with you."

"And my mother?" he said.

"She died in the fire. You must not think of her. It is not important, as you will learn."

He swung his feet off the bed and began pulling on his clothes. "Take me to Derak now," he said.

Lupe reached over and slid a hand between his bare buttocks. "So soon? We've just gotten started."

He stood up, moving back out of her reach. "You're wrong. We're finished. Let's go."

"You mean you had your fun and now you're through?" she said petulantly. "What about me?"

He glared at her. "You promised."

She patted the damp sheet beside her. "Come back. Once more, then I will take you to Derak and your lady friend."

He cinched the belt buckle tight and crossed to the door. "If you won't help me, I'll find them myself."

"Go ahead, if you think you can," Lupe taunted him from the bed. "But it will be much nicer in here with me."

"The hell with you."

He went out and slammed the door. The night surrounded him. He looked at the lonely cars crouching like abandoned beasts in the painted spaces. The lights were out now in all the rooms, except the one where Lupe waited. Malcolm felt terribly alone.

He walked back past the motel units to where the land sloped up into the foothills. Up there somewhere was Derak. And he had Holly with him. But where? How to find them in all that expanse of dark, rolling country? The boy's doubts made the night even colder.

Then he heard it. The howling.

Unmistakably, it was a call to him. Malcolm closed his eyes. He sniffed the air. Small, invisible changes happened inside his body. And the night was not so cold anymore.

When he opened his eyes, their green color had deepened. He started confidently up into the hills.

Chapter 25

Gavin Ramsay sat staring at the little digital clock on his desk in the La Reina County Sheriff's office. He caught himself counting the seconds as they ticked off, and angrily turned the face of the clock away from him.

All right, so Holly Lang had not called last night. That didn't mean anything. There were a hundred reasons she might not have telephoned him. Yeah, he told himself grimly, and about fiffy of them were bad news.

The new, slimmed-down version of Deputy Roy Nevins came into the office. His leather gleamed; his uniform was freshly pressed. He was shaved, trimmed, and looked maybe ten years younger than he had a year ago. Gavin marveled at the varying effect exposure to violence had on different people.

"Any action, Roy?" he asked.

"Not to speak of. Somebody used the deer-crossing sign for target practice again. I collared a speeder from L.A. trying out his new Porsche. Had to break up a couple of guys who had pulled off the road to do some smooching."

"Couple of guys?"

"I should have mentioned that they were from San Francisco."

"Oh. Well."

Nevins sat down to type out his report in two-finger machine-gun style. Ramsay sighed and turned the clock back around to face him. The hell with this. He was worried, and there was no use pretending he wasn't. He picked up the phone and direct-dialed the number of the Silverdale Motel.

The female voice that answered had a pleasant, foreign-sounding lilt.

"Is there a Dr. Hollanda Lang registered there?" he asked.

"Yes, sir. She in room twelve. I ring for you."

He listened while the line buzzed five times in his ear.

"Sorry, sir, she not answer."

"This is Sheriff Gavin Ramsay of La Reina County. I'd like you to take a look in Dr. Lang's room to see if she's all right."

"Is something wrong with lady?" The woman's voice rose several tones.

"There's no reason to think so," he said soothingly, "but I'd appreciate it if you would take a look."

"Yes, yes, I look. You want I call you back?"

"I'll hold on," Ramsay said.

There was a clunk as the receiver was set down on the other end. Ramsay counted seconds on the clock for five minutes. Roy Nevins had stopped hammering the typewriter and was watching him.

"Hello, Sheriff?" The sudden return of the voice in his ear startled him for a moment.

"Yes."

"I look in room. Nobody there. Lady's clothes put away all neat. Car outside. Maybe she walk down the road for breakfast."

"Yeah, maybe," Ramsay said. "Thank you."

"Trouble?" Roy Nevins said when he had hung up.

"I don't know. Holly was going to call me from Silverdale. She didn't. Now she's not in her room. It's probably nothing."

"Sure." Nevins went back to his report, but he continued to glance over toward Ramsay.

Gavin made a try at studying his calendar for the coming week. Talk to the Darnay Boys' Club, lunch with local Kiwanis, oversee motorcycle hill climb east of Pinyon, entertain police science class from La Reina College. It was no use; he could not concentrate.

He picked up the phone again and called Inyo County. The sheriff there was a man named Fielding whom Ramsay had met once or twice. A stolid lawman with good instincts but little imagination.

Ramsay identified himself to the switchboard and was put through to the sheriff, who sounded harried.

"Good to hear from you, Ramsay. What can I do for you?"

"A woman from Darnay, a Dr. Hollanda Lang, checked into the Silverdale Motel yesterday. She's still registered there, but the woman in the office couldn't find her. I'm a little worried."

"Any reason to think something might have happened to her?"

"Nothing concrete, except the business she was doing there."

"What business?"

"It had to do with the carnival."

Fielding exhaled a blast of air into the mouthpiece. "I don't know anything about your doctor, but I've got plenty of troubles of my own with that carnival."

"Oh?" Ramsay leaned forward.

"Couple of men died there last night under suspicious circumstances."

"Two men?" Ramsay said. "What happened?"

237

He could hear other voices talking excitedly in the background at Inyo County.

"I've got to go now, Ramsay," said Sheriff Fielding. "Give me a call back this evening and maybe I'll have something for you."

The phone went dead in Ramsay's hand. He hung up the instrument, then dug into the bottom desk drawer for the silver bullets that had rested there since he had last used them at Pastory's Bear Paw clinic.

He said, "Think you can manage things here for a day or so, Roy?"

"No problem," said Nevins. "Is Holly in some kind of trouble?"

"I hope not," Ramsay said, "but I think I'll take a run over to Silverdale to check on her. If you need me, call Sheriff Fielding, Inyo County."

"Will do," Nevins said.

As he drove through the Inyo Pass and started the descent through the hills to Silverdale, Ramsay began to wonder what he would say to Holly if he found her safe and sound in the Silverdale Motel. How would he explain galloping over here like John Wayne on the chance she might be in trouble?

Hell with that. There *was* trouble here. Two men were dead on the grounds of the Samson Supershow, and Ramsay would be damned surprised if Holly and the boy Malcolm were not somehow involved.

He had to pass the carnival grounds on his way to the motel, so Ramsay pulled off there first. identified himself to the Inyo County deputy who was posted at the entrance. In the tent that displayed pictures of "Grolo the Animal Boy" he found Sheriff Fielding and an agitated little man named Moskowitz, who seemed to be the owner of the carnival.

Fielding gave him a rundown of the previous night's fatalities. "One of the dead men was Bateman Styles. He ran this Animal Boy thing. Cause of death seems to be a heart

238

attack, but there were suspicious bruises. The other one was definitely not a natural death. Had his throat ripped out."

"Got a suspect?"

"A pretty good one," Fielding said. "It seems this so-called Animal Boy hasn't been seen since the killings. Nobody knows where he went. Not that they're telling, anyway."

"You're on the wrong track there, Sheriff," piped Moskowitz.

The lawmen looked down, surprised. They had forgotten for a moment that the little man was there.

"What makes you think so, Mr. Moskowitz?" said Fielding.

"The kid did a kind of wildman act, but that's all it was—an act. When he wasn't working he was just a shy, sweet-natured kid. No way he could kill anybody. Besides, he thought Bateman Styles was Jesus Christ."

Ramsay had a sudden thought. "What was the name of the second victim?"

Fielding consulted a notebook. "The name in his wallet was Wayne Pastory. A doctor, apparently."

The muscles tensed in Ramsay's upper back. "I know that one," he said. Briefly, he filled the Inyo sheriff in on Pastory's background in Pinyon.

"Could you take a look at the body and give us a positive ID?" Fielding said.

"Sure. But there's something I have to do first."

"Check on your Dr. Lang?"

"I'll get back to you."

Holly Lang's little Volkswagen Rabbit looked so natural and peaceful parked outside unit twelve that for a moment Ramsay felt his fears might be foolish after all. However, the apprehension returned as he knocked and waited for a response.

A woman with glossy black hair and mischievous eyes opened the door. She wore a motel bath towel wrapped around a sensual olive-skinned body.

"Sorry to keep you waiting," she said. "As you can see, I was in the shower."

Ramsay pulled his head back and checked the room number again. "I'm looking for Dr. Hollanda Lang. Maybe I have the wrong room."

"You have the right room," the dark woman said. "She's not here."

Ramsay fumbled out his identification. "My name's Ramsay," he said. "Sheriff, La Reina County."

"I am Lupe," said the woman. "I was told you might be along."

"Told? Told by whom?"

The woman shivered. "Do you mind if we go inside? I'm getting a chill standing here."

Ramsay stepped into the room. Lupe closed the door behind them. He looked over the impersonal motel furnishings, searching for some sign of Holly Lang. Aside from a blue overnight case beside the bureau that might have been hers, he could find nothing.

"Where is Dr. Lang?" he said.

"Why is everyone so interested in finding that woman?" Lupe said. "Won't I do?"

"I don't want to play games. If you know where she is, please tell me."

Lupe pointed up into the foothills that rose immediately behind the motel. "She's up there."

"Up there where?"

"She's with a friend of mine."

Ramsay took a step toward her. "Let's stop wasting time. I want to know where Holly is, and I want to know now."

Lupe clutched the towel to her breast in mock fright. "And what will you do to me, Sheriff, if I don't want to tell you? Give me the third degree?"

240

With an effort Ramsay brought himself under control. "I think we'd better talk to the local authorities. They're investigating a couple of deaths at the carnival, and they might want to ask you some questions."

The woman's green eyes lost their playfulness. "I don't think you want to have me arrested. Not if you want to see your Holly again."

Ramsay ground his teeth. "Where *is* she?"

"I told you—with a friend of mine. His name is Derak."

"Should the name mean something to me?"

"He is from Drago."

Ramsay stiffened. "And you?"

"Yes."

"Jesus." Unconsciously his hand brushed the jacket pocket that was heavy with the silver bullets.

"I see you are beginning to understand. She will not have been harmed yet, but if you want her to stay that way, you had better be nice to me."

"What about the boy, Malcolm? Is he with them?"

"If he is not, he soon will be," Lupe said.

Ramsay moved toward the door.

"Where are you going?"

"To organize a search of these hills."

"A search?"

"Men, helicopters, whatever it takes."

"That would be a mistake. Your men and helicopters did not capture Derak the last time. They are no match for him. All they can do is make him angry. And then what do you suppose he might do to your Holly?"

Gavin stood indecisively halfway between the woman and the door.

"There is another way," Lupe said in a throaty voice.

"Well?"

In a sinuous movement she pulled away the towel and let it fall to the floor. Gavin stared at the smooth naked body.

241

"Come make love to me and I'll tell you about it," she said.

"Are you crazy?"

The green eyes flashed. "No. I'm hungry. Last night I had a boy. He just gave me a sharper appetite for a man." She opened her arms. "Come. Let me show you what a woman like me can do for a real man."

For a moment Gavin was actually close to accepting the challenge. The woman's body was wonderfully inviting, and the faint musky smell of her made him feel a little drunk.

He shook off the impulse. "I'll bet you're something," he said, "but strange as it may seem to you, I'm not in the mood. See you."

He turned and walked to the door. As he gripped the knob she called to him.

"Wait."

He turned back. She reached down and picked up the towel but made no effort to cover herself. "I'll take you to them."

He eyed her suspiciously. "Why would you do that?"

"Because I do not want her to be one of us. That's what happens, you know, when someone is bitten and doesn't die. They become . . . what we are."

"So I've heard," Gavin said.

"Lately I have been Derak's woman. I don't want to share him."

"All right," Gavin said. "Get dressed and let's get started."

The first half hour was rough going as the slope grew steeper and there was no usable trail through the heavy brush. Lupe, in spite of her soft shoes and leather outfit, moved easily up the hill while Ramsay struggled. He was breathing hard by the time they reached a trail that angled up the hillside at a more gentle grade.

Lupe was waiting for him as he topped the rise onto the

trail. She contrived to brush her breasts against him. "Want to rest? Or something?"

"No, I'm fine. Let's go."

She made a face at him, but they continued up the trail.

After another hour they were making good time. The trail forked, each leg angling up the hill in a different direction. Ramsay turned to Lupe for a decision. She suddenly cried out and fell to her knees. She rolled to a sitting position, clutching her right leg.

"What's the matter?" Gavin said.

"It's my ankle. I stepped on a rock and I heard something pop in there. It hurts."

Gavin knelt beside her and took the leg gently in his hand. He eased the soft leather shoe off her foot. Lupe grimaced.

"Do you think you can walk on it?" he said.

"I don't know. It hurts really bad."

He ran his fingers gently along the skin of her leg from knee to instep. There was no irregularity that might indicate a broken bone. In spite of the urgency of the situation, he was aware of the smooth feel of her flesh.

"Maybe it's higher up," she said. "Above the knee. Why don't you feel there?"

He turned and saw she was grinning at him.

"Go ahead," she said. "Feel my leg. It's already getting better."

"Damn you," he began, but before he could say more, Lupe grasped him behind the neck and pulled his head down into a steamy kiss.

He pulled away, a little bit surprised at her strength. "Will you for Christ's sake cut it out?" he said.

She leaned back on her elbows, looking at him. "What's the matter? You do like women, don't you?"

"I like women just fine," he said slowly. "And I like sex with women. But I like it with the woman I choose and at the time I choose. Now quit crapping around and let's go."

Lupe did not move. Her eyes flashed angrily. "I'm not good enough? You've got to have a lady doctor, is that it?"

He opened his mouth to answer, but the words died when he saw what was happening to Lupe. Her mouth opened in a snarl to show strong canine teeth. Hair sprouted from her face. Her body jerked in a convulsion as she tore away the leather clothes. Claws pushed out of the ends of her fingers as the hands stretched and blackened. She rose, standing on the powerful hind legs of a wolf.

Ramsay looked up at the creature that now stood a good head taller than he. All resemblance to the beautiful, seductive woman was gone. What remained was a deadly, ravenous creature covered with glossy black fur. He pulled the revolver from his holster.

"Get back!" he said. "Silver bullets."

Lupe, or what had been Lupe, gave a deep-throated bellow that echoed faintly of the woman's derisive laugh. She came at him.

Ramsay hesitated for a near-fatal moment. He could not erase the image of the vibrant, sexy woman who had been there a moment ago. The oversized hands caught him, the claws digging through his jacket into the flesh of his back. The creature's jaws creaked open. The teeth came down toward his throat. Her breath stank of carrion.

Ramsay pulled the trigger. The sound of the gunshot was muffled against the huge body of the werewolf. She gave a shriek of mingled pain and shock. The grip of the claws relaxed and she staggered backward.

Blood pumped in a steady stream from a hole in the belly of the wolf. The green eyes fogged over and the creature fell, raising a puff of dust from the trail. The jaws opened a last time in a long, wailing howl, then the head dropped back lifelessly.

Ramsay stood for a long minute looking down at the dead thing that had been a woman. The revolver was still in his hand. He was surprised to see it shaking.

He put the gun away and turned his gaze up the trail into the hills. Finding Holly would be a tough job now without Lupe to guide him. But he knew she was up there, and he was not going to turn back. As he concentrated on choosing one of the two trail forks before him he heard a voice high in the hills and off to the left. Howling.

He knew now which direction to take.

Chapter 26

Holly Lang leaned her back against the rocky face of a cliff. The ledge where she sat was some thirty feet wide. Beyond it the trail sloped sharply down the hill through heavy brush. The silence was broken only by the chirping of birds off in the forest. Holly shivered with the chill of the morning. She hugged her knees and waited.

They were all waiting. Derak with his arms folded, his eyes on the spot where the trail came out of the brush, the rest of them sitting, standing, crouching. There was little conversation. They were waiting. Waiting for Malcolm.

Holly looked around, studying the people gathered on this rocky ledge in the Inyo Hills. There were men and women ranging in age from young to very old. Some were thin, others fat. To all appearances it was a group of normal people spending a day in the mountains. Their faces betrayed nothing beyond a mild anxiety. Nothing at all was remarkable about them. Nothing, except that they were all werewolves.

When Derak had taken her from the motel last night, Holly fully expected to die. Instead she had been brought here, given coffee and a candy bar for breakfast, and told to

246

be still and she would not be hurt. She understood now that she was the bait that would lure Malcolm back to these people. Whatever happened, they still might kill her. She simply could not let herself think about the possibility.

She had considered running and had actually made an attempt shortly after Derak brought her there and left her alone. When no one seemed to be watching, she had plunged down the steep grade toward the trees. They let her flounder thirty yards or so into the forest, then two of the women had simply come and gotten her and brought her back. These people moved in the wilderness with a natural ease that she could never hope to match. After the aborted escape attempt she had sat quietly like the rest of them. Waiting.

At noon he came. Malcolm walked straight up the trail with no attempt at stealth. His eyes flicked over the assembled people and came to rest on Holly. She thought he looked a little tired. And somehow older.

The boy started toward her, but Derak stepped into his path.

"The woman has not been harmed," he said.

Malcolm faced him coolly. "Why did you bring her here?"

"So you would come. I tried to make you understand that this is where you belong, but you were stubborn. Taking the woman was the only way."

"And now you expect to keep me here?"

"I expect you to stay."

"What if I don't?"

Derak's mouth compressed into a tight line. He looked over to where Holly now stood against the face of the cliff. "You are fond of the woman, I think."

"Are you saying you would hurt her?"

"What happens to her depends on your decision."

Holly spoke up then. "Don't let him destroy you, Malcolm. You can be helped. I'm sure you can."

Derak looked over at her with a bored expression and turned back to Malcolm. "You see, she doesn't understand the realities of our life. She doesn't know that there is no turning from the course that is set for us from birth. And she also doesn't know what we can do to her."

A muscle twitched in Malcolm's cheek.

"But you know, don't you, boy?" Derak continued. "You know, but you have been unwilling to face the truth."

"I was told you are my father," Malcolm said.

For the first time Derak's poise slipped a little. "Yes, but that makes no difference here. Don't expect any special treatment."

The slim young man and the stocky older man faced each other. Malcolm said, "If I stay with you, will you set Holly free?"

"I'm glad you've decided to be sensible."

"I want your word first."

Derak's face clouded. The green eyes glowed from some inner fire. "I don't make bargains with pups."

Malcolm pulled at his shirt collar as though it had suddenly grown too tight. "I want you to let her go."

"You *want*? *You . . . want*? Do you think it matters to me what the devil you want? You like this woman, do you? Maybe you would like her even better if she were one of us. Have you thought about that?"

"No!" Malcolm cried. He took a step forward and flexed his shoulders. The muscles bulged and pulsed until the shirt stretched tight across his upper arms. He spoke to Derak through bared teeth. "It's your fault that I've never known who I am . . . what I am. You're my father. You should have told me things. You withheld the truth from me."

"I was waiting until you were ready. That's the way it is always done."

"I *was* ready! You should have told me." The seams of his shirt split with a loud tearing sound. "There are things I should know. What am I? Why am I this way? How do I

248

control it? What can hurt me? You never told me the third way a werewolf can die. Fire, a silver bullet, and what else, father?''

Holly and the others stood in a semicircle, mutely staring at the confrontation. Malcolm's teeth began to grow, pushing out through the gums. His nose and mouth stretched into a muzzle. The dark fur sprouted as he ripped away his clothing.

''You fool!'' Derak growled. He pulled off his own clothes and laid them aside as his body began the shape change with a popping of bone and tendon. The fur that grew over the older man's flesh was sand-colored. His face twisted into that of a wolf. It bore the scars of old battles.

When he spoke his voice had deepened into a hoarse rumble. ''The third way we can die is never spoken of because it is unthinkable. It is the one unforgivable crime for our kind. We can die by fire, as you remember from Drago. We can be destroyed by a weapon of silver, as mankind learned long ago. And the third, most terrible way . . . one werewolf can kill another.''

There was a soft moaning sound from the others. They shrank back a step from the father and son. Holly's throat was dry as she watched the two figures evolve from men into huge and terrible beasts.

It was the first time Malcolm had completed the metamorphosis. As a wolf he was taller by a head than his father, but Derak was more muscular, more sure of his body. They circled each other warily.

The dark wolf attacked first. He lunged wildly at Derak and was batted aside by a clawed hand. He lunged again, and again Derak evaded him, dealing a painful blow as he did so. The son bellowed in anger and frustration. The father was watchful, conserving his strength.

For an hour the battle continued much in the way it had begun. Malcolm, younger and quicker, struck time after time, but Derak's experience and cunning made him miss repeatedly. Before long the blows struck by the older wolf were taking their toll. Malcolm's lunges became more clumsy, his own wounds deeper.

Holly bit into her knuckle as she watched. She had once seen two chimpanzees fight to the death during an experiment on the animals with PCP. It had been agony to watch, but this was more terrible by far. Not only was it beast against beast; it was father against son. And the son was losing.

As Malcolm slowed perceptibly, Derak began to go to the attack. He moved in with teeth and claws and drew howls of pain as he slashed through fur and flesh. Once Malcolm fell and Derak stood over him, teeth bared for the kill, but he backed off and gestured Malcolm toward him like a taunting prizefighter.

As Malcolm pulled himself erect, blood trickling from a dozen wounds, Holly had to look away. As she did so, she saw a man emerge from the brush along the trail. Gavin Ramsay. She ran toward the tall sheriff, ignored by the others, who were intent on the battle.

Ramsay stared at the two beasts. He opened his arms and gathered Holly in as she came to him.

"Are you all right?"

"Yes." Her voice was no more than a whisper.

Ramsay could not take his eyes off the wolves. He drew the revolver and leveled it at them.

Holly seized his wrist, forcing the arm down. "Don't," she said. "One of them is Malcolm."

"Jesus." Ramsay looked around at the others, who had now taken note of him. Normal-looking people, but in their eyes lay a threat. "Are they all . . . ?"

"Yes," Holly said. "You might be able to kill some of them, but the rest would get us."

"Jesus," Ramsay said again. He put the gun away, and the others returned their attention to their leader and the young challenger.

The battle continued. Big patches of dark fur had been ripped from Malcolm's body. A tooth was gone, leaving a bloody socket. One of his ears was nearly torn away. It seemed only a matter of time before the more experienced of the two would finish the fight.

Then with shocking suddenness, Derak sprang at him. The killer teeth of the older wolf tore through his chest. Malcolm fell, blood streaming from this last and deepest wound. Derak poised for a moment over his fallen son, then cracked his jaws wide and bent down for the kill.

But Malcolm was not quite through. With an effort that brought blood pumping from his chest, he twisted where he lay so that when Derak came at him, his own throat was seized in Malcolm's jaws.

The muffled crunch of bone drew gasps from those who watched. The powerful wolf body of Derak thrashed and bucked, but the teeth of the younger beast were sunk deep. With a last strangled cry from Derak, it was over. Slowly the jaws of the son opened. The father lay limp and silent. The fur of both creatures was matted with blood. Malcolm turned his battered head to look over at Holly. She reached out to him.

Dragging himself painfully a few inches at a time, Malcolm came to her. Ramsay started again to reach for the pistol but held back. Holly dropped to her knees as the beast that had been a boy reached her. He rested his great torn muzzle against her for a moment, then he died.

Holly stroked the tangled fur of his head, smoothing it down. After a minute she stood up. "It's over, Gavin," she said.

He looked back along the ledge and frowned. "Where are the rest of them?"

Holly followed his gaze. The two of them were alone. They and the dead beasts. "They must have slipped away into the trees."

"Should we report this back in town? Send out a search party?"

She looked deep into his eyes. "What do you think?"

"No," he said after a moment. "They'd put us away."

She nodded and squeezed his hand.

He said, "We'd better try to make it back before dark. Are you ready to walk down?"

"I'm ready," she said.

Gavin circled her waist with an arm and they started down the trail. From somewhere in the hills behind them they heard it one last time. The howling. They did not look back.